Love Will Always Remember

Also by Tracey Livesay

Love Will Always Remember
Along Came Love
Love On My Mind
Pretending with the Playboy
The Tycoon's Socialite Bride

Love Will Always Remember

TRACEY LIVESAY

AVONIMPULSE

An Imprint of HarperCollinsPublishers

An excerpt from *Along Came Love* copyright © 2016 by Tracey Livesay.
An excerpt from *Love on My Mind* copyright © 2016 by Tracey Livesay.

Digital Edition AUGUST 2017 ISBN: 978–0–062497765
Print Edition ISBN: 978–0–062497833

Cover design by Guido Caroti
Cover photographs: © GrandPix / Getty Images (couple); © Freedom_ Studio / Shutterstock (sheets)

Avon Impulse and the Avon Impulse logo are registered trademarks of HarperCollins Publishers in the United States of America.
Avon and HarperCollins are registered trademarks of HarperCollins Publishers in the United States of America and other countries.

FIRST EDITION

17 18 19 20 21   HDC   10 9 8 7 6 5 4 3 2 1

To my sweet daughter, Grayson Faith.
Nothing has ever compared to the relief we
felt when we knew you'd be okay.

Acknowledgments

As ALWAYS, A big hug and cup of coffee to my agent Nalini Akolekar of Spencerhill Associates for her support and guidance. In lieu of thanks, I offer unlimited coffee refills and my extra hours of sleep to Tessa Woodward, my amazing editor whose superpower is knowing how to make a story better. For real.

Thank you to several people who provided invaluable information to me for this book: Leigh Florio & Cassy Carillo for answering questions about ER procedures and patient intake; Jim Florio, for insight into the customs and norms of the Secret Service; and Fabiola Chenet & Claudine Martinez for being my French and Spanish in terpreters, respectively.

These next few you should know by heart . . .

To my LaLas: Sharon, Annette, Petra, Ashley, Leigh,

Nellie & Chrissy. We've been on this running journey for six years and I don't regret any mile spent in your company.

Running my first marathon with you convinced me there isn't any challenge I can't overcome when I put my mind to it.

To Mary & Alleyne, my writing crew. You continue to help me navigate this unpredictable publishing world with my sanity intact . . . mostly.

To my three children: Trey (who is now the tallest person in the family), Graysie (my sweet and talkative girl) and Will (my baller and ambassador of swag). Being your mother makes me a better person. Thank you.

And last, but never least, my husband James. The reason I can write the stories I do is because of you. You are the 'happy' in my happily ever after and the 'he' in every hero I create. My heart will always remember you.

Until the next one,
TL

Chapter One

LEIGHTON CLARKE KNEW the moment the Honorable Mr. Fred Ramsey from the State of Illinois saw her.

His pale eyes widened and he stiffened, the tumbler—containing more than a splash of amber liquid—abandoned midway on its journey to his mouth. His throat bobbed while his gaze darted left and right seeking an exit.

Leighton's lips quirked in a canary-eating grin. *Don't leave on my account, Freddy.*

Not when moments before he'd stood next to the makeshift wooden bar set up in the far corner gesticulating grandly, unaware or simply not caring that surrounding himself with younger men only made his graying hair and sagging jowls more pronounced.

She wrinkled her nose. He shouldn't be here—the

attendees simply too young to be his peers—but like a leech scenting a nearby blood supply, he was physically unable to pass up the opportunity to check out fresh meat.

And this annual celebration of DC's next generation of foreign policy leaders provided it. In spades. Leighton didn't miss being part of the incestuous dealings on the Hill with people who lived, drank and fucked politics. Been there, done that for years. No, she was here for a specific purpose, and once accomplished, she'd be on her way, well before the DJ replaced the string orchestra and the subsequent commencement of random hookups.

She navigated the space between her and Ramsey, embracing the telltale tingle of being watched prickling the nape of her neck. After a lifetime of living in the most powerful city in the world, as the daughter of a well-known diplomat, she was accustomed to the attention. When she'd been younger, the notion made her crave burrowing her head in the sand and hiding. Now, she knew how to use it to her advantage.

She nodded to several acquaintances, bestowed benign smiles on anyone brave enough to meet her gaze, but her stride didn't waver. Shoulders slumping, Ramsey succumbed to the inevitable and waved away the audience encircling him. He might be vice chairman of the House Subcommittee on Commerce, Manufacturing and Trade but she was an influential lobbyist. He might not like the fact that he *saw* her there, but he would *see* her.

When she was several feet from her quarry, a Mack Truck masquerading as a bodyguard blocked her path. "You can't approach him."

Members of Congress received twenty-four-hour protection at the Capitol, but only a select few rated private security detail away from the building. And of that select group, only a tiny percentage would be assigned protection by the Secret Service.

Fred Ramsey wasn't in either group.

Rocking the requisite ear piece, the guard might fool the average person, but he wasn't Secret Service. His inability to blend into the background was evident, not to mention the missing distinctive lapel pin that would identify him to other agents.

But she was counting on Ramsey's need to appear more impressive than he was. She'd dealt with men like him before.

Leighton didn't spare the rent-a-cop a moment of her attention. She shifted her weight to glance around his wide berth and stared at the congressman.

"It's okay, George," Ramsey said.

"Are you sure, sir?" George's dead eyes scoped her from the top of her head to the tip of her Manolos. He licked his thick lips. "She looks dangerous. I may need to frisk her."

Leighton addressed Ramsey. "What did he say? I speak four languages, but I'm afraid 'asshole' isn't one of them."

A muscle erupted in George's jaw, but he stepped aside.

Finally. "Congressman Ramsey."

Predictably, Ramsey's eyes scrolled down her body. Her hands tightened on her purse. Had these men never seen tits, hips and legs before?

"Miss Clarke, no one told me our little soiree would be graced with the presence of DC royalty. Tell me, do you intend to follow me all over the city?"

He projected his normally thin, reedy voice so it carried over the sedate string music. Several heads swiveled in their direction, followed by whispered asides and nods.

So *that's* how he wanted to play it: the big man on campus, in demand, and she was seeking his counsel.

She placed her Edie Parker clutch on the bar. "If that's what it takes."

He gulped his drink, the ice in his tumbler rattling against the glass. "We're in recess—"

"For a few more weeks."

"And when we return, the bill will be in conference with members from both houses. They're the ones who'll reconcile the differences between the two versions the House and Senate passed." He shrugged. "I may not get chosen for that committee."

Leighton eyed him while he signaled to the bartender for a refill. When a trusted source had disclosed Ramsey's presence at the gala, she'd instructed her driver to make the detour, despite being on the way to meet Thomas. She abhorred tardiness, but with Ramsey dodging her calls for the better part of two weeks, confronting him when he least expected it held a certain appeal.

And this little diversion has nothing to do with delaying where *you're meeting your fiancé or* who *else may be there?*

She squelched the penetrating thought and quickly amended her plan of attack. Scratch the idea of a simple, civil conversation. Ramsey would require a firm touch. Similar to how she'd dealt with Senator Kessler two years ago.

"Don't bullshit me, Congressman. You'll get chosen, but you think you'll lose me during the committee process." She leaned into his personal space, ignoring the alcoholic odor already seeping through his pores. "I assure you, you won't."

"It's out of my hands. If they strike your amendment—"

"It's your job to make sure that doesn't happen."

"How?" He shifted on the stool. "You have to understand. I'm in a difficult position."

Time for the hard sell.

"Really? Nothing about this should be difficult for you. We've done the research, put the presentation together. All you have to do is give it. Talk it up to your colleagues, support it. You've done this in the past. What's your problem now?"

Ramsey stared into his glass. "There's been talk about safety concerns . . ."

Though her insides morphed into a frozen tundra, she rested her hip against the bar and evinced a nonchalant air.

She'd worked hard to keep those issues concealed.

Concord Tires guaranteed they could correct the situation, but Leighton knew attaching the amendment to this bill was their only shot to get it passed. It wouldn't survive scrutiny on its own. So she'd pressed forward. This had to work. It was on her if it didn't.

She angled her head and gentled her demeanor. "You've seen the report. This device will change the automotive industry. You have the opportunity to ensure safer travel for millions of people."

"I know what the report says, but my legislative assistant is worried—"

Her irritation overrode her caution. "Who? Andrew? The pimply faced boy who just left elementary school, his breath smelling like baby formula?"

"He may be young," Ramsey conceded, "but if it's true—"

"One whiff of a safety hazard and you'll kill this deal. You're willing to fuck up a billion-dollar enterprise on the word of some kid?"

"If your client doesn't want that to happen, we can let the amendment fail in committee. That way no one will ever hear about the serious security issue. Concord Tires can still sell the device on the market and make some money." A nasty smile corroded his features. "Better luck next time, honey."

Red feathered the edges of her vision. She hadn't risen in the ranks to become a major player at Faulkner & Ingersoll, the city's top boutique lobbying firm, by losing her temper when things didn't go her way. But sometimes . . . It was the disrespect that angered her, so prevalent on the faces of the older white men who resented the fact that their mirror image wasn't sitting across from them.

She inhaled and studied her surroundings, using the moment to compose herself, and to allow him to wallow in his assumed victory. Hundreds of twinkling lights dotted the ceiling and gossamer-thin white tulle draped the crown of several doorways and cascaded down both jambs. A too-large full moon sat against a black velvet backdrop and more lights emblazoned the silhouette of a city skyline, its centerpiece: a ten-foot-high Eiffel Tower gleaming in amber uplights.

She'd come up with the *Midnight in Paris* theme, and these same decorations, eight years earlier when she'd chaired the planning committee for the State of Affairs gala. Apparently, imagination and originality, along with her idealism and naivete, had been abolished long ago.

The orchestra finished their set and a smattering of applause rippled through the room.

Her temper reined in, Leighton refocused on the task before her. Ramsey thought he'd won this round, that he'd gained the upper hand, but she was well-versed in the game of DC one-upmanship. Some might say she'd earned her doctorate.

"How's life back in Illinois's Fourteenth congressional district?"

He took another gulp of his drink. "Great."

"I'm glad. And your constituents are happy with your service on their behalf?"

He hesitated, his insouciant posture straightening, his bushy brows straining toward one another. "Of course."

Leighton slapped her hand down on the smooth lacquered wood of the bar. "Wonderful! Then you'll have nothing to worry about from Brad Bagley."

"Who?"

"Brad Bagley. Bagley & Sons Funeral Home. From your district."

He swallowed. "Why would I worry about some mortician?"

Leighton allowed one corner of her mouth to ascend. "Mr. Bagley just prepared his papers to declare his candidacy for your seat."

Ramsey shot to his feet. George the Bulldozer moved closer, but Ramsey indicated he stay put.

"How do you know that?" Ramsey asked in a furious whisper.

Leighton laughed, but not from any real amusement. "You'd be surprised at what I know. About your mistress, your gambling, and some of the gifts you've received."

With each complication she unmasked, his complexion grew paler and more waxy.

"A leaked picture, the release of an audio recording, any of those could cause you problems." Leighton shook her head and narrowed her eyes. "But that's bush league.

That's *not* how I operate. Besides, you'd probably talk your way out of any real trouble.

"Running for office can be so expensive," she continued. "You know what I'd do? I'd find the person running against you and back *them*. Put all of my considerable resources and expertise behind *them*. Flood your area with so much of *his* propaganda that even if I disclosed your indiscretions, no one would care because I'd rendered you irrelevant."

He slumped down hard on the bar stool, dropping his head into his hands. There was a time when she'd have been shocked by what she'd just done. That time had come and gone.

"So, we can count on you to push the bill through committee?"

His body stiffened, but without looking up, he nodded.

"And no more slanderous talk about safety issues?"

He finally lifted his gaze and though he shook his head in response to her question, his eyes telegraphed his impotent rage.

Too fucking bad.

This may be your first experience with disillusionment, but I tasted it years ago. Never again.

She adjusted the diamond cuff on her left wrist, a splurge with her first lobbying paycheck. The first time she'd made money in politics without her parental installed and approved blinders on. "Excellent."

Time to go. She'd cut it close. The DJ was setting up his station.

"You're nothing like Ambassador Clarke."

Refusing to acknowledge the twinge in her heart at hearing her father's name, Leighton arched a perfectly sculpted brow. "God, I hope not."

She'd idolized her father. Her entire life, Career Ambassador Eugene Clarke had proselytized, "*To whom much is given, much is required.*" The Clarkes had wealth and pedigree; her father had been vocal about his expectation that his only child follow him into public service. She'd been happy to oblige.

After his death six years ago, she'd learned he'd been less forthcoming with the truth that his long absences from home hadn't been a necessary sacrifice for his country, but rather a result of the international affair he'd been carrying on for over a decade. But thanks to her mother, no one had ever discovered her father's public persona didn't match the private one. Leighton still couldn't reconcile Beverly Clarke's actions. What kind of woman accepted, condoned and then covered up her husband's affair?

A woman who enveloped herself in an irrational shroud of love.

Something Leighton would never do.

Their actions cemented her reigning belief that people only acted in their own best interest. Effective insight for her line of work.

Considering her mission completed, she grabbed her clutch and—

"You're a bitch, you know that?"

She stopped on a dime. Did he think she would dissolve into a puddle of tears because he'd called her a name? But if he wanted to see a bitch . . .

She turned, braced her free hand against the bar and stooped to stare into his eyes. She lifted the veil off the emotions she usually kept in check and allowed him to see the full extent of her ruthlessness.

His chin trembled but she wasn't done.

"Did you mean to insult me? Better luck next time, *honey*," she said, tossing his words back at him. "You didn't, because bitches get stuff done. You should remember that the next time you want to measure your balls against my ovaries. I'll win every fucking time."

When she left the gala five minutes later, the humidity rose up and smacked her in the face like a harassed congressional intern. DC was beautiful at night, the glittering lights from the cars, restaurants, office buildings and monuments providing an ever-changing tapestry.

But in the summer . . .

Maybe Congress had it right, taking one of their many "recesses" during the months of July, August and September, while the city careened between throat-clogging heat and air-crackling thunderstorms that did little to offer relief once they'd passed.

The encounter with Ramsey had yielded the result she'd wanted but not without creating a bad aftertaste. A side-effect from thinking about her father.

She pulled out her phone and sent a quick text to her

driver letting him know she was ready to resume their trip. Thomas was leaving for London for an extended period of time tomorrow and he'd made a special evening appointment with their jeweler.

She spared her bare left hand a brief look. The engagement ring didn't matter to her, but it was essential for Thomas. As was everything about their wedding. Some grooms wanted no part of the planning. They showed up on the morning of the ceremony having contributed nothing to its preparation. Not Thomas. He wanted input.

"It's a display that will benefit us both."

Her wedding. Their marriage. A display.

She didn't care. He got the cachet of being associated with her family, the wedding of the season and their ascension to the top tier of DC power couples. She got one of the city's most eligible bachelors as a husband and the appearance of stability, something the partners at her firm desired before she could join their ranks.

She squinted ahead to check out the traffic. Bright red brake lights as far as the eye could see.

Shit.

She wasn't late. Not yet. But with the notorious gridlock of Friday night traffic snaking through the steep side streets and narrow lanes, the six-mile trip could take up to forty minutes. It'd require a miracle for her to get from this neighborhood to Shaw in time to meet her fiancé.

At his brother's restaurant.

She was unable to prevent the butterflies that soared

in her belly at the thought of the unbearably sexy Jonathan Moran and she cursed her body's traitorous response. She was constantly surrounded by rich powerful men and some of them were attractive. Did they cause her breath to quicken or send her heartbeat soaring?

Of course not.

But the first time she'd met Jonathan, his laughing, mocha brown eyes had swept over her, exploding tiny bombs of unreason and lust in her chest. Tall, dark and gorgeous, the resemblance between the two brothers was striking, though Thomas was slightly shorter and a tad stockier than his sibling. But somehow, the genetic combination of the younger Moran affected her in a way her fiancé's did not.

She'd been intrigued by him and the anticipation he'd inspired in her. He'd smiled and her gaze had wandered to his lips, imagined how they would feel against her own. Would his kiss be fleeting and soft or hard and fierce? Staring at him, she'd forgotten she was standing next to the man she'd planned to marry.

Horrified, she'd slapped a steel lid on those emotions and riveted it shut. Despite the example shown by her parents, she wouldn't use "feelings" to excuse a selfish and harmful decision.

It had been an unexpected, momentary lapse, never to be repeated. Now, she knew to be on guard. And as a bonus, Jonathan lived on the other side of the country. Since the brothers didn't get along, she wouldn't have much contact with him.

That all went out of the window when he decided to open a restaurant here.

Her driver pulled up to the curb in a black luxury sedan and she slid into the blessedly cool interior.

"You know how I feel about being late, Herb."

"Don't worry, ma'am. I'll get you there on time."

Leighton leaned back, closed her eyes and immediately opened them upon seeing Jonathan's red-tinged image imprinted behind her lids.

No, no, no!

She'd figure out a way to get past this. She'd been in meetings with some of the most powerful people in the world, had dined and interacted with European royalty, Hollywood celebrities and world-famous musicians.

She'd be damned if she'd allow an inconvenient attraction to her future brother-in-law to get the best of her.

Chapter Two

WHAT IRRITATED JONATHAN Moran more than the headache-inducing noise of five guys hammering, drilling and pounding wide-planked wood flooring into place was the knowledge he'd suffered through a similar installation a week before. He'd lost three days of access to his main dining room as workers had used concrete, stain and sealant to yield a floor similar to the one that graced his San Francisco restaurant, *Quartet*.

But when Karl, his designer, had breezed in from his red-eye flight, clutching a venti coffee and an artificial air of alertness, he'd taken one look at the floors of this new establishment, *Sedici*, and declared his vision corrupted. Unwilling to lose more time, Jonathan tried assuring him the floors were fine.

To which Karl had crossly replied, "Since you wouldn't

know an Aubusson from your asshole, please leave the flooring decisions to the experts."

Considering Karl had devised the award-winning interior for *Quartet*, Jonathan had heeded the other man's "advice" and signed the work order replacing a perfectly good floor with an entirely new one. After all, he had boatloads of time and an infinite supply of money.

Not.

Jonathan's chest tightened and he massaged the offending spot, dreading the "discussion" that would occur when Zach found out about the additional five figure expenditure.

But not more than he dreaded this moment, this conversation, hell, this entire encounter with his brother. Even after all these years, Thomas Moran was still an asshole.

"Aren't you worried?" Thomas asked, flicking back his jacket and sliding a hand into the pocket of his slacks.

Jonathan stared at his older brother, imperious in a custom-tailored suit. Jonathan never found it, but he was certain his parents had a baby picture of Thomas in a three-piece Hugo Boss, minutes after he'd been born.

If he'd sensed any sort of genuine concern on his brother's part, any indication he actually cared, Jonathan might have confessed his uneasiness with the rising costs, constant delays and unexpected restrictions plaguing his latest venture.

But he didn't.

"Not at all. *Sedici* will open in three weeks as planned."

It saddened him that he and Thomas didn't have a better relationship. Thomas had viewed his younger brother as a genealogical anchor and Jonathan had tired of being unfavorably compared to the Moran scion. He'd yearned to be his own man, to appreciate an experience without hearing how Thomas had done it first. And better. Going away had allowed him the time and space to mature. Coming home tested that growth.

Thomas curled his upper lip. "What in the hell is a *suh-dee-chee*?"

"It's the name of the restaurant," Jonathan gritted out.

"Interesting," his brother said in a way that screamed it was anything but, condescension glazing his features. "I was talking about the construction going on outside your front door, but yeah, I'd be troubled about opening on time with the amount of work you have left to do."

"Oh how I've missed these pep talks!" Jonathan lifted a crate of glasses and set them down beside the back bar. He shared a conspiratorial brow raise with his bar manager, who'd been concentrating on a group of bartenders-in-training. He re-focused on his brother. "What brings you by?"

"Besides the scent of impending disaster?" Thomas snorted at his own joke.

If he didn't have a year and a shitload of money invested in opening this restaurant, he'd turn around, go back to San Francisco and never worry about seeing his asshat of a brother ever again. Repairing his relationship with Thomas was one of the reasons he'd made the decision to come back home. Watching his best friends find love and strengthen their families had made him acutely aware of his own familial deficiencies—and intent on correcting them. But that decision had been easy to make with three thousand miles and infrequent contact glossing over the reality of his brother's disposition.

"Leighton and I are meeting a jeweler here in ten minutes."

At the mention of Thomas's fiancée, Jonathan's breath hitched in his chest and a bolt of pure lust shredded down his spine and settled heavily in his cock. If his brother's obnoxious personality wasn't enough of a reason to keep his distance, his unadulterated attraction to Leighton Clarke should do it.

"What part of 'my restaurant isn't open' didn't you understand? This isn't your satellite business office."

Thomas looked around him, brows lifted. "If you think I would ever consider this shipwreck my office, it's clear you have no idea what I do or how well I do it."

Arrogant bastard.

Jonathan clenched his jaw so hard his molars could've cracked a walnut. He forced himself to relax, then calmly asked, "Why are you meeting a jeweler?"

"Leighton needs to pick out an engagement ring."

She wasn't wearing a ring? Why hadn't he noticed?

Because you refuse to let your eyes move any farther south than her neck.

"You've been engaged for months." Irritation at his errant, inappropriate thought turned his voice sour. "Why haven't you given her a ring?"

"How is that any of your business?"

Thomas was right. It wasn't. But the restaurant, and what happened in it, was.

Jonathan shrugged. "You should've asked me first. I could've saved you the trip. Now isn't a good time."

Jonathan couldn't imagine two brothers more different. He was food, friends and fun. Thomas was suits, salary, societal status. But did that mean they couldn't get along? He'd hoped he'd magnified their differences in his mind. Maybe they'd grown out of it. The move, the restaurant, getting along with his brother; he'd come back determined to make it all work.

Then he'd met his brother's fiancée.

A nimble once-over on his part, taking in her creamy dark skin, razor-sharp cheekbones and lush, sensuous lips, and his body had risen to attention like a recent Naval Academy graduate. And when her tongue had darted out to moisten said lips, desire had grabbed his balls in a vise-like grip and refused to let go. He'd wanted to slide *his* tongue along her neck, nibble the lobe of her ear, grip the enticing curve of her hip and pull her close. He'd wanted to cook for her, feed her, fuck her. He'd never experienced a lust so overwhelming, so powerful, so instantaneous . . .

And there was nothing he could do about it. She was going to marry his brother.

When they'd shaken hands, the connection altered him on a cellular level. Fear and confusion had him retreating to the opposite side of the room, where he'd surreptitiously watched them together until he'd been inexplicably drawn back to her luminous presence. He'd cursed himself for his weakness, told himself that coveting her was a negation of his self-imposed exile and personal progress.

He needn't have bothered. Though stunningly beautiful on the outside, she'd been haughty and judgmental, a total snob.

And yet he couldn't banish the mental spectacle of those long, lean legs wrapped around his waist, his lips attached to the throbbing pulse in her neck and her heady scent surrounding him as he plunged into her until his knees wobbled and he could barely stand.

"My bad," Thomas sneered. "I forgot that nothing and no one is more important than your needs. Like when Dad had his retirement party and you couldn't be bothered to come home."

"Not on that day," Jonathan objected. "But I flew him and Mom out to San Francisco the week after."

"I had to move them to Florida by myself—"

"You picked the one weekend you knew I wasn't available." Jonathan was honored to be a judge at the annual Young Chefs of America competition. He'd participated every year for the past four years, issuing an open invitation for his family to join him in Palm Springs. His parents always accepted. His brother never did.

Thomas brushed aside his response. "I had to put the house on the market without you."

"You're keeping a tally?"

"Yes."

"Are you serious? I can't do you a favor because I'm busy opening my restaurant and suddenly *I'm* the bastard?"

"As a matter of fact, yes, that's exactly how it works." Thomas's sigh would've made a soap opera matron proud. "I should be used to it. You've always done what's best for you and fuck its effect on anyone else."

Irritation bubbled to the surface at the old refrain. "That's bullshit. You're thirty-six years old. Isn't it time you stopped bringing up things that happened when we were kids?"

"I'll stop bringing up our childhood when you stop being a child."

And like a fixed patio door, they slid effortlessly back into the acrimonious rhythm that had eventually poisoned their relationship.

The front door breezed open, halting the nasty retort on the tip of his tongue, and bringing with it the stifling humidity/heat combo of a DC summer night, the constant clamor of the construction happening directly outside his front door, and her.

The breath abandoned his body.

Leighton stood just inside the doorway, sheathed in a black and ivory form-fitting dress, the cinched waist emphasizing her sensuous figure. His heart shifted in his chest. She looked cool and poised despite the weather and late hour, her hair falling in a dark curtain around her shoulders and an impressive diamond bracelet glistening on her arm. He tightened his hands into fists at his side, in an effort to stem the tingling in his fingers.

Why her? DC was filled with gorgeous, accomplished women. Hell, roughly fifty-three percent of the population was female. Why couldn't he stop thinking about the *one* engaged to his brother?

"I'm not an expert, but I don't think requiring your customers to traverse an obstacle course to enter your restaurant will be good for business."

Her smoky voice stroked him like a velvet glove. What he wouldn't give for her to whisper dirty words in his ear while her hand stroked his cock in a similar manner.

A clattering crash jerked his attention away from temptation to the area behind the bar. A young man stood and placed several large jagged pieces of glass on the heavily veined marble counter.

His bar manager rolled her eyes. "If I catch any of you doing that *cocktail* shit, I will throw your asses out. That's not what we do here."

Exasperated at the broken glassware, but thankful for the interruption, Jonathan crossed his arms over his chest and scowled at the newcomer. "You're right. You're not an expert."

Her dark, tilted eyes, the color of espresso, flickered and dropped lower to follow his movements. His pulse rocketed and his skin heated where seared by her glance. She drew in her lower lip and it popped out wet and glistening, before she gave a tiny, almost imperceptible shake of her head and looked away.

What the fuck? Did she just check him out?

Thomas strode forward creating a physical and mental barrier between them. "Ignore him. Contemplating the possibility of failure has put him in a foul mood."

"Ignore me? In my restaurant? You can both leave, make it that much easier."

Thomas brushed a brief kiss at the corner of her mouth and squeezed her upper arm.

That's how he greeted her? If nine o'clock at night was the first time Jonathan had seen Leighton all day, he'd do more than peck her cheek. He'd tangle his hand in the thickness of her hair, claim those ripe lips and show her just how much she'd been on his mind—

If he liked her and she was his fiancée.

Which he didn't.

And she wasn't.

Not wanting to see if there was more to Thomas's welcome, Jonathan headed over to the guys installing the floor. "Why don't you call it a night?"

The foreman stood. "Are you sure? We could keep going."

While Jonathan's wallet appreciated the sentiment, his head couldn't take any more noise. And with Leighton here, he'd need to exert the maximum amount of mental focus. "You can finish in the morning."

"Alright, Chef." The foreman motioned to the workers, who ceased hammering and began putting their tools away.

When he tuned back in to their conversation, Leighton was asking Thomas, "What time is your flight?"

"Six tomorrow night. I'll go straight to the airport from my lunch meeting with the partners."

For the first time since her arrival, she smiled and it was a thing of beauty. "The fact that they're sending you is a sign of their confidence *in* you."

What the fuck are you doing to yourself? Why are you still here?

He was a glutton for punishment. He should be somewhere in the back checking inventory or helping Gib with the staff or doing one of the other numerous tasks on his punch list. But he wasn't. He was here, watching Leighton smile and wishing like hell it was directed at him.

It was a dick move to covet his brother's woman.

Still, he inserted himself into their conversation. "Where are you going?"

He didn't expect a real response, so he was surprised when Thomas exhaled loudly thorough his nose, but answered. "My firm is sending me to implement a new accounting system for our London office."

He was impressed despite his efforts to feel otherwise. "Will you be gone long?"

Brown eyes, identical to the ones he saw in the mirror

every day, save the thin white scar above the left brow, met his then darted away. "Six weeks."

The disappointment burned like a shot of cheap tequila. He rolled his lips inward and nodded his head. His brother would miss the opening. Why should he have expected anything different?

Thomas pulled out his phone and asked Leighton, "Did you get my message about the wedding planner?"

She nodded. "I did. I made the call and she's in."

"Excellent."

Not surprising. He'd been back in DC for over a year and he was already learning that whatever Leighton Clarke wanted, Leighton Clarke got.

You're just mad she doesn't want you.

"She'll call me tomorrow with her earliest available appointment."

"Everything is coming along as we planned," Thomas said, the glee in his voice invoking the image of an evil mastermind rubbing his hands together.

"Where's the jeweler? He's late," Leighton said.

Jonathan checked his watch. "Only a few minutes."

"*Our* time is valuable," Thomas said, his implication clear.

"So is mine," Jonathan challenged. "Yet here you are."

"You don't need to be here," Thomas said. "We wanted the space, not you."

Fucker.

It's the same thing he'd told himself minutes ago, but still . . .

Leighton's gaze flew to meet his and the frost melted from her countenance. With a lingering look at him, she touched Thomas's arm and spoke in a low voice.

Jealousy gnawed the edges of his heart.

Thomas's lips firmed into a straight line and he gave a brisk nod. Facing Jonathan, but staring at something over his shoulder, his brother said, "We appreciate you allowing us to use the restaurant."

Jonathan looked from Thomas to Leighton, who stood in profile to him, her arms folded stiffly in front of her, her gaze somewhere near the entrance to the kitchen.

"You're welcome."

He didn't need his brother's gratitude, didn't want it. But he took it.

Because *she'd* offered it.

All three turned at the sharp knock on glass. An older man holding a silver aluminum briefcase stood just outside the front door, eyeing the metal scaffolding as if he were being forced to cross a large open field with buried land mines.

Jonathan opened the door a bit. "Can I help you?"

The visitor adjusted the wire-rimmed glasses on his round face. "I'm Samuel Bridge from Walker-Grant Jewelers. I'm here to meet Leighton Clarke and Thomas Moran."

He pushed the door wider in invitation. "I'm Jonathan Moran. Please, come in. They're expecting you."

Bridge shook his outstretched hand. "It's a pleasure,

Chef. I'm a fan. My wife and I dined at *Quartet* when we were in San Francisco last year. The roasted squab was incredible."

Pleasure blossomed in his chest. He'd never tire of hearing how much people loved his food. "Thank you."

Thomas's features tightened at the admiration. As the oldest, he wasn't used to being the subordinate of the two Moran brothers. "I'm Thomas Moran and this is my fiancée, Leighton Clarke."

Bridge's face flushed red in a mottled pattern that would be concerning in a different situation but was probably par for the course with Leighton. "A pleasure."

They shook hands. Leighton had a strong handshake, no limp wrist or lady fingers for her.

"Thank you for agreeing to meet us here after hours," Leighton said.

"No problem at all. Like I told Chef Moran, I love his food. I couldn't pass up the opportunity to get a sneak peak at his new restaurant."

Was it wrong that he got enjoyment from the waves of irritation emanating from Thomas?

Jonathan smiled. "You just have to give me your word not to tell anyone what you see, okay?"

Bridge's posture straightened. "Oh, of course."

"My man! Can I get you something to drink?"

"No, thanks, Chef. I can't stay long."

Thomas glared at him. "Don't you have floors to sweep or sous chef's recipes to steal?"

Jonathan shrugged off the insult. "Nope, I'm good."

His gaze was drawn to Leighton—*again*—and he caught the amusement on her face before she hid it.

"First, congratulations on your engagement." Bridge approached the bar and lifted his case. "May I?"

"One second." Jonathan excused his bar manager and the trainees for the evening. "It's all yours."

Bridge placed his case on the counter and pressed his thumb over a small panel that glowed a dull red. The light turned green, the case clicked and with a *whoosh* the lid sprung open. He removed a black velvet cloth.

Thomas placed his hand on the small of Leighton's back and urged her closer. Jonathan stayed where he was, but shifted so he had an unobstructed view of the case's contents, and Leighton.

"Mr. Moran indicated you would only be interested in diamonds in the four to five carat range." Bridge pulled out a black velvet tray containing twelve conical ring holders, six in each tiered row. Ten of the holders were occupied. He indicated some on the first line. "These are the most expensive."

They were certainly sparkly.

Bridge pointed to the first ring. "The three rows of smaller diamonds on each side draws attention to the large center diamond, creating a halo effect. A total weight of 5.26 carats."

Describing the middle one, he said, "This is an art deco–style ring set with a central radiant-cut diamond surrounded by over two hundred and forty round and baguette cut diamonds. Total weight, 4.9 carats."

And finally, "This is a popular design, a substantial oval cut diamond with a double diamond halo. It's also the largest, with a total weight of 5.47 carats."

A buzz followed Bridge's explanations and the instrumental version of "Diamonds are a Girl's Best Friend" blared in the space. Bridge fished his phone out of his pocket. "I have to take this. Feel free to look at them, even try some on. Hello, dear . . . Yes, it won't be much longer now . . ." He walked over to the hallway that led to the bathrooms and disappeared from sight.

Thomas slid the largest ring off its holder. "I like this one."

Why didn't Thomas just whip his dick out and piss in a circle around her? It'd be cheaper.

Leighton wrinkled her nose. "I'm all for making a statement, but I'm not a Kardashian or a reality housewife. My value isn't tied to the size of my ring. There's no reason it needs to span from the base of my finger to my knuckle!"

"Any ring would look ostentatious when paired with that cuff. Take it off."

She hesitated, then unclasped the delicate platinum and diamond-encrusted bracelet from her left wrist and placed it on the bar.

Nope, not better.

Thomas's phone rang and he checked the caller ID. "It's my office, I have to take it." He headed to that Bermuda Triangle near the restrooms where callers ventured never to be heard from again.

Stay where you are, Jonathan! This has nothing to do with you, Jonathan!! She's your brother's fiancée, Jonathan!!!

He sidled up next to her, staring at her patrician profile as she studied the selection. Her hair caressed her cheeks. He wanted to brush the strands behind her ear, then traces the hills and valleys of the shell with his tongue.

Ahhh shit. So much for staying north of her neck. From this position he had an amazing view of her breasts, lovingly displayed by the bodice of her dress. Clearly more than a handful, the tops were plush and soft, like freshly rising dough.

Why had he thought about positions? About twenty, featuring the two of them, flashed into his mind, like exhibits from a sex museum.

"Do you like any of these?" Her voice was low and serious.

Fuck yeah. Especially the one where those long legs are draped over my shoulders and I'm sliding inside of you while you thumb your clit—

It didn't take long to realize his error. But because the blood had forsaken his brain only seconds earlier, he replied, "Does it matter? I'm not marrying him."

She withdrew slightly, as if disappointed by his response.

She'd expected something else? Maybe a mature, thoughtful reaction.

He gazed at the rings and his attention was caught by a solitaire in a classic setting. He picked it up. "What about this one?"

"Oh!" she breathed.

On a whim, he captured her hand and slid the ring on her finger. She inhaled audibly and contentment settled over him. Despite everything being wrong with this scenario, nothing had ever felt so right. The rose gold color of the band and the simple oval cut diamond suited the long, slim, elegant digit. She held her hand away from her, then brought it closer to her face.

"Do you like it?"

"Yes." Her voice was filled with surprised wonder. "It's the one I would've picked out."

"Great minds think alike," he said in a voice barely above a whisper, conscious of her and their closeness. She smelled incredible, like sunshine and toasted spices.

"I guess so."

She lowered her hand and lifted her head.

They were so close. A tiny mole near her temple marred the boring perfection of her forehead. The pulse at the base of her neck throbbed and he yearned to kiss it and her. Expressions flittered across her face faster than he could read them, but she didn't move away.

And he couldn't.

What would happen if he touched her? Just once. Brushed his thumb along her parted lips, slid his fingers through her hair? Would she let him? And if she did, could he stop there? Or would he want to do more? Like take her juicy bottom lip between his teeth and tug? Would she allow him to do that? Or more? Would she touch him?

"Did you see something you . . . Oh!" Bridge skidded to a stop.

Jonathan shifted smoothly away from Leighton, grabbing a nearby towel and setting to work scrubbing a non-existent spot on the bar. His heart pounded so loudly in his chest it drowned out any other sound. What was he *doing*? Things may be difficult with Thomas now, but if he'd done what he'd been thinking . . . There would be no coming back from that.

Bridge's interruption was both the best and worst thing to happen. His biggest problem was he honestly didn't know which.

Chapter Three

THAT MEETING HAD been a total waste of time.

Not that the executives of Rappahannock Pharmaceuticals knew it. Leighton had been so prepared, she could've given that presentation while completing the *New York Times* crossword and playing Double Dutch. She had no doubt they'd retain her firm and request her specifically for the account.

But while her mind had been able to provide information, it hadn't been capable of accepting it, which meant her assistant would have to find a surreptitious way to get it later. All because she'd been mentally berating herself for her behavior the night before.

She'd ignored her own pep talk. She'd gone from refusing to succumb to this inconvenient attraction to eye-fucking Jonathan while her fiancé—his brother—

stood nearby. Thank God Thomas hadn't come out and seen them. It was bad enough Mr. Bridge had, but he'd been too much of a professional, and a gentleman, to comment on it. In the end, she'd decided to pass on the selection he'd brought. The one Thomas had liked was a bit much and the one Jonathan had . . .

Cursing herself and her Moran sensitivity—similar to gluten, only more disruptive—she slid on her sunglasses and exited the office building, one of the many housed in Tysons Corner, one of the largest business districts in Northern Virginia. She needed to keep her distance. She didn't like the way he made her feel: flustered, hot and needy.

None of this was helped by the fact that the man was the walking, talking, breathing personification of sex. Everything about him teased her. Taunted her. Called to her. If she gave in, his essence would lift her off the ground and draw her to him, like an old-style Looney Tunes cartoon. It had been *that* compelling. And it had taken a massive amount of self-control to resist it.

His dark hair had grown a little longer and a little shaggier and the gleaming strands contained a wicked wave, giving him a disheveled I-will-fuck-you-long-hard-and-oh-so-well look. He'd worn a dark green t-shirt that had draped itself across his chest and broad shoulders like a possessive lover. A tattoo on his bicep had played peek-a-boo with her, guaranteeing her eternal curiosity, while jeans sat low on his hips and highlighted strong thighs and a bite-able ass.

She'd noticed his every movement—where he stood, what he was doing—and she could feel him watching her, his gaze leaving invisible love marks on her skin. She could barely look him in the eye, afraid that what she was feeling would show. Or even worse, that looking at him would intensify those feelings. Feelings that reminded her of her father's deception. Feelings that she'd amputate and cauterize if she could, because the last thing she wanted was to be like her father.

Her need to escape Jonathan's presence had been so great that she'd left her diamond cuff behind. She'd call Thomas later and ask him to retrieve it for her.

That was all the mental energy she planned to waste on Jonathan Moran. She needed to get back to DC.

Speaking of . . .

She shifted her Goyard St. Louis tote on her shoulder, pulled out her cell and placed a call to her office.

"How did it go?" her assistant asked in lieu of a greeting.

"Great. Rappahannock should be contacting us within the next few weeks."

"That's wonderful." Nicole hesitated. "And Ramsey?"

That's right. Leighton hadn't been in the office this morning. "He'll do it."

Nicole blew out a breath. "Ramsey agreed to champion the bill through committee?"

Leighton pictured the incredulity on the stylish young woman's face.

"I'm offended. You doubted my skills?"

"Will you fire me if I say, 'a little'?"

Would she? This was Leighton's third assistant in two years. Her co-workers would blame it on her exacting standards, but Leighton never asked her assistants to do anything she wouldn't—or hadn't—done herself.

"It'd take too long to train your replacement. But I might decide to revoke the additional two days off I authorized so you could go on your cruise next week."

"I should've known better." Nicole's response was offered without equivocation. "I won't make that mistake again."

"Good, and I'm kidding." This time. "I'm on my way back. I'll be there in time for my appointment at two."

"Did you grab lunch? You're back to back all afternoon."

"I will. Make sure all my notes are uploaded to my tablet and I need you to block off an hour for us to conference tomorrow morning."

"Any reason in particular?"

"Ramsey brought up the safety issue."

Nicole cleared her throat. "Is that a problem?"

"Absolutely. I took precautions to make sure it never got out."

Which meant there was a leak in the office and she needed to find out who it was.

Over a year ago, her boss assigned her to the Concord Tires case. The company had improved on the current process used to self-inflate tires on commercial and military vehicles, finally making them viable for consumer vehicles. They'd realized the potential but lacked the access and know-how to make it happen.

That's where Leighton came in. She'd urged, pushed and persuaded members of Congress until she'd amassed a cadre of support, including one to sponsor a bill that would make the external air valve, Concord's new invention, a requirement for all automobiles that travel on interstate roadways.

Plainly speaking, every tire on every car to be sold in the US would be required to carry the Concord valve. Billions of dollars of profit were on the line.

"And if word got out you knew about the problem, did nothing and people got hurt—"

"I'd be subpoenaed to appear as a witness at the biggest congressional hearing since Jack Abramoff was investigated for defrauding his own clients."

"That would be . . . unfortunate," Nicole said.

Unfortunate? Understatement of the year.

"Concord will have time to fix the problem before the rollout begins. Until then we need to quash any whispers of danger that may arise."

But discovering the mole and establishing a strategy for damage control would have to wait until another day.

"You got a call from *District Life*," Nicole informed her.

District Life magazine was the premier guide to affluence, influence and sophistication in Washington. Their associate editor was a sorority sister who called on Leighton if she needed a quote from a Washington society insider or an identification of someone photographed for their "Gallery of Galas" section.

"Were they looking for a quote or an ID?"

"Neither. They're doing a story on the merger and they're considering a small profile on you."

She pumped her fist and gained a wink from a passerby. "Fantastic."

This could be great timing. And if they scheduled the interview soon, the article would come out just after the bill passed.

"They mentioned the possibility of the cover . . . if you could get your mother to pose with you."

Resentment squeezed the air from her lungs and she let her hand drop to her side. Her first instinct: tell them to fuck off! But the publicity would only help to raise her profile. And the higher her profile, the better it was for work. She could interact civilly with her mother to achieve that outcome.

"She's out of the country, but she should be back in a couple of months. She's guest lecturing at Howard University for the second semester. See if that's amenable for another article at a later date."

"Have you told her yet?"

She knew what her assistant was asking. Nicole had a soft spot for Beverly Clarke and couldn't understand Leighton's remoteness. Not surprising since the Clarkes excelled at projecting the perfect image. "No."

"What are you waiting for?"

"She'll find out when she gets the *Save the Date* card. Same as everyone else."

"Leighton."

She gritted her teeth against Nicole's censorious tone. It wasn't any of her mother's business. If she didn't need to know the pertinent details about her parents' personal lives, her mother didn't need to know about hers.

"Anything else?"

"Kimberly Reed called."

The wedding planner. "What did she say?"

"She offered two options. She could meet you next month or, if you didn't mind, she could see you after hours, tomorrow night at her office."

Next *month*? Unacceptable.

"Where's her office?"

"On Eleventh and N Street."

That was only two blocks from *Sedici*. Two birds, one stone.

"Call her back and tell her I'll meet her at her office."

"Will do. I'll see you back here soon."

Leighton disconnected the call and started to call Herb when a familiar profile several yards away caught her attention. Although Leighton couldn't see the woman's full face and people streamed between them on the busy street, she'd know that patrician nose, strong jaw and severely cut silver bob anywhere.

She hurried toward the older woman who'd taken on the role of her unofficial mentor when she'd first started on the Hill. When she was close enough that she could reach out and touch her shoulder, she said, "You promised me you'd quit after the last campaign!"

Andrea jumped then coughed and a plume of smoke wafted from between her lips. She turned, her expression warning a cutdown was coming, but a smile immediately smoothed out her features.

"Leighton! You scared the hell out of me!"

"What are you doing here?"

"You know . . ." The hand wielding the cancer stick twirled in the air. Andrea wrinkled her nose and dropped the lit cigarette, stomping it with her heel. "Need to cut out these filthy things."

Like Leighton hadn't heard *that* before.

"I stopped for a while," Andrea said, blowing out a noisy breath, "but you know how it is when I get stressed."

"Why are you stressed?"

Andrea shrugged. "Never mind. I'm fine. How are you?"

"I'm doing well."

"Clearly. I've heard talk about the tire bill you've been shopping around. Oh, and I understand congratulations are in order."

Leighton shrugged. "Thanks. If we can get pull it together, we're thinking of getting married in the spring."

Andrea frowned. "Wait, you're engaged?"

"Yes."

"To who?"

Really? "Thomas Moran." A thought occurred to her. "If you didn't know about my engagement, why were you congratulating me?"

"I was talking about the list."

Leighton froze. "The Top One Hundred Lobbyists?"

Every year, policymakers on the Hill curated a list of the city's top lobbyists. It was a prestigious listing and hard to crack if you were under fifty. Year after year, most of the same names appeared. She'd never made public her desire to be on the list, but she'd wanted the recognition.

Badly.

"How did you find out? They aren't releasing it until next month."

But she already knew the answer to that. Andrea Ferris was an institution in DC politics. She knew everyone and everything that happened in their small, incestuous world.

"So, I made it?"

"You made it, doll."

Leighton pulled Andrea into a hug, laughing as happiness spilled forth from her.

"It's just an honor to be considered," she finally said, with a small, knowing smile.

"Bullshit. You've wanted to be on that list ever since you started working as a lobbyist."

"You're right. I did."

Andrea's face withered into sober lines. "Now, about this engagement—"

"You don't approve." It wasn't a question.

"I don't," Andrea said plainly. "He's not the one for you."

"That's an interesting position to take considering you introduced us."

"He's the managing director for a large, distinguished investment firm. He was fine to date, especially when you wanted a suitable escort to events around the city. But long term?" Andrea shook her head. "He isn't in your league. You need someone to challenge you, someone to arouse your passions—"

Unbidden, an image of Jonathan flashed in her mind. The way he'd stared at her mouth like it was a gourmet feast and he hadn't eaten in a month. She lifted her chin. "The last thing I'll ever consider when it comes to my future is passion."

"I've seen you together. You don't love him."

She brushed that off. "In DC, people get married for lots of reasons." Power. Access. Branding. "Love is way down on the list."

"Don't you want more for yourself? Do you want to wake up five years from now and realize you've made a mistake? That you settled out of disappointment, hurt and anger?" Andrea's tone could just as easily been used to soothe a skittish mare.

Leighton adjusted her stance, shifting her weight onto her back leg and crossing her arms. "Marrying Thomas will give me exactly what I want."

"Which is what?" Andrea narrowed her eyes. "I used to know."

A way to build her own legacy. She no longer thought it enough just to be the daughter of Gene and Beverly Clarke. Though the world didn't know it, the association, especially given what she now knew, sullied her soul.

"What are you doing over here?" Leighton asked, seeking to change the subject. "You're a long way from Capitol Hill."

Andrea looked away, running an unnecessary hand over her smooth hair. "I was having lunch with a friend."

"Have you started dating again? Good for you."

Andrea's wife died two years ago from breast cancer. She still wore her wedding ring.

The door to the restaurant swung wide, surprising both women. A tall, middle-aged brunette stepped out.

"That must be an extremely long cigarette, Andrea." The woman's eyes widened when they landed on Leighton.

Oh. My. God.

Leighton was sure she mirrored the other woman's expression.

"Governor Wittig, it's a pleasure to meet you. My name is—"

"Leighton Clarke." Wittig took her hand. "I know who you are. Andrea speaks of you constantly."

"She does?"

"You have a fan in her."

Leighton shot a look at Andrea. "The feeling is mutual."

"I've met your parents. Good people. Your father was a brilliant man."

Leighton didn't even flinch. "Thank you."

"How's your mother?"

"Good. Traveling."

"One of the perks of retiring from public office. I plan to take full advantage of it if I ever decide to follow suit."

Leighton glanced at the signage above the restaurant. "I thought you were allergic to seafood, Andrea."

Wittig answered for her. "We weren't here for the cuisine."

The two women shared a look.

It clicked then.

The smile that crossed the governor's face confirmed when she knew that Leighton had figured it out. "It's off the beaten path, and at this point, secrecy is of the utmost importance."

"I understand."

Wittig turned to Andrea. "Are you considering her for the team?"

"Possibly." Andrea winked at Leighton. "I'll try to convince her."

Wittig nodded. "That's good. With the people you know and the connections you have, you'd be an asset." She clapped her hands together. "Make it happen, Andrea, then come back inside. I only have fifteen minutes before I have to leave. It was a pleasure to meet you, Leighton."

Wittig re-entered the restaurant.

Excitement hummed in Leighton's body. "The rumors are true? She's going to run?"

"Nothing's been decided—"

"Oh, come on. How many times have I listened to your stories recounting the beginning of a campaign? And since you haven't worked on a state race since your early days . . ."

"We're talking. We have another year before she

needs to declare anything. Right now, we're just laying out a strategy." Andrea reached into her fitted suit jacket and pulled out a pack of cigarettes. She shook one loose. "Are you interested?"

"In what?"

"Say something was happening—and I'm not saying it is. Would you be interested?"

There was a time when she would've jumped at the opportunity. But that was before she'd been able to see past the illusion of service and learned it was all about power.

"Thanks for the offer, but no."

"Working on a national campaign is something you've always wanted to do."

"Not anymore. Besides, as you mentioned, my career is flourishing, especially with this big client I've taken on."

"Concord Tires." Andrea shook her head. "You know that's not going to end well, right?"

Leighton narrowed her eyes. "What are you talking about?"

"You've managed to keep it hidden, but you have to be concerned about their safety, with the tires over-inflating and explod—"

"Do you have the entire city under surveillance?"

"Do you want to be called in front of a judicial committee?" Andrea fired back.

"No! And I won't. By the time the rollout begins, Concord will have fixed the problem."

"You hope."

"I'm a lobbyist, not an engineer. If there are mechanical issues, they have nothing to do with me."

"This isn't like you."

"It's not how I used to be. It's who I am now."

"I know when you found out about your parents—"

Resentment thickened her throat. "I don't want to talk about it."

"I respected that for a while and maybe my leaving you alone with regards to Thomas and your parents, not saying my piece, did you more harm than good."

Leighton's blood simmered. "I said I don't want to talk about it."

"Have you talked to your mother?"

"Andrea, you want to stay my friend? Stay the fuck out of it!"

Andrea's mouth dropped open. Raising both brows, she nodded and held her hands up, palms out. "Fine." She lit her cigarette, inhaled and blew out a stream of smoke. "As for Wittig, you don't have to make up your mind right now. Take some time. Think about it."

"I don't need to think about it. I'm not interested." Leighton glanced at her watch. She'd have to call Herb now if she didn't want to be late for her afternoon meetings. Who did *she* have to lobby to get another couple of hours added on to the day? "I've got to go."

"We're not done talking about Thomas and your engagement."

"Yes, we are."

"Doll, I love you like you're my own daughter and I'm

concerned about you. The engagement, Concord Tires . . . Are you sure you want to go down this path?"

The image of the intense look on Jonathan's face when he slid the engagement ring on her finger flashed in her mind. Her heart thrashed against her ribcage. She smothered the image.

"My life is exactly how I want it. I wouldn't change a thing."

Chapter Four

JONATHAN SHOVELED HIS hands through his hair and pulled. He'd trade a non-vital organ for a moment of quiet.

The restaurant's front door opened and a short, stocky guy poked his hard-hat-covered head in, bright orange construction headphones hugging his neck.

Anticipation galvanized Jonathan's pulse. "Wayne, you guys finished? Are you finally ready to take the scaffolding down from in front of my door?"

The metal poles had been there so long it was starting to look like an architectural feature of the building.

Karl hadn't been enthused about *that* design detail, either.

The construction had been going on outside his restaurant for the past three months. He'd thought opening *Quartet* had been tough. He'd thought garnering three Michelin stars had been hell on earth. Both had been child's play compared to trying to open a restaurant in the nation's capital. Between permitting delays, updating the historic building to make it a viable space to house a restaurant, and a legal dispute he had to settle between an adjacent property owner and the previous owner of the space, a restaurant that should've launched two months ago was still struggling to open.

In the beginning, as he'd faced interruption after interruption, he'd been furious. Now, the inevitability of another setback had reduced his anger to a dulled acceptance. He'd gotten to know the crew pretty well by now.

Wayne scratched his temple. "We were close . . ."

"But—" Jonathan prompted, hands on his hips.

"There's a broken water main half a block down. The city sent a crew to fix it, but they have to dig up the pipe and, well . . ."

Jonathan's rage threatened to bubble back to the surface, but he took a second. Inhaled. It wouldn't help to yell at the man. This wasn't his fault. "Tell me."

"The street out here is going to be a war zone for the next four days. Once they're done, we can assess the damage and give you a better idea of when we can finally be done."

He shook his head. There wasn't anything he could do about it. Just another situation in the odyssey to open this godforsaken restaurant.

"Just let me know as soon as possible. You need to be

outta here by next week, so we can get to work on the signage."

"We'll try." Wayne looked around the space. "It looks great in here. Things are finally coming together."

"Thanks." Jonathan gripped the back of a nearby bar stool so tightly, his knuckles whitened. "Are you done for the night?"

"About another half an hour."

"Make sure you stop around back before you go. I'll have one of the prep cooks make up some boxes for you and the crew."

"Thanks, Chef. You're the best."

Jonathan's reluctant smile faded when Wayne disappeared back outside. Fuck non-vital organs. Were there semi-vital organs? What about his pancreas? Yeah, he'd give his pancreas for peace and no more complications with this restaurant.

He could leave, but where would he go? His new house? It was a beautiful place, a smart investment, but it wasn't home. His restaurants were home. His kitchens were home. Plus, there was no way in hell he could be anywhere else when the time to open *Sedici* was winding down with an alarming quickness.

"What about that space in Adams Morgan? No, the other one." Zach Dalman, his business partner in the newly formed D&M Restaurant Group, pushed through the swinging door into the dining room from the kitchen.

It looked like that "discussion" about the expensive floor change would happen now.

"I need those numbers as soon as possible." Zach ended the call and slid his phone into the front pocket of his slacks. He settled his hand on his hips and glanced around. "It's looking good."

Jonathan shook his head. "No it's not."

"No, it's not," Zach parroted, "but there's activity and people buzzing around, so that's a good sign. Is it going to be done in three weeks?"

His voice seemed to suggest he thought the possibility was unlikely.

"What if we aren't?"

Zach hefted a blond brow. "Excuse me? September 9. That's the date. We can't miss it. Failure is not an option."

They were opening a restaurant, not starting out on a black ops mission and Jonathan wouldn't open if the restaurant wasn't ready. He'd only get one chance to make his first impression to the city. And with all he'd already accomplished, much would be expected from his DC debut.

"What would it cost us to defer a week?"

"Over and above the two million we're already spending?" Zach scratched his cheek. "It doesn't matter. We can't postpone the opening."

"But if we have to?" Jonathan persisted.

"We have eight hundred reservations. If you cancel them, you can forget about getting them back."

Zach was right. Jonathan sighed. "It'll be done. Even if I have to do everything myself."

Zach motioned toward the front door. "What's going on outside?"

Jonathan explained the situation.

"We've had the worst luck trying to open this place! What the fuck did you do to get on DC's bad side?"

Lust after his future sister-in-law?

"Maybe the city is trying to tell you something."

Stop picturing Leighton Clarke naked? Keep your hands to yourself? "It'll work out."

"It'd better. Because this is it."

"I know, I know."

"No, I mean it."

Something in Zach's voice chilled him.

They'd designed their partnership so their roles were clearly defined: Jonathan handled the management of the restaurant; Zach handled the business. But the essential component of their successful association was the respect each had for the strengths the other brought to the table.

"What's going on?" Jonathan rubbed his temple.

Zach's gaze was steady. "If we don't open on our date in three weeks, we don't open."

"Why?"

"A clause in the contract. Do you know how many restaurants open in DC? How many close? The sale of the building was contingent on the restaurant opening before a date certain. September 14 is that date."

"Why would you agree to that?"

"Because the minute you saw this space, you wanted it and nothing else would do. There's no way we could've foreseen a need to delay the opening twice."

"That wasn't our fault!"

"It doesn't matter. The money we've put in, the money we got from Adam and Mike, it's all gone. Do you want to go back to them and ask for more money for another space?"

Fuck no.

Zach looked around. "Probably not a good time to decide to put a new floor in when nothing was wrong with the original one."

And there it was.

He didn't have the time or the patience to deal with this right now, especially on top of everything else that was happening.

"I didn't decide shit. That was Karl."

"Uh-huh." Zach's phone rang. He pulled it out and checked the caller ID. "I have to take this."

Jonathan clenched his jaw, but nodded.

Zach plugged one ear with his finger. "Talk to me," he barked into his phone while moving several feet away.

"Chef?" Robby, the front-of-the-house manager, hurried over, carrying two clothing options for the wait-staff. "The mockups of the uniforms came in. Which do you prefer?"

Now that Jonathan saw them in person, the choice was obvious. He pointed to the winning garment.

"I'll put the order in for these right now," the manager said. "If I hurry, I can catch them on the West Coast before their business office closes."

Zach rejoined him, nodding to the departing manager. "I've got to fly up to New York, but I'll be back on Monday. I have faith in you. Let's get this done."

He squeezed Jonathan's shoulder and headed out the front entrance, dodging the pandemonium of the construction, his phone already re-attached to his ear.

"A moment, Chef?" His sous chef, Nyah Gibson, stood in the entryway to the kitchen, one hip bracing the swinging door open.

Fuck it. Forget about non-vital or semi. Vital it was. Kidney or liver? Which one could he give away for the greatest amount of peace?

He pinched the bridge of his nose, closed his eyes and inhaled. Although the peace he sought failed to materialize, he focused on his second in command. "What's up?"

She jerked a thumb over her shoulder. "We've got a problem."

Clenching his jaw, he hurried into the state-of-the-art kitchen he'd lovingly crafted. The gleaming stainless steel, industrial grade ranges, grills, ovens and coolers. He may have trusted Karl with the front of the house, but the conception of the kitchen was all him.

Members of his cooking staff gathered around the main attraction.

Elaine, one of his *entremetiers*, jabbed a finger at Miguel, a *rotisseur*. "—get your shit together."

"Girl, please. My shit is soigné," Miguel said, motioning as if to brush dirt off his shoulder.

"Asshole, *please*." Elaine mocked him and swept a tattooed arm in the grill's direction. "Chef sent back three of your veal chops because they were over. I had to refire my swiss chard and my mushrooms. That fucks up my flow."

Miguel grabbed his crotch. "I can get you flowing right."

A chorus of "oohs" inflated the air.

Elaine pushed her bottom lip forward in a pout. "Not even with your momma's mouth."

Laughter, wolf whistles and claps of appreciation. Elaine executed a bow.

Heat blossomed on Miguel's tanned face. "Don't talk about my mot—"

"Enough!" Jonathan settled his hands on his hips and blew out an impatient breath.

Everyone froze. Then, like a scene played in reverse, respect reinforced postures, erased glee from faces and urged cooks back to their stations.

The reaction didn't surprise him; his presence demanded it. His staff understood the importance of granting him the deference an executive chef was due in his kitchen.

"You two done?"

Though Elaine's almond-shaped black eyes clashed with Miguel's round brown ones, they both smartly kept their comments to themselves and said, "*Oui*, Chef!"

Emphatic. Definitive. In unison. The way it was done in the kitchen.

He studied the offending cooks. "This is prep. It's

only going to get harder. If you can't cut it now, you won't make it to opening night. Are we clear?"

"*Oui*, Chef!"

He sent Elaine and Miguel back to their respective stations, then turned to look at his sous chef. "You couldn't handle this?"

Gib crossed her arms over her black tank top. "Of course I could. Who do you think *has* been handling it?"

"This isn't the first time?"

She gave him a look like he'd just grown a brussels sprout–sized head from the side of his neck. "This has been going on for weeks."

"Fuck."

"Exactly." She used her forearm to wipe the sweat from her brow, her mop of curls clinging to her temple. "That's part of the problem. They're getting bored, restless."

"This is a restaurant, not the setting for a fucking soap opera!"

"Come on, Chef. You know better than that."

That was his business side talking, but the cook side of him did know. And understood. Working long hours in quarters where there was no such thing as privacy or personal space yielded a thick as blood camaraderie, but also led to personality clashes of epic proportions.

"Thanks for bringing me up to speed. I'll take care of it."

"I didn't tell you because I need you to 'take care of it.' I told you so you'd know you aren't the only one affected by this delay. We may lose some of these people and that would be a shame. Despite what you just saw, they're all really good."

High praise from Gib. Many glimpsed her petite stature and big doe eyes and committed the unpardonable sin of underestimating her. Some even exacerbated the initial error by mistaking her kindness for weakness. It was a miscalculation they all lived to regret. He'd once seen her excoriate a burly line cook with her sharp tongue and superior knife skills.

For four years, she'd worked for him at *Quartet*, progressing through the ranks from prep cook to *entremetier* to *rotisseur*. When he'd decided to open the restaurant in DC, he'd approached her with the choice of being *Quartet*'s new sous chef—an opening that would arise when he promoted his current sous chef to chef de cuisine—or following him across the country to be his sous chef at *Sedici*.

Her decision told him a lot about her goals, her ambition and her mindset and confirmed that he'd made the right decision selecting her. Understanding that the possibility was high for him to venture into opening more restaurants, she knew she'd rise to chef de cuisine much faster here than if she'd stayed in San Francisco and waited her turn.

"I hear you." He checked his watch. "Tell Isaac to put together some food for the construction crew, then have everyone finish up in here and head home. You and I can meet in the morning and go over the punch list for the next three weeks."

"*Oui*, Chef." Gib smiled and bumped her shoulder against his side.

He pushed out of the kitchen, a smile expressing his unexpectedly buoyant mood. His restaurant might not open on time, he might lose the space, but he was confident Gib would develop into an amazing sous chef.

He heard steps in the main dining room. What *now*? If Wayne was coming back to tell him the work would be more extensive than they thought and they needed to tear up the entire block, taking *Sedici* with it, Jonathan was going to fucking lose it and it wouldn't be pretty.

Leighton stood there, looking around, a portion of her lower lip restrained by her teeth. She wore a simple ivory fitted dress that showcased her breasts and ass in a way that made him want to drop to his knees and thank whichever deity had created her. How in the hell was he supposed to resist her when she showed up like a pretty package he couldn't wait to unwrap?

You can do it, man. Don't get sucked in. She is not for you.

Would the Jedi mind trick work if he didn't wave his hand?

"Hey."

Her eyes shot to him and she exhaled silently between parted lips. "Hi."

He moved closer. "Are you meeting Thomas here? I thought he was in London?"

"He is." Her tongue swept across her bottom lip. Fuck! "I left my bracelet here the other evening. I'm meeting our wedding planner at eight and her office is nearby. I thought I'd stop in and pick it up on my way."

Considering he was harder than the marble counter on his bar, he'd only heard "bracelet . . . here . . . meeting . . . eight."

Her bracelet? Right. "I don't have it. I sent it over to Thomas's office yesterday morning."

"Oh." She fumbled with the handle on the large leather bag that hung from her wrist. One of those expensive ones that women in this city seemed to love and that probably cost tens of thousands of dollars.

He didn't have what she needed, in more ways than one. He should smile and send her on her way. That was the safest, wisest course of action.

He glanced at his watch. "It's only seven-thirty. Why don't you stay and have a drink?"

What the fuck was he doing?

"I don't know . . ."

That's right, Leighton. Save both of us. Do the right thing. Lord knows he wasn't capable of it.

"Okay. But just one."

He gestured for her to precede him to the bar. Bad move. Her ass, in that dress . . .

They were tempting fate and he knew by the way she frowned and continued to fidget with her purse that he wasn't the only one to recognize this. While he wasn't willing to pull a one-eighty and abruptly ask her to leave, he could put them back on the footing with which they were both more comfortable.

"Isn't eight at night a little late to be meeting your wedding planner?"

"She's in demand. Kimberly Reed is *the* premier planner for the under-forty crowd in DC. She's done the weddings for some of the oldest families in the city, as well as some of the younger senators and even the secretary of state's oldest son."

Jonathan rolled his eyes.

"Not impressed?" Surprisingly, she didn't sound offended, only amused.

"The idea of hiring a society wedding planner makes me break out in hives." He grasped the back of one of the wheat colored tufted leather swiveled bar stools Karl had lost his shit over. "Have a seat."

She did and her scent tickled his nose. When he turned her to face the bar, his fingers skimmed her bare shoulders and she shivered. He closed his eyes briefly, gathered his self-control like a shield then headed behind the bar.

She cleared her throat. "Never getting married?"

"I don't know. But if I do, I might consider what my two best friends did. They had these small, intimate celebrations. I liked those."

Small and intimate hadn't meant inexpensive. Mike and Indi had flown twenty of their closest friends and family to Koh Som, a small private island in the Gulf of Thailand. By comparison, Adam and Chelsea's wedding could've been deemed tame as it was held at their home in the San Mateo mountains. However, a decadent menu, luxurious flowers and a lavish, personalized decor, made the event anything but bland, landing it on the cover of *People* magazine four months ago.

"What can I get for you?"

An elegant brow lifted. "You're going to serve me?"

"I do it all." He reached beneath the bar for a towel and slung it over his shoulder.

"I bet you do," she murmured.

He stiffened. Had she actually said that or had his fantasy life taken over for a brief moment? He glanced at her, but her cool expression gave nothing away.

"Special service from a James Beard Award–winning chef. I'll try to contain myself."

"I'm sure my brother didn't waste his breath extolling my achievements, so you've been checking up on me?"

He braced his arms against the bar and her eyes followed the motion, lingering. He could barely breathe. He had to force the oxygen into his body. No other woman had ever affected him in this way. Why her? He didn't understand it.

She averted her gaze. "I check on everyone who comes into my life."

He frowned. "I was just joking."

"I wasn't." She placed her purse on the bar stool next to her.

Interesting. That type of vigilance made for a very lonely existence. And it wasn't natural. Something had happened to make her believe such action was necessary. However, he didn't get the feeling she would be amenable to sharing that information with him.

He straightened. "Now, about that drink . . . a cosmo, apple-tini, strawberry daiquiri?"

She exhaled and her lips quirked. "I appreciate you offering me some of *your* personal favorites, but I'll take a Macallan 21 on the rocks."

He hesitated. "You drink whiskey?"

It was rare, but he did know a few women who enjoyed the smooth spirit. He suspected his disbelief would annoy her.

He was right.

"Sexist, much?"

"Maybe, but it's borne out by my fifteen years in the restaurant business."

"Isn't it wonderful to still be able to discover something new after all that time? An old dog can still learn . . . something." Her sweet smile had him struggling to contain his grin.

He grabbed a lowball glass off the stack, added a couple of ice cubes and poured the drink. "M'lady."

She took a sip. Her lashes fluttered and her jaw moved laterally as she coated her tongue with the flavors. The blood rushed straight to his dick again—it must have an E-Z pass—leaving him momentarily light-headed. Thank God he was standing behind the bar.

She set the glass down on the black cocktail napkin

he'd provided. "What do you drink besides your be-loved apple-tinis?"

She had jokes. One corner of his mouth tipped upward. That's all he'd allow her. "Macallan's good, but I prefer bourbon. Jefferson's Presidential Select."

"I've heard good things about Jefferson but I've never had the opportunity to try some," Leighton said. "The stock is limited, right?"

"Yes, but I tracked down a case of the Seventeen." He smiled, recalling the night he'd shared a bottle with Adam and Mike last year. "I'd be willing to part with a little bit."

Silence met his offer. Then—"Maybe I can get Thomas to try it. He tends to stick to craft beers."

His brother.

Her fiancé.

Right.

Big guilt keep on churning . . .

He turned to put the bottle he'd used on the back bar shelf where it belonged. "Yeah, well, my brother's taste has always left a lot to be desired."

Only after the words were out did he realize how they sounded. He turned back in time to see the hurt on her face morph to anger. "I'm sorry. That's not what I meant."

Her expression cut into him like an extremely sharp gyuto knife. She held up a hand as if to halt his words. "Then it's a good thing your opinion makes no differ-ence to our life at all."

"No seriously. Leighton." He rushed around the bar and reached for the hand that had fallen to her lap. He didn't question his need for her to understand his words weren't aimed at her. He dipped his head until he forced her to meet his eyes. "I swear, I wasn't talking about you. My brother should be on his knees kissing someone's ass every day, thanking his lucky stars that you've agreed to marry him."

She stared at him, stone faced, and he feared he may have ruined whatever accord they'd managed to form.

Which was probably for the best.

But when her features began to soften and forgiveness seemed to follow, relief made him giddy and he couldn't have stopped what he did next even if his very survival depended on it.

One taste. That's all he needed.

He touched his lips to hers.

Time stopped.

He'd been wrong. He'd need much, much more.

He deepened the kiss, tasting, nibbling then moaning when her lips parted and she let him in. Her soft tongue glided against his and desire roared through him.

Her arms snaked around his waist and clutched his ass. She scooted forward on the stool, spreading her thighs and pulling him between them. His fingers skimmed along her jaw and slid through her hair, like air moving against silk.

His heart was pounding so loudly it drowned out any protests his rational mind tried to put forth. He didn't care who she was, who he was, or why this could never be. He'd never experienced this kind of raw passion with anyone and in that moment, his only concern was giving her as much pleasure as she was giving him.

"Chef, do you want us to leave you—" Gib's voice acted as fingers on a chalkboard, jarring and cringe-worthy.

Leighton's eyes flew open, and fear and disgust contorted her features. She pushed against his chest, catching him off guard, and he fell back into a neighboring bar stool.

Before he could process what was happening, she'd jumped from the stool and was running—quite a feat in her heels—to the front door.

He hurried after her. "Leighton!"

She pushed out into the night and paused looking left and right.

He saw the metal scaffolding falling and a roaring filled his ears.

Oh no! No! GODDAMMIT!!

He started to run. "Leighton, wait!"

He was too late.

Chapter Five

As LONG AS he lived, Jonathan didn't think he'd ever forget what he saw outside of his restaurant.

Even now, hours later, as he shifted on the torture device known as the hospital waiting room chair, he couldn't prevent the images from playing on a loop in his mind.

The metal scaffolding crashing down on her head.

The way her body seemed to liquefy and melt to the ground.

The feeling of absolute helplessness that swamped him when no latent superpowers roared to life, enabling him to get to her before she fell.

What happened after he reached her—crouched next to her motionless body—was a blur: the babble of the construction workers surrounding them, shouting orders at Gib, the sirens of the various emergency response vehicles, riding in the ambulance with Leighton.

Never once did she regain consciousness. He'd clasped her limp hand between his and fervently bargained to any higher power listening that he'd give everything he owned for her to wake up and verbally kick his ass one more time.

Turmoil and confusion reigned when they'd gotten to the hospital. From the moment the ambulance doors opened and his feet hit the ground, the ER doctor and nurses bombarded him with questions:

What happened?

Did she lose consciousness immediately after the accident?

For how long?

Does she have a history of seizures?

Had she been drinking?

Had she taken any mind-altering drugs, like marijuana or cocaine?

He was able to answer the ones pertaining to the accident, but the ones about her personal life . . . He'd realized he didn't know much about her.

Except the way she tasted.

He answered as best he could, especially once he heard the EMT refer to him as the patient's fiancé. Had he told them that? He must've, and his admission that he was with her, as well as his behavior toward her, had probably bolstered his assertion and explained the access and information he'd been thus far granted.

His phone rang. It was about fucking time. Unfortunately, his brother's face wasn't the one staring at him from the caller ID screen.

Mike Black's voice boomed through the connection. "I know it's late your time, but I figured with the restaurant hours you keep, you'd be up. How are things going? Still opening in three weeks?"

Jonathan stood, stretched out the kinks and withdrew to a small alcove to take the call, away from the other people in the waiting area. "That's the plan. I know I've changed it twice before, but this is it."

He had no other choice.

"I remember what you went through with *Quartet*, so I'm not surprised at all of the delays."

"I thought I was prepared, but opening *Sedici* has been a nightmare. Still, with it being so close to Indi's due date, I don't expect you guys to come."

"Now that's some shit! You're revoking my invitation?"

"Don't be an asshole."

Mike laughed. "I'll be there, and despite my best efforts to convince her otherwise, Indi's determined to join me."

What? "I thought it'd be just you and only for the evening?"

"Not if Indi comes."

"That can't be safe for her. You're going to let her do that?"

"Have you met my wife? Do you think I *let* her do anything?"

Fair point. "And her doctor agreed?"

"Dr. Kimball isn't enthused, but this is our first baby

and likely to be late, anyway. We won't be able to fly commercial but that's not a big deal. We'll come over with Adam and Chelsea on a private plane and Dr. Kimball has already referred us to an area doctor when we get to DC. We'll cover our bases and make sure everything is okay."

Jonathan rocked back on his heels and almost rolled his ankle. Startled, and a bit shaken, he stared down at the clogs on his feet and realized he hadn't changed from his kitchen footwear back into his regular shoes.

For fuck's sake.

He pressed his thumb and forefinger over his closed eyes and attempted to rejoin the conversation.

"You're going through a hell of a lot. You don't have to do this."

"Adam and I were there for the opening of *Quartet* and we'll be there for *Sedici*. We're making it a tradition. We vow to attend the openings of every new restaurant you add to your portfolio."

"But Indi and the baby—"

"Indi said she'd be pissed forever if we stayed home and nothing happened. And a forever-pissed Indi? Not interested. We'll be there."

Relief stealthily quieted his nerves. "Thanks, man."

When Adam, founder and CFO of Computronix, the country's fastest-growing tech firm, had introduced the HPC to the world, Jonathan had flown back west to be at the presentation. Ditto for the celebration where Mike, Computronix's COO, had announced the company's new deal with telecommunications giant, TTL, to purchase exclusive rights to their cable programming. The opening of *Sedici* was just as important to his career as those announcements had been to theirs and selfishly he wanted his friends by his side. It wouldn't be the same without them.

Above him, the intercom system sounded.

"Paging Dr. Carillo. Dr. Carillo to trauma room four, stat. Dr. Carillo to trauma room four, stat."

"You're not at the restaurant." Mike's controlled tone decayed with worry. "Where are you?"

Jonathan sighed. He'd hoped to avoid this conversation. "I'm at the hospital."

"Is everything okay?" A sense of urgency joined the worry. "Are you hurt?"

"No, not me."

"Who then? Your parents? Thomas?"

"It's Leighton." His throat tightened and he forced the words through the obstruction and out into the air. "She was in an accident."

"Leighton? The lobbyist? Your brother's fiancée?"

"Yeah."

"Shit! Is she going to be okay?"

"I don't know. I'm still waiting to hear from the doctor."

A pause. "*You're* waiting? Where's Thomas?"

"He's not here."

"I'm confused." A state he knew Mike detested. "Leighton was in an accident, but *you're* at the hospital with her, not Thomas."

"She was with me when it happened. At the restaurant."

When Mike didn't immediately respond, Jonathan rushed on. "Thomas is in London. Leighton stopped by the restaurant to get her bracelet and . . . I said something I shouldn't have and I . . ." Fuck! Why did he have to kiss her? He'd known it was wrong, but he'd done it anyway. And now . . . "She ran out of *Sedici* and that's when it happened."

"I'm sorry." Mike's sympathy served the twin roles of making him feel better—because he knew he had his friend's support—and making him feel worse—because he knew he didn't deserve it. "Are you okay?"

Not really. "I just wish I knew how she was doing."

"You know this isn't your fault, right?"

"Mike—"

"You said it yourself: it was an accident. Don't let your brother get to you."

"I won't."

Mike continued as if Jonathan had never spoken. "If he got a paper cut he'd blame you because you use paper, too."

Any other time he would've laughed. But not this time. Not about Leighton.

"Can you blame him? She got hurt while she was with me."

"Is she a woman or a puppy?"

Jonathan's gaze flicked skyward. "You know what I mean. She's his fiancée and I . . ."

You just had to taste her. Mouth whatever platitudes necessary, but they're only excuses for you doing what you'd wanted to do from the first moment you saw her.

"Dude, did you intend to hurt Leighton?"

His heart clenched in his chest. "Of course not!"

"Adam would say a key component of the definition for *accident* is that there's no intent. No plan to cause harm. You didn't mean to hurt Leighton. So don't let Thomas blame you, okay?"

That sounded exactly like something Adam would say. He fought the smile that wanted to break free. "I'll try."

"Let me know if you need anything. And I'll call Adam so you don't have to recite the story again."

"I appreciate that."

"Keep us updated."

Jonathan disconnected the call and slid the phone into his pocket. He crossed his arms over his chest, his feet at the ankles and let his head fall back against the wall. He closed his eyes and tried to block out the sounds around him. The people scurrying past, the murmur of voices from the waiting room, the drone of the TV, the whine of children who didn't want to be there.

"I feel you," he said to the baby crying somewhere nearby.

His phone rang again. Either Mike had more advice for him or Adam had decided to get the information straight from the source. But when he saw his brother's information on the caller ID, his chest tightened.

Slow your roll. No need to go into panic mode and spill your guts. You don't know anything.

"Hey."

"What happened?" Thomas's voice was stern and brusque.

He took a deep breath. "Leighton was in an accident."

"Oh my God. How serious was it?"

Thomas's tone mingled with Jonathan's own feelings of responsibility and reduced him to a little boy being questioned by his big brother.

"Pretty serious." He nudged a seam in the vinyl flooring with the toe of his shoe.

"What about the driver? Hank? Harold? Something like that. Is he okay?"

"It wasn't a car accident. She was leaving the restaurant and some metal piping fell on her head."

"Are you kidding me?"

He could hear the disbelief in his brother's voice, and the weighty pause as his mind worked to find the connections that would somehow make this Jonathan's fault.

"No. It was a freak accident."

"The only kind that always seem to happen when you're around."

And there it was.

"Oh, come on," Jonathan said, incredulous that Thomas was bringing up the time he'd jumped from a tire swing, forcing the tire to rebound and hit Thomas in the eye.

Hence the stitches above his brow. "You really want to bring that up now? We were kids."

"I'm not bringing up anything. I'm just saying that I've been with Leighton for almost two years and she never got hurt while she was with me."

Heat suffused him. "Since we're drawing thin lines of fault, what about yours? She shouldn't have been with me. I couriered you her bracelet yesterday morning before you flew to London. Any reason you failed to mention that when you talked to her? Maybe if you had, she wouldn't have needed to stop by the restaurant and she wouldn't have gotten in the accident."

Yeah, because if she'd never been there, you wouldn't have kissed her and she wouldn't have run away from you, failing to pay attention to where she was going.

"You're an asshole," Thomas said, his words dripping with irritation. "Where is she?"

"They're still examining her. I've been waiting for a while." Which reminded him—"What took you so long to return my call?"

"What?"

"I've been calling and texting you for the past two hours. Why didn't you get back to me?"

Another heavy silence and then—"I was busy."

"But I said it was urgent and asked you to call me back."

"And I would've if you'd told me Leighton had been in an accident."

The subtext was clear. At first he hadn't understood

why Thomas wasn't returning his calls. Then he'd figured it out: Thomas had thought he'd been the one in trouble and helping Jonathan wasn't worth his time.

He tried not to let the callous behavior hurt, but it seared through him, flesh, bone and marrow.

"It's not the sort of news you deliver via text or leave on a voice message. I actually thought it would be better to come from me. Of course, once I realized you were screening my calls, I was left with no other option."

"Surprisingly, this isn't about you."

"What the fuck is *that* supposed to mean?"

"Nothing. Look, the situation here is worse than anyone knew. I just got here. I can't fly back now."

"Your fiancée has been in accident. I think everyone would understand."

"They wouldn't." Thomas gasped. "Shit! What about Leighton's meeting with Kimberly? Did she make it? Did you call her?"

"What is wrong with you?"

"She'll think we stood her up. I'll need to call her." The sounds of typing on a keyboard clicked in the background. "She's booked solid for the next two years. The only reason she agreed to see us is because of Leighton. She'd be devastated if we lost the opportunity to work with Kimberly. I hope she understands."

Jonathan couldn't tell which woman he was referring to.

"Maybe you should worry more about your fiancée and less about the damned wedding planner."

"Mr. Moran?"

He turned to see a young man in scrubs standing in front of oak colored double doors, their smooth surface marred by two narrow rectangular strips of glass. He hurried over.

"Is that the doctor?" Thomas barked in his ear.

Jonathan put the phone on speaker mode.

"How is she?" he asked.

"What's going on?" Thomas burst in.

The doctor frowned and shot a look at the phone.

"Family," he mouthed.

The doctor nodded but spoke to Jonathan. "She's stable for now, but we do have some concerns."

His throat thickened. "What kind of concerns?"

"You told the first responders that she lost consciousness immediately. I'm afraid that state remains unchanged. She's in a coma."

The attitude leached from Thomas's voice. "Oh my God."

Jonathan's bitterness toward his brother wasn't far behind. The shock and agony he felt was probably a fraction of what his brother experienced.

"We've conducted a CT scan and an MRI and there aren't any lesions or lacerations on her brain, although there is some slight swelling in the medial temporal lobe. We've done what we can to alleviate the pressure."

The words slithered into his body and stole his breath. Swelling in the brain? That sounded serious.

Oh God, what had he done?

"Is she going to be okay?" Thomas asked.

Jonathan had misplaced his ability to speak.

"We don't know, but since she isn't in any distress, we'll transfer her to the ICU and keep an eye on her." The doctor squeezed Jonathan's shoulder. "Just give us some time to move her and I'll have a nurse inform you when you can see your fiancée."

Right.

"Doctor"—ah, there it was—"I'm not—"

"What he means is we're not able to thank you enough," Thomas said, his voice booming through the speaker.

The doctor, having delivered his news and ready to move on, nodded and headed back to the double doors. He swiped a small white card against a silver square on the wall and disappeared from sight before the sluggish panel completed its opening.

Jonathan took Thomas off speaker. "What the fuck was that about?"

An older woman glared at him and clutched her purse tighter to her chest. He gave her his best charming smile and headed back to the alcove he'd recently abandoned.

"You know how I said the situation was worse here than I expected?" Thomas said.

"Yes. I'm not an idiot. You just mentioned it."

"It's really bad."

Was Thomas really trying to justify a decision not to come home? His brother was unbelievable.

"Did you hear what he said?" Jonathan flung an arm

toward the double doors that had swallowed the ER doctor. "Leighton is in a *coma*. With a *swollen. Brain.*" He emphasized the pertinent words, in case his brother hadn't initially understood their importance.

Thomas cleared his throat. "I can't come back."

Shock freeze-dried his insides.

"You mean they'd prefer it if you stayed but you'll explain the situation and hop your ass on the next available plane so you can be here with your fiancée."

"I can't. The new system needs to be in place before the end of the fiscal year."

"They can have someone else handle it."

"If they send someone else, I can kiss this partnership goodbye. I've given that firm ten years of my life. That partnership is mine."

"Your fiancée is here, fighting for *her* life. You need to be here with her, helping her, not in London."

"Leighton knows how crucial this assignment is. I'll get valuable face time with some of the partners. She'll understand."

"How can she understand? I don't understand. The woman you love, the woman you want to spend the rest of your life with, is in a coma. How can you even think about anything else?"

"You don't know Leighton and you don't know shit about our relationship."

"Enlighten me."

"Not that it's any of your goddamned business, but I asked Leighton to marry me because I respect and admire her, and because we have the potential to become an influential couple in this city."

He'd swoon if he wasn't horrified by what his brother was saying. "I see. And do an acre of land and three cows come with this transaction?"

Where was the love? The passion? And why in the hell would Leighton agree to settle for this eighteenth-century bullshit?

"Spare me your judgment. I know her better than you do. She would support this decision because she knows it's important to my career and what's important for my career is important to our marriage."

Jonathan shook his head. Despite their differences, he'd thought his brother was a better man than this. For years, he'd felt like he was lacking when he compared himself to his brother. But he wouldn't abandon the woman he'd pledged his life to when she needed him most.

Thomas cleared his throat. "I need you to do something for me."

The balls on this guy! Jonathan's top and bottom molars met and tangoed. He tilted his head back. "What?"

"Stay there. Visit her. Do what I would do if I were there."

"You *should* be there!"

"It's impossible."

"Time travel is impossible. Licking your elbow is impossible. Returning home from a business trip when your fiancée is in a coma is very fucking possible."

"Her mother is in Europe. I'll try and get in touch with her, but who knows when she can get back. She has no siblings—"

"Lucky her," he mumbled.

"—and I don't want her to be alone," Thomas concluded.

"But not enough for you to cancel your trip.'

"The doctor called you her fiancé."

He swallowed. "About that . . . I had to tell them—"

"It doesn't matter. Don't correct them. You can be there while I'm gone. When she wakes up, explain the situation. I promise, Leighton will agree this was the right thing to do."

Was he insane? How could he even consider this?

The image of Leighton slumping to the ground.

Her warm body pressed against his, their heated breaths co-mingling as they kissed.

How could he not?

And the thought of Leighton being in the hospital all alone, waking up with no one there . . . It was a fiery poker to the gut. Still—

"I have a restaurant to open in three weeks."

Sensing a crack in the ice, Thomas set about enlarging it. "It's just a couple of hours a day. You stop by. You see how she's doing. You give the hospital your number so they can call you when she wakes up. And when she does, you tell her what happened. I'll have a better chance of getting the time off in a week."

"A week?"

"Two at the most."

Jonathan rubbed his jaw, the scruff bristly against his palm. "I don't know."

"Please. Don't do it for me. Do it for Leighton."

If his brother had said anything else he would've gladly told him to kiss his ass.

But for Leighton . . .

Because Leighton was somewhere in this hospital seriously injured because of him.

Because seeing her hurt had taken a decade off his life.

Because even with everything that happened, he didn't regret seizing the opportunity to kiss her.

And that made him the worst kind of bastard.

Jonathan closed his eyes and exhaled. "Okay, I'll do it."

Chapter Six

SHE WENT FROM unaware to aware in a nanosecond.

Blackness.

Sounds invaded her consciousness first. A rhythmic, high-pitched note. Angry, insistent beeping. Indecipherable voices, whose tones gradually increased in volume only to recede out of her hearing.

On some level came the awareness that she may be able to control the darkness she experienced. She fluttered her eyelids and slowly attempted to open them. The task required a near herculean effort, but she immediately capitulated when assaulted by the piercingly bright light.

She inhaled deeply, her nose twitching at the antiseptic smell, and tried again, prying her eyes open, her body tensing for the anticipated luminous onslaught. This time, the experience wasn't as excruciating, so she squinted her lids without fully closing them. After some time, she let them expand and took in her environment.

She was lying on her back, semi-reclined. Above her, the ceiling consisted of large white squares with what appeared to be dozens of holes in them. Several of the tiles had been swapped out with flat lighting fixtures. Pale colored paint covered the walls and a wood-grained board floated across the foot of the bed. Beyond that, a closed door boasted a rectangular pane of glass that offered a limited view of the space beyond.

Was she in a hospital room? Her left index finger felt slightly compressed. The back of her right hand felt tight. She balled that hand into a fist and felt a pull at her skin.

An IV?

A taped loop of clear tubing ran from her hand, up her forearm . . . She turned her head to see where it led and pain burst through her skull.

Sweet Jesus!

A sound, like that of a wounded animal, erupted in the room.

Was that her?

She tried to lift her arms, to press her hands against her head in an effort to lessen the pain, but she couldn't. Without moving her head, she glanced down and noticed brown leather cuffs, cushioned by white cotton, encircling her wrists. A strap and buckle led from each cuff to somewhere over the sides of the bed, in effect, restraining her.

What in the hell was going on? Forgetting the lesson she'd just learned, she wrenched her head to the side and—

Oh My God!

What happened? Why did her head hurt?

She searched her brain and . . .

Nothing.

Panic seized her lungs, making breath a precious commodity. She concentrated on sucking in as much oxygen as possible even as a more insistent beeping and shrill, grating tone filled the room. She opened her mouth and that wounded animal sound saturated the air before the door opened and a woman, wearing navy blue scrubs with neon green butterflies, strode in. The nurse cupped a light brown hand and moved it under the dispenser mounted on the wall next to the door. A dollop of white foam pooled in her palm. She rubbed her hands together and journeyed over to the bed, the end of her stethoscope bouncing against her ample bosom.

"Good afternoon, Ms. Clarke. Did you enjoy your nap? Here, let me turn this off."

The nurse bent over her to press a button on the machine. It went blessedly silent and she was able to read the name tag clipped to the neon green piping on the woman's scrub top.

Ujala Rajan.

"I'm Nurse Rajan"—she pronounced it *rah-JAHN*—"and I'll be taking care of you today. I need to check your vital signs and your dressing."

Nurse Rajan pulled the clip off her index finger and pressed another button. Something hugged her bicep. Just when the sensation grew uncomfortable, the pressure lessened and another beep sounded.

"Excellent," Nurse Rajan said, uncoiling the stethoscope from around her neck. "I want to listen to your lungs."

She wanted to take her cue from the nurse's confidence and unhurried manner, but each time she tried to access anything regarding why she was in this specific situation, she was met with a void.

Which elevated her stress, making it impossible for her to achieve any level of relaxation.

The nurse ran fingers around her hairline and for the first time she was aware of a dull throb in her forehead.

"The dressing looks good. There's no bleeding or seepage."

She had a bandage? She lifted her arm to feel it and the bite of the cuff reminded her she was being held against her will. She jerked against the restraints, the metal buckles banging against the bedrails.

Nurse Rajan patted her shoulder. "I know, but I can't take those off you yet."

Why in the hell not? She hadn't done anything to warrant this type of treatment.

Had she?

"Everything will be okay, Ms. Clarke," the nurse said, her brown eyes soft, her smile reassuring, "but I need you to calm down."

Didn't the nurse know she *wanted* to calm down? She wanted to—Wait, why did she keep calling her Ms. Clarke?

Was that her name?

A glimmer of recognition, just out of reach. It sounded familiar . . . She reached out a mental hand and—

Yes! Clarke. Her name was Leighton Clarke.

Leighton opened her mouth to share her discovery and even that was difficult. Her mouth felt like something really nasty had died and its rotted corpse had been wrapped in sandpaper and buried in her throat.

Nurse Rajan poured a cup of water and inserted a straw. The head of the bed whirred, raised, and then the nurse was holding the straw to her mouth. Leighton took a sip, the coolness a balm for her tongue. She swallowed and tried again to use her words.

"What—"

The nurse set the cup down and smiled. "You're going to be okay. You were in an accident."

An accident?

She tried to access those memories, but there was no glimmer to reach for.

"Don't—"

"I know." Nurse Rajan walked over to the computer perched atop a rolling cart and began typing in information. "We've been through this several times today."

Several times? Today? So this nurse had been in her room and they'd had this conversation before? What did that mean? Why couldn't she remember?

She tried to ask that question. "Can't remember."

"It's a side effect of the accident."

Nurse Rajan pressed more buttons on various machines around the bed, then input information into the computer.

Leighton had managed to get some answers, but they didn't settle anything for her. They only led to more questions. She started to freak out.

What was going on? Why couldn't she remember?

"Don't know how—"

"I know this is very scary for you, Ms. Clarke, but it's going to be okay," Nurse Rajan repeated. "I've paged your doctor and he'll be along shortly."

As if on cue, the door opened and an attractive blond man walked in, wearing a white lab coat over a light blue shirt, yellow tie and gray slacks.

"You're awake again. That's good. It's happening more and more frequently." He went through the dispenser and white foam routine and moved to her bedside. "I'm Dr. Faber, a neurologist on staff."

He held out his hand and she lifted her arm, drawing his attention to her confinement.

"Needed your approval before they could be removed," Nurse Rajan said.

Dr. Faber nodded and stepped back. "I think it's safe for now. But leave them attached to the bed in case we need them later."

Need them later? Why? What had she done to warrant them in the first place?

As the nurse released her, she rotated her wrists and shrugged her shoulders, trying to take inventory of her movements without jostling the IV in her hand or making any motion with her head.

"Why—"

She swallowed, and this time, instead of offering her the straw, Nurse Rajan surrendered the cup. Leighton took it, enamored with the cool liquid flowing down her throat. After her third long pull, she found her mouth sufficiently lubricated to allow her to speak with less difficulty.

"Why did you restrain me?"

Dr. Faber patted her blanket-covered foot. "It was strictly for your safety, not to punish you. The first couple of times you regained consciousness, you tried to pull out some of the lines we'd inserted for your care."

Leighton rolled her head on the pillow and looked at the doctor. "She said we've talked before. I don't . . . remember."

"I promise to explain everything," Dr. Faber said, his soothing voice as much of a balm as the water, "but first I need to do an examination. Just answer me the best you can."

He wanted to ask her questions? It should be obvious that she didn't know anything. She let her lids close and exhaled her impatience.

"Hey." Another tap on her foot.

Opening her eyes, she met Dr. Faber's direct gaze. "Please?"

She nodded.

"Good. Let's begin. What's today's date?"

Was he joking? "I don't know."

"Where are we right now?"

"The hospital?"

"Which city?"

She let her eyes sweep the room, looking for any identifying information. Finding none, she was helpless to stop the tears from pooling in her eyes.

"Do you know your last name?"

This one she knew. She dashed away the moisture rolling down her cheeks. "Clarke!"

"Can you tell me your full name?"

Yes she could. "Leighton Clarke!"

He dipped his head and smiled. "We're almost done. I'm going to give you three words to remember and I'm going to test you on those words in five minutes. You ready? Dog. Book. Ocean."

Dog. Book. Ocean. She repeated the words silently to herself.

Dr. Faber pressed a button on his watch, then reached into the pocket of his lab coat and pulled out some laminated pages. "Can you read this sentence?"

She did.

"And the one beneath it."

He also had her read the paragraph. Then he asked her to close her eyes, stick out her tongue, point to the door, point to the floor and point to the source of illumination.

The last one took her a moment, but then she pointed to the ceiling light as an insistent beeping emanated from Dr. Faber's watch.

"Do you remember those words I asked you before?" He made notes on his tablet.

She nodded. "Dog. Book. Ocean."

"Good." Blue eyes, enhanced by the color of his shirt, twinkled. "That's really good, Leighton."

She'd recalled three words. Big whoop. She could also see, hear and breathe. None of them felt like monumental accomplishments.

"Why can't I remember what happened or how I got here?"

Dr. Faber closed the cover of his tablet and set it on the rolling overbed table. "We believe you have a condition called retrograde amnesia."

Amnesia? "That's a real thing?"

From the other side of the room Nurse Rajan laughed softly and Dr. Faber smiled. "Yes, it is."

"How? I know who I am. I can remember some things."

"There are different types of amnesia. We determine the type you have based on how your memory has been affected. You can remember how to talk?"

"Obviously."

"Do you recall how to brush your teeth and tie your shoes?"

She paused. "Yes."

"'That's called procedural memory and it's the remem-bered ability to perform tasks." He pointed to his tie. "What color is this?"

Heat flooded her face. "I'm not an idiot."

"I know, but I need you to answer the question."

"It's yellow."

"And the capital of Virginia?"

"Richmond," she answered, beyond annoyed with the pop quiz.

"That's semantic memory, the recollection of facts or information that's common knowledge, not to be con-fused with episodic memory, which is recalling events from your own life."

There was so much information, and trying to take it in, process it and respond was draining. She wished she could go back in time to when she first opened her eyes. The darkness, the quiet, it was much better than this unknowing.

"I don't understand."

"Knowing that basketball is a sport is semantic memory. Recalling what happened at the last Wizards game you attended is episodic memory."

"What does any of this have to do with what's wrong with me?" By the last word, she was shouting.

And paying the price when her head revolted in agony.

"Calm down. Getting upset won't help you and it could make your situation worse. Let's delve into what you recall from your own life. Your parents. Do you know their names?"

A glimmer. She reached for it and saw her mother's beautiful smile and regal dreads, and her father's signature salt-n-pepper goatee and distinguished features. "Gene and Beverly Clarke." A heaviness settled on her chest. "My father recently passed away."

"And what city do you live in?"

Another glimmer. "Washington, DC."

"Do you remember what you did on the morning of Friday, August 18?"

Nothing. "No."

"What about that evening?"

Again, try as she might, there was no glimmer, no spark of recognition. "What's so important about the eighteenth?"

"That was the night of your accident, the night you were admitted."

What had happened to her? She closed her eyes, squeezed them tight, tried to recall the details, but she couldn't. Filled with despair, she pounded her left fist on the bed.

"Do you remember what you did for New Year's Eve this year?"

She knew what New Year's Eve was: images of a crowded Times Square, a cork popping from a bottle of champagne, Harry running to Sally at the end of the movie. But when she tried to insert herself into any of those scenarios . . .

Tears leaked from the corners of her eyes. "No."

"How about the year before?"

Nothing.

"What's the last New Year's Eve you remember?"

A glimmer and then a memory where she was holding a champagne flute and standing on a balcony. In front of her water and fireworks discharging in the sky.

"One year, I celebrated with some friends at their condo overlooking the Potomac in Alexandria."

"That's real good, Leighton. Do you recall what year that was?"

She tried to focus in on certain parts of the memory, as if it were a photograph.

What do you think this is, some CBS procedural?

Feeling foolish, she thought about the friends at the party and how she knew them.

"It was 2010."

"Do you remember anything about 2011?" At Leighton's blank stare, he asked, "Or 2012? Do you remember what you did that New Year's Eve?"

"No."

Dr. Faber exhaled. "So we have some parameters to work from. It appears that your memories from the past six years have been compromised."

Six years? That was a long time. How would she ever figure out what had happened or what she'd done?

"How do I fix it?"

"Unfortunately, there's no cure for amnesia. Your earlier memories, before this six year gap, may be fuzzy but they'll start to come back. You're already accessing some of them now. As for the more recent six year gap, we can treat it with occupational and cognitive therapy, some hypnosis, but we don't know. Those memories may return spontaneously or never at all."

No! That was unacceptable! How was she supposed to live her life not knowing what she'd done during the past six years?

The door opened and an obscured figure spoke from the corridor. "They told me at the nurses' station that she regained consciousness again?"

Leighton's breath caught in her throat. The low pitch of his voice caressed her skin like a fine cashmere blanket, evoking a sense of serenity and certainty.

Who was that?

Nurse Rajan glanced at the doctor, who offered a sharp nod. "She did. Please come in."

When he stepped into the room she gasped, the inhalation acting like a shot from a starter pistol, setting her heart sprinting. Tall with broad shoulders, wavy dark hair and a sexy bit of scruff that emphasized his square jaw—his dark eyes swept over her, his piercing gaze scorching her skin each place it landed.

She couldn't imagine a more attractive man. And she was confident with that assessment, even with her "compromised" memory.

"You," she whispered.

The man stilled, his brows racing to meet above the straight line of his nose.

Dr. Faber swung his attention to Leighton. "Do you recognize him?"

Nurse Rajan placed a stabilizing hand on her shoulder and pressed her back. Leighton flinched, unaware that she'd physically responded to the magnetism he'd exuded, an allure that called to her spirit and made her yearn to be close to him.

"Yes." When no glimmer emerged to buttress her confidence, she lowered her gaze and brought her non-IV'd hand to her forehead. "Maybe. There's something about him . . ."

A flash of blue beyond him as several people ran down the hallway. The man peered over his shoulder, then strode farther into the room and closed the door.

For such a big man, he carried himself with an assured grace. He appeared confident in his own skin, fluid, coordinated, as if aware of everything going on around him. Even his hands, large and veined, with long, slim fingers that curled around the knob, looked capable, efficient. Experienced. Heat stirred low in her belly and she pressed her thighs together.

"Leighton?"

She forced her scrutiny away from the man across the room and back to Dr. Faber.

"You said there's something about him. What is it? Is it a memory?"

She was mistaken. She couldn't possibly know him. There was no way she could ever forget this man. He crossed his arms over the masculine contour of his chest, making his black cotton t-shirt earn its keep and revealing the geometric tail of a tribal tattoo peeking beneath a sleeve.

She swallowed, amazed at the sudden buildup of moisture after being parched only moments before. Had something happened to her in the past six years? Had she reverted to a virginal teenager, stammering, blushing and unable to form a coherent thought in the presence of every good-looking man who crossed her path?

No, that couldn't be true. Dr. Faber was handsome, but his proximity hadn't sharpened her awareness or incited her pulse to soar with anticipation the way Mr. Tall, Dark and Silent had with his mere entrance.

"Not a memory. A feeling . . ."

The man averted his gaze, and brackets formed on either side of his perfectly sculpted lips.

Dr. Faber nodded. "Definitely something we'll want to explore."

Had she missed something when she'd been ogling her visitor? "Why?"

"I find it interesting that you don't *remember* him but you *respond* to him."

"Do I know him?"

Nurse Rajan winked. "I'd say so."

Dr. Faber shot the nurse a censuring look then replied, "Yes, Leighton, you do. He's your fiancé."

Chapter Seven

LEIGHTON HELD THE phone to her ear while her gaze hopped around the hospital scenery that had grown way too familiar in the past three days. She needed to get out of this room. And her daily trips to therapy didn't count.

"You don't remember anything?" Beverly Clarke's voice had an intriguing *je ne sais pas* quality, after decades of dividing her time between the United States and France.

It had felt good to hear her mother's voice. It brought a measure of assurance she didn't get from anyone else. Except him. Jonathan. Her fiancé. No memories had surfaced yet but she felt like she knew him. Wanting to remember him and their relationship was the only thing that kept her fighting to reclaim her life during the times when she'd prefer to live in the past to escape her current uncertainty.

"Not from the prior six years." Even after the barrage of questions she'd fired at her doctors, she was having a difficult time wrapping her mind around this whole amnesia thing. Pun intended. "I've been working with a team of therapists trying different treatment options. I'm able to recall most of my older memories, but that six-year period, nothing."

Her mother's sigh was a force of nature. "I wish someone would've contacted me earlier, instead of almost a week after it happened."

Speaking of that . . . "I'm surprised you didn't know something was wrong. We talk several times a week. Weren't you worried when you didn't hear from me?"

Silence on the other end of the phone. "We haven't . . . talked very much . . . lately."

Leighton frowned. Why not? She adored her parents. As an only child, they'd spent a lot of time traveling together and she'd been inspired by their passion for justice and their resolve to do the right thing. There was no one she respected more. She grew up listening to them preach the value of public service and giving back, especially when they'd been blessed with so much. It was one of the reasons she'd chosen to pursue politics instead of going to a big firm after law school.

"You want to know what's weird? Logically I know it's been years since Daddy died, but emotionally . . . for me, it was just six months ago."

"Oh, Leighton . . ."

Tears stung her eyes and she rubbed the skin over her

heart. Her father's death had been a devastating blow, the void he left in her life immeasurable. She'd been a Daddy's girl, had thought him the best and smartest man she'd known. In the months following his passing, she and her mother grew closer than ever, clinging to each other as they both navigated the turbulent waters of losing the biggest love of their lives.

So she found it disturbing that she'd stopped communicating with her mother to the point that their not speaking for over a week wouldn't set off any alarm bells.

"Why haven't we talked, Mom? Was it work?"

Congress would come back from recess soon. Maybe she'd been busy analyzing bills that were due to be voted on. Several times a year, members of Congress tried to attach a slew of riders and provisions to must-pass pieces of legislation in an attempt to sneak through items they could never introduce on their own. Groups needed to keep a vigilant eye on certain bills to make sure the constituency they represented didn't lose their rights while no one was looking.

"What are your therapists saying about your missing memories?" Beverly asked instead.

"They tend to believe they are still there, being stored somewhere in my mind, but that the injury to my brain may have disrupted my ability to recall them. When my brain heals, I may regain access to them." She shrugged though her mother couldn't see her. "Or not. Despite all they've learned, there's still a lot they don't know."

A gut wrenching sob assaulted her hearing and Leighton jerked the phone away from her ear. "Mom! What's wrong?"

"Nothing." Beverly hiccupped. "I . . . I'm just so happy to talk to you."

Having no children of her own, Leighton couldn't imagine what her mother was going through. But if Beverly had been in an accident and Leighton hadn't known about it until a week after the fact . . .

"Mom, it's okay. I'm going to be fine."

A soft curse, some sniffling, a shaky breath and Professor Clarke was already re-emerging. "My plan was to head back to DC in a couple of months to begin preparing for my winter seminar. Maybe I should come now?"

"No. Stick to your plan, or at least, give me a few weeks. I can't wait to see you, but I need some time to regain my strength. I'll need to defend myself when you turn into Mommy ninja," she said, trying to lighten the atmosphere.

Beverly Clarke was a fierce protector, unafraid of taking on anyone or anything that threatened her family.

"I will for now, but I reserve the right to change my mind at a later date. When are they releasing you from the hospital?"

Beverly's lawyer-speak made Leighton smile. "In a couple of days."

"But who's going to take care of you?" Her mother's voice rose sharply.

A good question. One she'd asked herself.

"Jonathan, I assume."

"Who's Jonathan?"

Leighton laughed. "Ummm, my fiancé."

"Your fiancé?"

Her mother couldn't have sounded more shocked if Leighton had told her she'd planned to quit her job and become a bucket drummer outside one of the metro stations.

"You didn't know I was getting married?"

"No." Instead of the anger she would've expected, her mother sounded crushed.

Leighton pinched her lips together. What was going on? First she learned that she hadn't spoken to her mother in a while and now she found out she hadn't told her mom about her engagement. That thought about the bucket drummer job had been a joke, not a recovered memory, right? She hadn't really done that, had she?

Dammit. She wanted her memories back. Now!

"Is there something you know that you're not telling me?"

"Leighton—"

"Something must've happened. Did I do something to disappoint you, to make you mad?"

"No, of course not, honey."

"So you just stopped talking to me because the sun was shining?"

"I wouldn't stop talking to you for any reason."

"So I stopped talking to you?"

"No, that's not what I said." Beverly sounded defensive. "I don't want to get into this over the phone. Maybe I *should* come home early."

There was a brief knock on her door before it opened. Jonathan stood there in dark jeans and a navy V-neck t-shirt, the shadow of a stubble lending him a wicked presence. Their eyes locked. Moisture flooded her mouth and her heart thundered in her chest. She swallowed.

The man was walking sin. And he was all hers.

"No, don't come home early. We'll talk about this later," she said to her mother, continuing to watch Jonathan.

Beverly sighed. "I love you, honey."

"I love you, too." She hung up the phone, placing the handle back in its cradle.

Jonathan's gaze flew from the telephone to her face. He shoved his hands in the front pocket of his jeans. "Who was that?"

"My mom."

His shoulders lowered and he nodded. "How you feeling today?"

Leighton raised self-conscious fingers to skim the bulky white bandage on the back of her head, above her left ear. "Physically, I feel pretty good."

"You look good."

His gaze skimmed down her body and she heated from the inside out. And that was just from a look. How had she responded to his touch?

She studied him, trying to catalogue his expressions. "I didn't think I would see you again."

"I've stopped by every day but usually you're in therapy or they're running more tests. Didn't they tell you?"

"They did, but I'm still getting adjusted. Right now, a day feels like three or four to me."

"I'm sorry. I wish I could be here more often, but my restaurant opens in a couple of weeks and—"

She leaned forward. "You own a restaurant?"

"I do. Actually, this is my second one."

He must be doing well. If you paid attention—and she did—you couldn't help but notice the man exuded affluence without flaunting it. In addition to his TAG Heuer watch, his jeans carried a well-known high end insignia on the front pocket and the shades tucked into the neckline of his shirt were quality, as were the distressed leather belt and shoes he wore.

"Have I eaten at your other restaurant?"

She wanted to keep him talking, not just for the opportunity to learn something about her life from those missing years, but also to keep him here. Questions overwhelmed her brain, but Jonathan's presence calmed her, muzzled the noise in her head. Made her feel hopeful about their relationship even though she couldn't remember it.

"*Quartet*? No. That one is in San Francisco."

"I love San Francisco." At least she used to. "Is that where we met?"

"No. We met here in DC."

"Oh. How?"

His lips tightened into a grim line. "At a dinner party."

He stood as far away from her as he could, while remaining in the room. She frowned.

"Do we know the same people, have the same circle of friends?"

He shoved a hand through his hair. Her fingers tingled, jealous, wanting to feel the thick, silky strands themselves. "We met through mutual . . . acquaintances."

She glanced away, smoothed the material of the thin hospital blanket. "I'm sorry."

"Why are *you* apologizing?"

"I don't mean to interrogate you but you're the only person I know, the only person I have access to, who knows what my current life is like. What I've done, who I've met, all of it has been erased."

He moved a little closer. "That must be scary."

"It is. I'm a person who likes certainty, at least I used to be, and now I feel so uncertain." She looked at him. "The only thing I'm confident about is you. Or rather, the way you make me feel."

They stared at each other. He was so tall she had to lean back to look up at him. He had gorgeous eyes, dark and thickly lashed. Women would kill each other in a steel cage death match for those lashes. But instead of making him look feminine they made him sexy as hell. She licked her suddenly dry lips and his eyes blazed to life.

Holy hell.

Just when she thought he was going to come closer, the door to the room swung open. A food service worker wearing maroon scrubs backed in carrying a tray with a covered plate, a small bowl, a dessert cup and a drinking cup, all in the same beige hue.

"Knock, knock."

Leighton tamped down her irritation and dredged up a smile. "Hi, Shaniece."

The younger woman's visits had become the highlight of her day. Shaniece's bubbly personality made up for the fact that the hospital had her on the senior citizen dining plan, feeding Leighton when it was barely five-thirty.

"I've got your dinner, Ms. Clarke. No one saw me, but I grabbed an extra chocolate pudding for you."

Shaniece turned around and stumbled when she saw Jonathan. He moved quickly and took the tray from her before its contents were fed to the floor. Although, honestly, Leighton wouldn't have minded that outcome.

Shaniece's overly lined eyes widened. "Aren't you Chef Moran?"

Jonathan sat the tray down. "You know who I am?"

"You're kidding, right? The whole city is buzzing about your new restaurant opening."

He dipped his head. "Good to know I'm getting my promo money's worth. You work in the kitchen here?"

"Yeah, but there's not as much cooking as I thought. More like reheating."

He shoved his hands in his pockets. "You want to cook?"

"Since I was a little girl. I learned from my grandmother. But I don't want to work in a neighborhood joint. I want to work in fancy restaurants."

He nodded. "Have you applied to any?"

Shaniece waved a dismissive hand. "I can't do that."

"Why not?" he asked, sharing a quick, amused look with Leighton.

"I didn't go to culinary school."

"You don't have to go to culinary school to work at a fancy restaurant. And *fancy* is your word, not mine."

Shaniece put her hands on her trim hips. "Did you go?"

"Yes, but—"

Shaniece pursed her lips. "I knew it."

"But not at first," he said. "In the beginning I worked at restaurants and got as much experience as I could. Then I met a chef who saw something in me and took me under his wing. After a while, he suggested I go to school."

"That's great for you, but I don't have a fairy god-chef."

"I know lots of chefs who worked their way up in the kitchen and received their education on the job. If you have a good head on your shoulders, are disciplined, and have a willingness to learn and a drive to get better, you can definitely succeed without going to culinary school. Cool?"

Shaniece's nod set her micro braids swinging and her sunny smile broke through the doubt that had clouded her expression. "Okay, Chef, I hear you."

"On your next day off, I want you to come by the restaurant."

"I thought you don't open for another couple of weeks."

"We don't."

Her dark brown eyes widened. "Are you serious?"

"Yes. I'll introduce you around. You can talk to some of the cooks and ask questions, then I'll give you an opportunity to show me what you can do. If after that, you still want a job, we'll see."

Shaniece ran over to Jonathan and hugged him tight. "Thankyouthankyouthankyouthankyou."

He looked startled but then he smiled. That smile was warm enough to melt her insides and coax her lips into curving upward in response. Was that when she'd first fallen in love with him? The first time she'd seen that smile?

"You got a good one here, Ms. Clarke. Don't let him go."

"I don't intend to," Leighton said softly.

The door closed, breaking the spell.

"Thanks for saving my dinner." Leighton looked down at the tray and frowned.

"What's wrong?"

"The food. I may not know if my tastes have changed, but I know I don't like this."

He lifted the lid and she resisted the urge to turn her nose up at the chicken patty, mashed potatoes and broccoli on the plate.

"This is the second time I've seen this meal," she said. "I guess we're starting over in the rotation."

He laughed. "I'll be right back."

"I'll be here," she called to his back, taking the chocolate pudding cup and pushing the rest of the tray away.

A few minutes later he returned with bags of cheesy tortilla chips, plain potato chips, chocolate covered peanut candies and a ham and cheese sandwich.

Her mouth watered. "Where did you get *that* deliciousness?"

He smiled. "The vending machines in the visitor's waiting lounge."

"I'll take all of it," she said, her arms outstretched to reach for the items.

He opened the bags of chips. "No."

"Are you kidding me? Did you bring that food in here so I could watch you eat it? Are you trying to torture my memories back? You're too cute to be so cruel."

He smirked. "And you are too beautiful to be so dramatic."

She placed her hands over her warmed cheeks. He thought she was beautiful?

He pulled a plastic cutlery set out of his back pocket, tore open the package and extracted the knife. He divested the sandwich of its bread and began chopping the ham and cheese into uniform pieces.

The deep concentration on his face fascinated her. He gave the task at hand his sole attention and the passion practically vibrated off him in waves. Had he looked like that when he focused on her in bed? Right before he fucked her silly? God, she would give money for that memory.

Finally, he handed her the plate of food and sat at the foot of the bed. "Just a little something."

"And what do you call this?"

His lips were tilted in a smile, but his eyes crinkled at the corners with anxiety. "Ham and cheesy nacho supreme with a chocolate crumble."

She took a bite.

The flavors danced on her tongue, the crunchy texture enhanced by a mixture of salty and sweet. Her eyes rolled back in her head in ecstasy.

"Oh my God!"

"You like it?" A look of relief ghosted over his face.

"I love it. It's so good. I don't know how you managed to get this meal out of what you had. You should be on *Top Chef*." She paused. "Were you on *Top Chef*?"

His dark eyes watched her devour the food. "No."

"If you were, you'd win." She set her fork aside and wiped her mouth with a napkin. "Come here."

His nostrils flared and he hesitated for a moment, before leaning toward her.

She smoothed her palm on his cheek and felt the bristles of his early evening stubble against her hand. She stared into eyes dark with simmering heat and pressed her lips against his.

Her heart pounded against her ribcage, like a rebellious teenager trying to break curfew, and she pulled away before she succumbed to the longing to pull him down on the bed with her. "Thank you."

His gaze searched hers. "It's just a meal."

"No, it's more than that. You're a very busy man and the fact that you've stopped by every day means the world to me." She stole another quick kiss. "I want to remember everything about you."

Something shifted in his expression and he backed away from her. She swallowed her disappointment at his distance. The accident had happened to her but it affected both of their lives. Maybe he needed some time.

She sat back and took another bite of her food. "Do you have any awards for your cooking?"

"I've won a James Beard award."

"That's impressive," she said. But she wanted to give him a hard time, see how he'd react. "So have others."

He stared at her down the length of his nose. "*Quartet* has earned three Michelin stars."

Three Michelin stars! That was fucking amazing! "That's nice."

He narrowed his eyes. "I've cooked for the governor of California, several Grammy award-winning bands and the cast of the latest *Star Wars* movie."

She shrugged. "Well, you just hang in there. You might make something of yourself."

She lowered her head and held herself still, wondering how long she could hold her amusement at bay. After several long, *quiet*, seconds, she risked a glance from beneath her lashes and gave in to her laughter when she saw the wide smile splitting his face. She reveled in the brief relief of the tension that always seemed to hover between them.

"Wait, there's a new *Star Wars*?" she asked, through lingering giggles.

"Uh-huh. And it's good. Better than the prequels."

"I have to catch up on a lot." And she knew where—or with whom—to start. "You said your first restaurant is in San Francisco. Are you from there?"

"That's where I lived for the past fifteen years. But I was born and raised here in DC."

"So we met after you moved back here?"

He paused before continuing. "Yes."

"And did you move back here specifically to open this new restaurant?"

He leaned back against the footboard. "Among other reasons."

A critical thought occurred to her. "Are we staying here?"

"What do you mean?"

"You've lived the past fifteen years on the other side of the country. Are you going to stay here in DC or go back to San Francisco?"

"Initially I assumed I'd be bi-coastal."

"And now?"

He met her eyes. "Now, I'm not sure what my future plans are."

Because of her. Her and this stupid accident.

The door opened and Dr. Faber walked in.

"Hello." Dr. Faber shook Jonathan's hand then walked over to the bed and squeezed Leighton's shoulder. "I'd heard Mr. Moran was here, so I thought this would be a good time to drop by."

She wondered what he needed to say that would make having Jonathan here a prerequisite for the conversation.

"Good news. Your last MRI showed the swelling of your medial lobe had reduced significantly. Other than that, everything looks normal."

"Then why hasn't she gotten her memories back?" Jonathan asked.

Dr. Faber shrugged. "Not sure. But there's no reason to keep her here." He addressed Leighton. "We can release you tomorrow."

Tomorrow? While she was exceedingly happy to leave the hospital behind, she was panicked about her next step.

"Where do I go?"

"Do you live with someone?"

She looked at Jonathan, who swallowed and shook his head.

"I guess I can go home."

"Not if you live by yourself," Dr. Faber said.

What was she going to do? Maybe she needed to call her mother and ask her to return early, as she'd suggested.

Jonathan spoke up. "She'll come home with me."

Leighton touched the base of her neck. "Are you sure?"

"Of course. I'll take good care of you," he said, his words a solemn vow.

"Perfect," Dr. Faber said. "The nurse will come in with some instructions for home care. We should be able to get you out of here tomorrow afternoon. After your release, you'll still need to come back daily to continue with your therapy, at least for the next few weeks, okay?"

As Dr. Faber pulled Jonathan aside to go over a few more items about her impending discharge, Leighton sagged back against the pillows and smiled. She was getting out of this hospital before she had to endure another rotation through the hospital menu or she succumbed to the urge to purchase scrubs to wear in her daily life.

That didn't mean she wasn't worried about existing in the real world. Despite the food and the confinement, she appreciated the simplicity of hospital life. Decisions were made for her. Everyone she communicated with knew about her medical condition; internal debates about who she should trust and how much weren't necessary. Outside hospital walls, the chaos of the world awaited.

Speaking of chaos . . .

She stared at her fiancé and goose bumps sprung to life on her arms. Good Lord, how lucky was she? She'd be staying with him. Living together would give her the opportunity to spend time getting to know him and learning about their relationship. Though she instinctively trusted him to take care of her, she'd always been good at reading people. Those same instincts went on high alert when he averted his eyes and kept his distance.

He was keeping something from her. He may not believe it relevant to her recovery or their relationship, but if he truly knew her, he had to know she wouldn't rest until she discovered what he was hiding and why.

Chapter Eight

"DID YOU RECENTLY move in?"

Leighton stood in the middle of a living room with very little furniture, though it was exquisitely adorned with crown molding, a fireplace and an intricately carved ceiling medallion.

Jonathan paused in the act of sorting through his mail. "No."

Not even his affronted scowl could detract from the masculine beauty of his features. Was there any expression that could achieve that feat?

Hugging herself, she dragged her gaze away from his profile and directed it out the bay window, the actual scenery conflicting with her recollections.

The neighborhood featured historic Victorian row homes bordered by park benches occupied by older black men feeding pigeons, and sidewalks teeming with millennials toting yoga mats and messenger bags. It bore little resemblance to what she remembered, an up-and-coming area still struggling under the "unsafe" label due to overt drug use, prostitution and homelessness. She'd blinked and Logan Circle had evolved from a sketchy community to one of the trendiest sections in Northwest DC.

She turned from the view and found him watching her, his dark eyes intense and unblinking. Focused. Heat pooled between her thighs and her nipples pebbled against her arm. Leighton knew that look. It'd been directed her way numerous times before and was usually followed by the grip of strong hands pulling her close for a kiss.

Except Jonathan stayed where he was, positioned next to the antique credenza in the hallway, at least fifteen feet away from her.

Why?

He blinked and the heat disappeared from his gaze, as if it had never existed.

Dammit!

Why did she feel like her life was a long-running, award-winning Broadway play and she was some random woman plucked off the street and shoved onto the stage without a script? Everyone knew what they were doing except her.

She cleared her throat. "How long have you lived here?"

He returned his attention to the envelopes in his hand. "About a year."

She motioned to the sectional couch and large flat screen TV, the only items in the room. "But it's so empty!"

"I'm barely here. I spend most of my time at *Sedici*."

That explains it, I guess.

Still—

"Is that why we don't live together?"

He dropped the mail into the wooden decorative bowl placed on the credenza for that specific purpose, judging by the envelopes already there.

"Why would you think that's the reason? Maybe you decided to wait to move in until after the wedding?"

"Did you keep leaving the toilet seat up? Or are you one of those cap-off-the-toothpaste men?"

"Maybe it was you? You could be a secret slob." A tiny smile hovered at the corners of his mouth.

"Nope. Try again."

"What if we decided to wait until after the wedding for . . . other things, too?"

The way his tongue darted out to touch his lower lip when he said *other things* . . .

Is that why he was keeping his distance? Had they decided to wait and have sex after they were married?

If so, what in the hell had she been thinking?

She rolled her eyes. "Even if I can't account for the past six years, I'm pretty sure I wasn't concerned about protecting my virtue from you."

"No, I guess not." His smile wavered. "We're both busy people. Our careers are very important to us."

"My vulnerable virtue notwithstanding, I appreciate you letting me stay here."

Their eyes did that meet-and-bond thing again and this time, her heart skipped a beat. The connection between them was palpable.

"Of course." He severed their connection and scratched his cheek. "I went to your apartment and brought some of your things back here."

She gestured down to the slim black pant and blush pink sleeveless top she wore. "Is that where you got these clothes?"

His jaw tightened but he nodded.

He'd made the right call. The dress she'd worn the night she'd been admitted to the hospital was gorgeous, but dirt and blood had rendered it beyond salvageable.

Another thought occurred to her. "Do I still live on Capitol Hill?"

"No. In Foggy Bottom. A condo on Virginia Avenue with great views of the Potomac River."

Her stomach clenched in disappointment. She loved her apartment. She and her mother had gone house hunting for six months before she found that place. It was the first time she'd lived on her own.

"If you'd rather stay there, we could make the appropriate arrangements. Hire a nurse."

No!

Dr. Faber had informed them both that memory couldn't be recovered from being told personal experiences or from being in a familiar environment surrounded by personal belongings. Being in her apartment now would be akin to staying at a hotel. Except if she stayed at her place, she'd ignore her doctor's advice. She'd be compelled to roam around the rooms, touching various tchotchkes like they were supernatural talismans, waiting for the memories to flood over her.

Not to mention the pocket-sized part of her that feared recalling her missing years might bring some unexpected and unwelcome revelations.

"No, I want to be here." *With you.* "Staring at objects I don't recognize and hoping for a eureka moment seems depressing." She gestured to their sparse surroundings. "From the look of things here, that won't be a problem."

"Alright, I get it. You're not impressed with my decorating skills." His dark brown eyes sparkled.

God, he was gorgeous. And so damned sexy. It wasn't fair what he did to a simple t-shirt—white this time—and a pair of jeans. And his tattoo? She wanted to trace the pattern with her finger. Or her tongue. See if it only curled around his bicep or spiraled farther . . .

She swallowed.

Had she discovered a way to navigate the unmistakable tension between them? Some mental waders to don when longing thickened the space between them? Or had time and proximity lessened its effect? She couldn't imagine an occasion when she wasn't hyper aware of him, but there had to be more to their relationship.

And since she didn't plan on sitting around and playing "Marco Polo" with her old memories, she needed to ascertain what that was.

The day after she'd awakened, she'd gone all existential. If memories helped a person understand who they were, without them, who was she? It'd been a weird period of time and had jumpstarted her determination to use the therapy available to her, but that depression had stuck with her and she didn't intend to revisit it. Jonathan was living, breathing proof of her existence during the time she couldn't remember, and the way he made her feel was the only tangible thing tethering her to sanity.

"How are things going at the restaurant?"

"A million things on my checklist and only time to complete about half."

Her stomach knotted. His visits to the hospital probably hadn't helped.

Dipping her chin, she clasped her hands together and sat down on one end of the couch. "What made you decide to come east?"

His brows met like long lost lovers. "What?"

"Our conversation in the hospital. You'd been living in San Francisco and running your restaurant there when you decided to move back to DC. I asked if you came back to open *Sedici* and you said 'among other reasons.' I just . . . wondered what they were."

"Oh." He shifted his stance, pulling his head back and pushing his shoulders forward. "I wanted to reconnect with my family. I spent a lot of years in San Francisco and I missed them."

"Is your family still here?"

"My parents live in Florida now."

"Are you an only child?"

He shoved his hands in the back pocket of his jeans and the motion pulled his shirt tight across his chest. "No. I have an older brother."

Why did he suddenly look on edge?

"I always wanted a sibling," she said. "Don't get me wrong, I liked having my parents' undivided attention but, when they were working, it could get pretty lonely. It would've been nice to have a brother or sister to spend time with."

"That's the idea." His expression hardened. "But the reality doesn't always live up to that promise."

Oh. So the brothers didn't get along. She wondered why.

"What about me? Does your family like me?"

"Yeah, you could say that."

His dismissive snort didn't engender confidence and his posture screamed "Proceed at your own risk." Nothing good would come from prying deeper. At this time.

"You said you grew up here?"

He relaxed a fraction. "I did. Across the river, in Alexandria."

"My parents took me to Old Town quite a few times when I was a kid. When I got older, and my friends and I grew tired of Georgetown, we'd pile in a car and head over to walk down King Street, shop in those cute boutiques." She smiled up at him. "I wonder how many times we may have crossed paths as we were growing up?"

He laughed and the sound uncorked bubbles of happiness inside of her. "Somehow, I can't imagine we ran in the same circles. If we had, you wouldn't have given me the time of day. You probably would've looked right past me."

She pictured a young Jonathan, all unruly hair, gangly limbs, beautiful eyes.

Not notice him? Not a chance.

"You're right. We probably never met. Recent experience has proved that I would've remembered you."

His nostrils flared, and his hands clenched into fists then uncurled and flexed. The potency of his heated look scorched her skin and threatened to liquefy her insides. He wanted her. Why wouldn't he act on it? He didn't have to tongue her down, but a hug, a touch, something.

He shook his head, as if extricating himself from a trance. "Come on. Let me show you to your room."

He gestured for her to precede him up the dignified staircase. Her fingers trailed along the burnished mahogany balustrade that gleamed against the pale gray color of the bare wall. A wall that called out for artwork, decor or family pictures.

"Are you a control freak?"

He laughed. "In the kitchen, definitely, but I haven't been accused of it elsewhere. Why?"

"*I* chose not to add any finishing touches? I assume

we didn't live together, but I spent time here, right? Where are the lamps and side tables? The throw rugs and ugly ceramic vases?"

"I thought we'd moved beyond my lack of decorating prowess."

"We have, but now I'm starting to question mine. If I was going to live here, I'd get some plants, hang some pictures. There would be pillows on the couch, treatments on the windows—"

"Like I said, we're both very busy."

Apparently. "You with opening your restaurant and me at my job?"

"That's right."

No, something wasn't right at all.

"What about when I spent the night?"

At the top of the stairs, his hand warmed the small of her back when he applied pressure to indicate she should turn right. "This way."

Aware that he hadn't answered her question, but not sure why, she walked into a large light-filled room boasting the same view as downstairs.

Her pulse instantly steadied.

Unlike the rest of the house, this space was beautifully appointed. The wardrobe, nightstand, desk and chaise lounge played supporting roles next to the simple and delicate white four poster bed, a natural focal point in its place against the exposed brick wall. A suitcase and an overnight bag sat nearby.

Her steps echoed against the hardwood floor only to

be silenced when they met the patterned trellis area rug. It was gorgeous, but—

"I had my own room?"

"I had this done while you were in the hospital. I thought you'd appreciate your own space."

Lightness radiated through her. Not pausing to think or worry about the consequences, she closed the distance between them and slid her arms around his waist. "Thank you."

His body was hard and muscled and it burned hot beneath her touch. She burrowed her nose into the crook of his neck and inhaled. He smelled incredible, crisp, spicy, heady. She couldn't name his fragrance but she knew she'd always associate the scent with him.

He stiffened and her pulse stuttered.

Please don't pull away from me.

She closed her eyes and clutched the fabric of his shirt.

Maybe her accident changed things. Maybe he was no longer interested in her because she no longer resembled the woman he'd wanted to marry. That could explain his cool behavior toward her.

The duration between one second and the next stretched eternally, and just when her brittle nerves threatened to snap, a tremor ripped through his body and his arms closed tightly around her, one hand on her lower back, the other cupping the nape of her neck.

Thank God!

She sagged against him in relief, realizing only in that moment the sheer terror she'd been harboring of his rejection. The longer they stood there, the calmer she felt. Her life was the very definition of chaos, but his arms were the eye of the hurricane.

She could've stayed enclosed within them forever, but he detangled himself from her embrace. "I need to go over to the restaurant."

Her breath caught in her chest. "I thought we were staying home."

"You are staying here, but I need to check in."

Panic clawed her insides, shredding her prior composure to pieces. "Can't you check in tomorrow? I just got home. I thought we could spend some time together."

He flinched and the chill returned. "I won't be gone long. The restaurant is only a few blocks from here and I programmed my number into your phone. If you need anything, call."

"I need *you*."

The words were hard for her to say, the idea of making herself even more vulnerable not something she relished.

"I'm sorry, Leighton. My restaurant is opening in two weeks and—"

"I'm keeping you from it," she finished softly, wrapping her arms around her waist.

He had a restaurant to open and he needed to get it done without worrying about her. Plus, she didn't want to give him a reason to regret sticking by her side. She strode over to the window, intending to save herself the anguish of watching him walk away from her.

"Fuck." The curse was a barely whispered utterance. A moment later, he rested his hands on her upper arms.

"Go ahead. I'll be fine."

She hadn't expected to feel so needy. She'd gone from wanting to figure out what he was keeping from her to just wanting him. Her independent spirit had deserted her, leaving someone more fragile in its place.

"I'll only be a few hours, I promise. There's food in the fridge. All you have to do is heat it up." He hesitated. "You know how to heat up food, right?"

One corner of her mouth tilted upward. "Yes. That's procedural memory, like riding a bike and brushing my teeth."

"Good. Leighton, I . . . I'm glad you're okay and that you're here." In that moment, his concern for her was obvious as was his reluctance to admit it.

What aren't you telling me, Jonathan?

She'd have to wait for his response. He pressed a whisper-soft kiss against her hair, and then he was gone.

Chapter Nine

JONATHAN STOOD AT the pass in his kitchen and surveyed the people assembled. Everyone, from the food runners to the prep cooks to the pastry chef, watched him with either wide eyes or crossed arms.

Chef.

The most important position in the kitchen. Where he led, they would all follow.

Despite the prominence of his current status, he'd worked every job in the kitchen and he truly believed everyone was essential to its success. Being a first class establishment depended on delivering exceptional food in a timely manner.

If a customer were to peek in the back during the prime of a dinner service, it would look like a well-rehearsed dance routine, where everyone knew their moves and understood when to leap to the forefront or fade into the background. If one station was off—overcooking the fish resulting in a returned plate, or being late in delivering the vegetables—hampering the other station's flow, it could impede or disrupt the choreography.

He was the face of the restaurant; he'd receive the praise if service went well or the criticism if it didn't. But Jonathan knew he didn't do it alone.

It was his job to inspire that greatness. To get them to work their hardest and produce the best food possible while working very long hours.

It would start today.

He leaned against the counter and curled his fingers around a stack of warm plates. "Gib gave you guys the menu two days ago. Does everyone have it memorized?"

A few nods, but mostly dropped or averted gazes, slumped postures, shuffled feet.

He closed his eyes and counted to ten. In French.

He'd created an ambitious menu for *Sedici*. The cooks needed to know the sides and garnishes for every protein. They couldn't work the line looking at fucking menus. Preparing the food the way he wanted and at the pace demanded for a busy dinner service would require lots of practice.

Do your job, Moran.

"If you read over the menu, you probably retained more information than you think. Hedy"—he pointed to his pastry chef—"what's on the dessert menu?"

"Dark chocolate flourless cake, classic Grand Marnier soufflé, cardamom poached pear tart, chocolate pot de creme, assorted sorbet and an artisanal cheese plate," she recited, clearly and without hesitation, while maintaining eye contact.

A triumphant smile split his lips. "That's what I'm talkin' about!"

The adrenaline rush made him light-headed. When he was in chef mode, he never doubted his skills or his worth. Nothing mattered except putting out the best damn plate of food possible, every single time.

And yet the remembrance of Leighton's body pressed against his, the flash of electricity that skated across his skin when she touched his cheek, zoomed through his body like a mental aftershock.

No!

He grabbed a plate and pressed it between both hands, fighting the heaviness that wanted to set up camp in his dick. He was here to work. As long as his staff did their part and allowed him to focus on the food, he could keep his mind on *Sedici*, where it belonged.

"Tell me about the agnolotti." He brought the plate up and tapped it against his chin.

"It's filled with braised short rib and horseradish." Elaine stood with her hands clasped loosely behind her back.

He nodded. "And how is it garnished?"

"Brown butter and . . . a squeeze of lemon juice?" Her voice tap-danced up the octave scale, and she twisted her lower lip.

Almost.

"Brown butter and *bread crumbs*," he said, enunciating the last two words. "The agnolotti isn't creamy enough to warrant the hit of acid."

In fact, if he'd garnished the dish as she'd instructed, it would've been ruined.

The oh so sweet and salty taste of her full lips pressed against his as she thanked him for that dish he'd whipped up for her at the hospital . . .

He cleared his throat. "Which protein goes with the fingerling potatoes, mushrooms and tarragon mayo?"

No responses.

"Anyone?"

Elaine looked around and then tentatively raised her hand.

It did him no good for one person to recite the entire menu. "Anyone else?"

An unnerving stillness filled the space.

"Roasted chicken?" came a small voice in the back.

Chicken? *Chicken?* He didn't even have chicken on his goddamned menu!

Leighton gazing up at him, her dark eyes wide and vulnerable, pleading with him to stay . . .

"*I need you.*"

A toxic brew of frustration and anger torpedoed from his belly and scalded the back of his throat. The plate in his hand soared through the air and smashed against the far wall, shattering into pieces.

Some of the cooks flinched. Others straightened, tilting their chin up.

"What the fuck, guys? You had two days. Two. Days. And you couldn't fucking memorize the menu? I didn't have to be here. I could've been—" He shook his head. "I don't have time for this amateur bullshit in my kitchen. You call me when you're ready to act like the professionals you're supposed to be."

The front of his restaurant had been deemed the scene of an accident, the interior looked like an abandoned renovation and his kitchen staff still didn't know the menu. How in the hell was he going to open his restaurant under those circumstances?

And none of it was helped by his sporadic absences because of her.

Leighton.

He stormed into his office and sank down at his desk, letting his head fall into his hands. He'd gone from wanting to keep his distance to inviting her to stay in his house. But what other option did he have?

She had amnesia!

He'd visited her several times when she'd been in a coma. The sight of her hooked up to monitors and machines, had unnerved him more than he'd expected. One day when he'd been sitting there, staring at her still body and feeling fucking useless, a nurse had come in and told him he could talk to Leighton.

"Studies show that hearing the voices of loved ones really can help those in a coma wake up sooner," the woman had said. "Plus, your voice stimulates circuits in the brain, helping trigger that first glimmer of awareness."

So he'd talked about cooking, about San Francisco and *Quartet*. He'd talked about her and how they met. His best friends and their wives, his parents . . . Thomas. He even threw in a couple of insults, naively believing he'd make her angry enough that she'd regain consciousness just to smack him.

Nothing had happened.

The day he'd checked in at the nurses' station and they'd informed him she'd come out of the coma, relief had almost brought him to his knees. She was going to recover. Everything would be okay. But sorrow soon followed. Now he had to tell them the truth. He'd have to admit he wasn't her fiancé. He'd have no more reasons to visit her, no excuse to spend time with her.

He'd walked into her room, excited to see her conscious, dreading the moment she saw him. She *would* smack him. Curse him out, blame him for her injuries and rightly so.

But the expression on her face hadn't been anger. It'd been warm, curious and desirous. She'd looked at him the way a woman looks at a man she finds extremely attractive. To his shame, his body had responded.

And when he found out she'd lost her memories of the past six years of her life, his shame had multiplied tenfold.

He heard footsteps and glanced up to find Gib standing in the doorway.

"What do you want?"

She didn't respond. She came in and closed the door

behind her. Plopping down in the chair against the wall, she crossed her arms and stared at him.

He scrubbed a hand over his face. "I know. I'm sorry."

She raised a delicate brow and cocked her head to the side, like a smug pixie.

"What happened after I left?"

She stretched her legs out in front of her and finally deigned to speak. "Nothing much. I handed out another copy of the menu and gave them an hour to work on it."

"Did anyone walk out?"

"For that penny ante shit?" She gestured with her head back toward the kitchen. "You flung one empty dish at the *wall*. Some of them have had plates full of hot food tossed near their *heads*. They'll be fine."

It was true. Generations of chefs had been bullied, yelled at and publicly humiliated all in the name of mentoring. Unfortunately, many of those same chefs viewed the abuse as a rite of passage to inflict on those cooks beneath them, assuring the moronic cycle of cruelty would continue.

"Yeah, but you know that's not how I run a kitchen."

"I know," she softly affirmed.

"I could've handled that better."

"Chef, everyone who's ever worked for you loved the experience. Even those chefs who envy you. You foster a great working environment, you don't play games and you're a straight shooter. You were having a bad day and you let a plate fly. They'll get over it." She pointed at him. "You have to get over it, too."

He held out his fist and smiled at her answering bump. "Thanks, Gib."

"Anytime, Chef. Now, let's talk about what's really bothering you." She leaned forward and planted her elbows on her knees. "You've been gone a lot this week."

"I have a lot on my plate."

"What's more important than opening the restaurant on time?"

A few days ago, he would've said nothing. But now . . .

He exhaled and dropped his head back on the headrest. "Why do I feel like my life is some cosmic joke?"

"What's going on? What can I do?"

As his sous chef, Gib was his lieutenant. When he gave orders, it was Gib's job to ensure those orders were executed. It was a magical, everlasting bond, forged by spending more than seventy hours a week together, and built on a trust he shared with very few people.

"Leighton Clarke was released from the hospital this afternoon."

"That's good news. Your brother must be happy."

Fucking Thomas.

Jonathan hadn't actually talked to his brother since their call in the ER waiting room. His subsequent calls hadn't been answered and his text regarding Leighton's current condition had been met with Thanks for the update. So much for Thomas's promise to come home in a week.

"Who knows what he's feeling."

Gib tugged on her ear. "Am I missing something?"

He nodded and filled Gib in on the situation.

Her hazel eyes widened to rival the size of saucers. "Why in the hell would you agree to that stupid-ass scheme?"

"What should I have done?" he asked, hyperaware of the prickling heat of embarrassment marching across the nape of his neck. "He was going to leave whether I agreed to his plan or not."

"Then he would've left. And when she'd recovered, they would've dealt with the consequences of his departure on their relationship. Now you've inserted yourself in the middle of it."

I should be in the middle of it. It was my kiss that made her rush out without seeing where she was going.

"That's not the worst part."

"There's more?"

"We assumed she'd wake up and be fine. Thomas assured me she would understand the reason behind our ruse. We'd never anticipated she'd lose her memory. Who would've thought of that? Now *she* believes I'm her fiancé. I don't know what to do."

Gib's mouth had fallen open. "This is like the soaps my nana used to watch. You've got to change your name. ThornCliff or StoneRidge," she suggested, laughing into her closed fist.

He clenched his jaw. "This isn't funny."

She sobered instantly. "No, it isn't. You need to tell her the truth."

"I tried." The day she'd awakened, in fact. "Her doctor shot down the idea."

"It's too late," Dr. Faber had said, a deep groove growing between his brows. "She's already latched on to the truth, used it to begin re-building her self-image."

"But isn't that why it's not too late, why I should tell her now before things go any further? Because it's not the truth."

"Imagine her mind is like a Jenga puzzle. From the moment she realized she was missing memories, her mind began creating new ones, or rebuilding, to give her a basis for her new self-image, which is necessary for her to function in society. If you pull a block from the very foundation she's building, it could set her recovery back considerably."

"But I'm not her fiancé!"

"Do you care about Ms. Clarke?"

The exhilaration of sparring with her, the addictive quality of her kiss, the sheer terror of seeing her collapse on the street . . .

Jonathan nodded.

"Then give her some time. Let her regain her strength. Build her tower a little taller, if you will. Then we can work together with her therapists to determine the best time and approach to amend what you've told her."

Gib stared at him. "Then you have no other choice—you've got to go along with it."

Yeah, he knew that. He just wished his conscience would accept it and give him a fucking break.

"Thanks for listening to me babble." An unfamiliar invoice on his desk caught his attention. He grabbed the corner of the paper and pulled it closer. "Bringing you over here was one of my better ideas."

"I have another one I hope you'll love as much."

He blinked. His truffle supplier was trying to increase his price by four percent. Not going to happen. "Yeah?"

"Take care of your life at home. Let me handle this."

His head jerked back. "Excuse me?"

"It's obvious your attention is divided and now I know why. Even when you're physically here, you can't focus because you're thinking about her, your 'fiancée.'" She used her fingers to make air quotes.

"About that, despite what you saw the night of the accident, I am not—"

"Uh-uh." Gib held up her hands, palms facing him. "Don't. Want. To. Know."

"Fine, but I can't leave. We have to open in two weeks."

"We'll get there. You've done most of the heavy lifting. I can handle the kitchen staff. That's my job, after all."

He threaded his fingers together behind his neck. "What about the million other things we have to do? We have a big food shipment due in the morning. I'll need to go through it and—"

"Provence roasted squab. Braised short rib agnolotti. Wagyu beef tenderloin with winter black truffles. Yellowfin tuna carpaccio. Crispy black bass and braised veal cheek."

"Why are you listing dishes off my menu?"

"Because unlike those asses out there, I know it, inside out. I can check the orders as they come in. I can train the staff on the way you like things done."

"Gib—"

"And do you see this thing?" She held up her cell phone and waved it from side to side. "It's a funny little invention. I press a button and look what happens."

The muffled sound of his ringtone rumbled from his pants. He narrowed his eyes.

Smart-ass.

"If anything comes up that requires your attention, I'll use this newfangled device to contact you."

It would definitely solve a few of his problems but—

"How about this? It's Friday. Why don't you take the weekend off? I got this and I can call you if I need you. No matter what, you can come back early on Monday morning, re-focused and ready to scream holy hell. You'll still have two full weeks."

Gib presented a tempting offer. Taking a few days off would help him fulfill his promise to watch after Leighton. It had been easier to meet his obligation when she was in the hospital and he could come to the restaurant secure in the knowledge that she was taken care of. But now that she was home? Who would take care of her when he wasn't around?

He couldn't ignore the fact that the restaurant *needed* to launch on time. With an extremely long punch list to tackle, any hours spent away from the restaurant heightened the odds of not meeting their deadline.

Being a chef was his calling. He cooked because the longing to do so coursed through his veins. From the first moment he'd stepped in front of a stove, and turned on the burner, a feeling of peace had steadied him and confirmed he was on the right path. And that, more than anything else, aided him in making his final determination.

"I appreciate the offer, but no."

Her lips tightened briefly, but she nodded and met his gaze. "Okay."

"And it has nothing to do with my faith in you or your abilities."

"I know."

"This restaurant is my baby. There's nothing more important to me than making *Sedici* a success. I can't turn it over to someone else. Not yet."

"I understand."

"Alright." He stood and rubbed his hands together. "Let's see if they've got this menu memorized."

She checked the clock that hung on the wall above his desk, next to the painting of a hectic kitchen scene. "It hasn't been an hour."

"What do you think this is—a culinary pre-school? We can't fucking hold their hands."

Gib smiled and followed him out of the office. "*Oui,* Chef!"

Chapter Ten

LEIGHTON SAT ON the bed with her back against the headboard and her knees drawn up to her chest. Every click, knock, bang and creak sent her heart bursting from her chest, leaving her behind to seek safety.

It was easier to be strong when she was in a hospital surrounded by doctors, nurses and staff, or even when Jonathan had been here. Her bravery went on strike as the sun set and she found herself alone, surrounded by strangers, in an unfamiliar neighborhood, in a house she didn't know, unable and unwilling to contact the only person she could call.

That's right, Veronica Mars, maybe before you set out to discover what Jonathan isn't telling you, you solve the mystery of your missing courage.

Something buzzed near her and she almost leapt out of bed. It took several seconds before she understood it was a phone and another one before she realized it must be hers. Her eyes followed the sound until she found its source sitting on the chaise lounge where Jonathan had placed it. She didn't want to move, feeling relatively safe in her spot where she had clear views of every entry into and exit from the room, but curiosity won out. She crawled across the thin sky-blue blanket and reached for the device.

It was large, almost twice the size of what she remembered. The name Andrea Ferris flashed across the screen. Leighton blinked several times in succession and stared at a picture of the woman many considered to be one of the most influential political consultants in the country.

"Hello."

"Oh Leighton, thank God! I'm so glad you're okay."

It was *the* Andrea Ferris. She'd had the privilege to meet this woman when she'd been invited to a luncheon for young women in politics at Andrea's home in Falls Church. She'd believed they'd hit it off, but this outpouring of affection seemed a bit excessive.

"I was so worried when I heard you were in the hospital. How do you feel?"

She squinted. "Better."

"I couldn't stop replaying our conversation. If that had been the last time I'd seen you, the last thing I'd said to you," Andrea said, speaking so fast Leighton had to concentrate to follow her, "I never would've forgiven myself."

Leighton's head recoiled slightly.

"Thank you for coming. We must get together soon."

Those were the words Andrea regretted?

"How bizarre is it that I saw you the day before your accident—"

Leighton stilled and focused on the other woman's words. "You did?"

"Yes," Andrea said haltingly. "Remember . . ."

Ha! Wasn't *that* the word of the year?

". . . you saw me in Tysons Corner? You caught me sneaking a cigarette."

Leighton pressed her index and middle fingers against her left temple. She'd been so caught up in determining how *she* was going to handle her new normal that she hadn't given any thought to how she'd explain her situation to others. Assuming she planned to tell them anything.

"Are you okay?" Andrea asked.

Andrea Ferris was a well-respected person whose services were in demand. Despite that, she'd taken time to call and her concern seemed genuine. Leighton didn't know the extent of their relationship but the other woman might possess information about the life she'd forgotten. She took a deep breath. "Do you know what happened to me?"

"Not the specifics. No one does. All that's going around is that you were in an accident and had to be rushed to the hospital. That was a week ago. No one has heard from you since then. I couldn't even get in touch with your fiancé."

Had her tone changed when she mentioned Jonathan?

"I'm not in the hospital anymore. I was discharged today."

"That's good news! Your assistant called me when you didn't show up for work on Tuesday. She wasn't too worried when you didn't come in Monday; she thought you might have decided to work from home. But when she didn't hear from you on Tuesday, she became concerned. Especially since she would be out of the office for the rest of the week. Something about a cruise."

Leighton took a deep breath. She hoped she wasn't making a mistake. "You asked if I remembered seeing you in Tysons Corner. I'm sorry, but no. I don't."

"Oh, doll." Andrea's voice wobbled.

"My doctor says it can happen with the type of injury I sustained, though it's unusual. Still, I expect to make a full recovery."

"I've heard of that. People can forget what happened right before the accident. It's like the body's way of dealing with the trauma. Andrea sighed. "I feel like a grade-A ass, calling you and blathering on about that day."

"It's okay. How could you have known?"

"Does your mother know?"

Andrea Ferris knew her parents? Of course she did. Anyone in politics at her level would've had dealings with the Clarkes, even if it was just socially. "Yes. I talked to my mother yesterday."

"I'm sure she's happy to know you're okay."

A sense of urgency cascaded through Leighton. Here was a person who contained some of the pieces missing from the puzzle of her life. She needed to take advantage of the situation. "Can you tell me about that day when I saw you?"

"It won't hinder your recovery, will it?"

"It's fine," Leighton said.

"Well, I think you were coming from a business meeting when you saw me."

"What did we talk about?"

"We had a conversation about your work and my next project." She hesitated. "You don't remember *any* of this?"

"No."

"What memories are you missing? Is it the hours before the accident or that entire day?"

The air stilled in the room as if even the molecules waited with bated breath to hear her response.

What should she do? Did she dare admit any more to this woman? What if she meant her harm? Maybe something had happened during the years she was missing and this woman was no longer someone she held in high regard, but her foe? God, is this what every day would be like for her? Every encounter a distressing exercise in parsing the true intentions of everyone she met?

Her instincts had screamed at her regarding Jonathan and they hadn't led her wrong. Maybe she'd listen to them regarding Andrea, too.

"I don't remember anything from the past six years."

The silence was heavy. "What are you saying?"

"I have amnesia."

"You're shitting me."

"I'm not. It really exists and apparently, I have it."

"But you remembered me."

"In my mind, we just met at the luncheon you hosted."

"All we've been through, our time together, our conversations, everything . . . it's gone?"

She winced at the dismay in Andrea's voice. No matter what she did, she managed to disappoint everyone. "I'm sorry."

"You have *nothing* to apologize for. This happened to you. And we'll get through it. I'll do whatever I can to help you, okay?"

The sting of tears burned her eyes and stole her voice.

"Well that explains why I hadn't heard from you. Is it fair to assume you haven't contacted anyone from your job?"

How could she when she didn't know where she worked? She hadn't gotten her cell phone until the morning she'd been released.

"Do I still work at the Women's Defense Fund?" Leighton asked.

"That was your first job on the Hill."

Her *first* job? "Where do I work now?"

"Faulkner & Ingersoll."

She was a lobbyist? And not just any lobbyist. Faulkner was one of the best lobbying firms in DC. "They're big league. I must be doing well."

"Depends on your metric for 'doing well.'"

"You don't seem to approve."

"It's not my life. I will say that you were satisfied with the decisions you'd made to get to that point."

On the surface it sounded good, but the woman's manner and carefully worded statements suggested the opposite.

"You said our conversation upset you."

"That was before I knew—"

Leighton leaned forward on the bed, gripped the phone tight in her hand. "Please. I need to know."

"Maybe it's better if you remember on your own."

"Why? You can tell me what happened, what was said."

"It's not that simple. Anything I remember, all of my impressions, will be from my own point of view, filtered through my thoughts. They wouldn't be fair to you or what you were thinking."

"You know what isn't fair? That I can't remember any of my recent life. Choices I've made, who I work for, who my friends are. None of it. It's like time stopped for me for six years. I'm still living in 2010, but life has moved on. Help me. Leaving me in the dark is like torture."

"What do you want to know?"

She exhaled, unaware, until that moment, of how tense she'd been. More puzzle pieces. "We met at your luncheon, but we seem to have a personal relationship, right?"

"That's right."

"When did that happen?"

"Not long after the luncheon. When I came into the

industry, I didn't have anyone looking out for me. It was always my intention to give back by mentoring."

Leighton understood the importance of mentoring, especially when you were the minority in your field of choice. Politics was still an old boys' network and it was critical to see someone who looked like you succeeding at what you wanted to do. That mirroring lent credence to the belief that it was possible to achieve your dreams.

"A couple of weeks after the luncheon, I called and asked you to meet me for coffee and the rest is history."

A history I don't remember.

"I became your mentor."

"Really?"

"That's what you said. Though I feel I've learned just as much from you as you have from me."

It appeared that Leighton's instincts toward the woman had been spot on. "So what happened that night?"

"We talked about your engagement."

Jonathan.

"So I *am* engaged?"

"Yes."

She pressed the palms of her hands against her eyes. Jonathan was her one constant right now. She needed to know she could still believe in him. In them.

"What else?"

"I congratulated you on making the top lobbyist list—"

Pride firmed her posture. "I did?"

Everyone who worked on the Hill knew about that list. It was huge, it—

"Wait, is that still a big deal?"

"Oh yeah," Andrea said, the smile in her voice clear.

"And then?" At Andrea's apparent hesitation she urged, "Don't stop now."

"I'm not sure I'm doing the right thing."

"Based on what you've said, we have a close relationship. I don't understand why we were arguing that day."

"We got into a discussion about where you were heading with your life."

"It sounds like I was going in the right direction. But you had a different opinion?"

"I did." Andrea sighed, the sound weighted, as if she'd concluded some inner argument with herself. "From the moment we met, you've been a straight shooter and you've expected the same from me. In this city, in this business, that type of trust is valued but seldom found. It's one of the things I love about our relationship. I'm going to assume that even though you're missing some memories, you're the same woman underneath. So no, I wasn't happy with the direction your life was taking."

Her stomach tightened into knots. "Why not?"

"Because I felt like you'd let the things that you'd discovered change your perspective and affect the decisions you were making."

"What things?"

"Now *that* I'm not going to tell you."

"What happened to all of that 'straight shooter' talk?"

"It's not my story to tell. Besides, you deserve the

chance to recover your memories on your own." Andrea swallowed. "And your fiancé? How has he been throughout your ordeal?"

Leighton pictured Jonathan standing in the room, talking to Shaniece, making her food.

She shivered in pleasure. Knowing he'd been there when she'd been in the coma and that he'd stopped by to see her almost every day since she'd awakened made her feel supremely cared for. She wanted to know everything about him, recapture every memory she'd lost.

And she would.

It would take time, but that appeared to be something they would have a lot of in the foreseeable future.

"He's been great. Having him by my side has made this whole situation bearable."

Andrea cleared her throat. "Then it appears I may have been wrong. You probably don't remember, but I hate to be wrong. In this instance, I don't mind."

"Thank you for calling."

"I'm glad I did. I needed to know for myself that you were okay."

Leighton looked around the room and closed her eyes. "I wouldn't say I'm *okay* . . ."

"Considering what I'd been imagining, I think you're doing incredibly well. I'll call your assistant and let her know what happened."

"Don't tell them—"

"I won't give them any details," Andrea assured her.

"I'll confirm you were in an accident, and that you'll need some time to recuperate. You can call them when you're ready."

"Thank you."

"Anytime, doll." Andrea hesitated. "Do me a favor? Give me a call before you head back to work, whether you get your memories back or not."

The woman had done a lot for her. Leighton had more insight into who she was before the accident, even if she didn't like what she'd been hearing.

"I will. I promise."

"Take care of yourself."

Leighton ended the call, swirling in a vortex of her thoughts. Since she'd awakened from her coma, she'd assumed the solution to her situation was to regain her missing memories. Naively, she'd believed the life she couldn't remember had been perfect and once she was made whole, everything would fall into place and she'd continue on as if nothing had ever happened.

First the feeling that Jonathan was keeping something from her and now this cryptic phone call from Andrea Ferris . . .

For the first time Leighton considered the notion that getting her memory back might be the beginning of her problems.

Chapter Eleven

IT WAS AFTER midnight and the house was dark when Jonathan returned home from *Sedici*.

Six hours. He hadn't meant to be gone that long. The cooks had finally memorized the menu and he'd been able to put them through their paces. The kitchen wasn't anywhere near what he'd envisioned, but after this evening, he had faith they could get there.

And that wouldn't have happened if he hadn't gone in. So his unseemly desire for Leighton wasn't *all* bad. It had gotten him out of the house before he'd done something stupid, like confess his sins or kiss her until he could recall her taste on demand. But he wasn't in the clear yet. That's why he planned to go straight to bed—do not pause at her door!—before his ever present stupidity reared its dumb head.

He shut the door behind him, tossed his keys in the

wooden bowl on the credenza and tripped over something on the floor by the entryway.

"Dammit!"

He flipped the light switch on the wall and was surprised to see Leighton's bag from the hospital sitting where he'd dropped it when they'd first come home.

Why was it still there?

Did it matter? It wasn't like it contained anything she needed. It only held the dress she'd been wearing the night of the accident and the few personal items she'd acquired during her hospital stay. Not like her purse—he peered into the living room . . .

Which still lay, like petrified remains, on the chaise portion of his sectional where she'd initially deposited it.

He fought the unease that prickled his scalp.

You're letting your guilt from leaving her alone drive you to Crazytown. She's fine.

The pep talk didn't work.

He strode down the long, narrow hallway to the kitchen, disturbed by the deathly still atmosphere that greeted him. Tumbleweed rolling aimlessly across his slate floors wouldn't have been out of place.

Nothing had been moved.

There were no dishes in the sink, no containers in the trash. He opened the refrigerator and saw the food he'd put there earlier.

Untouched.

What the hell?

He retraced his steps, reaching the stairs and taking them two at a time.

Setting aside propriety, he flung open the door—

And rubbed the spot on his chest over his heart.

Her room was shadowy, save for the streetlight that shone in from the window, highlighting the huddled figure on the bed. Leighton lay facing away from him, her back curved, head bowed, arms and legs drawn up to her torso. There was an even tempo to her breathing, a steady rise and fall that indicated she was asleep.

He leaned against the doorjamb, closed his eyes and pinched the bridge of his nose. He hated his brother in that moment, but no more so than himself. Why in the hell had he ever agreed to this? Her need for love and support from her fiancé was obvious and yet he *couldn't* provide it.

He'd had to employ every trick in his disciplinal arsenal to keep his distance from her. It'd been much easier in the hospital. Nothing like the scent of antiseptic, the sight of machines and tubing and the sound of heart monitors and children crying to depress his libido and remind him of the inappropriateness of his carnal thoughts.

But seeing her in his house, looking like she belonged: tall, lush, beautiful, with skin like dark satin?

His willpower had failed him and his hands had transformed into sentient beings, tingling with the need to touch her, to hold her. He'd had to restrain himself—

literally—holding his mail, crossing his arms, shoving his hands in his pockets, anything to keep them from straying to where they'd craved to be.

With his hands on lockdown, his eyes had picked up the slack. The looks that passed between them set the blood boiling in his veins and threatened to demolish the wall he'd spent the better part of a week erecting. And then she'd walked into his arms and breached all of his defenses.

Initially, he'd planned to stay home and keep an eye on her. Watch a movie or something similarly low-key. But after that embrace, any thought of staying was out of the question. He needed space. And three levels of living in thirty-five hundred square feet wouldn't be enough.

Leaving her had been a dick move, but giving in to what he'd been feeling would've been unpardonable. So he'd inoculated himself from shame, told himself she'd call if she needed to, and he'd dived headfirst into last minute preparations for the restaurant.

When he'd finally looked up and seen it was after midnight, a bitter taste had coated his tongue. He'd checked his phone but found nothing from her on his missed calls log. No missed texts. Maybe he'd misread the situation.

Maybe she'd wanted some time by herself.

But seeing her now . . .

He was a fucking idiot.

She whimpered and the sound ripped him apart.

He perched on the edge of the bed and shook her shoulder.

"Leighton."

She jerked awake and turned wide espresso-colored eyes to him. Her distress constricted his already-battered heart.

Which took another beating when the light accentuated the faintest trace of tear tracks on her cheeks.

"Hi." Her voice emerged low and a tad rough.

"Why didn't you call me?"

She shrugged. "I didn't want to bother you."

"I gave you my number for a reason. You wouldn't be bothering me."

"I wasn't sure, since you were in such a hurry to get out of here."

Her words scored a direct hit. He sighed. "I'm sorry."

"Why?" She sighed and rolled back to face the window, laying her head down on her arm. "You didn't sign up for this and you don't have to be here. You can go."

Her body was rigid, her shoulders curling over her chest, sorrow and anguish emanating off her in waves.

Listen to her, Moran. Go. Right now.

That's exactly what he should do. Her earlier embraces, the kisses in the hospital . . . she wasn't responding to him. Hell, she didn't even like him. She was probably reacting to subliminal feelings she had for Thomas. And when she'd been told that Jonathan was her fiancé, she'd transferred that affection to him.

He couldn't allow himself to trust it was real or to do anything to bolster the belief that they were a couple. Thomas would return soon or she'd get her memories back. Either way, Jonathan only hoped they could move past their previous hostilities and try to get along. Having spent time in her company, with her guard down, he could finally acknowledge what his brother found attractive about her, physical beauty aside. Although—

I asked Leighton to marry me because I respect her and admire her, and because we have the potential to become an influential couple in this city.

Had Thomas ever seen the vulnerable side of his fiancée? If he was here, would he give her the affection she so desperately needed?

Considering he'd left the country when she'd been in a coma, Jonathan didn't think so.

Fuck it.

Before he could second guess his decision, he kicked off his shoes and lay down on the bed. He curved an arm around her waist and pulled her back until she was nestled against him, her head resting on his outstretched arm.

His soul appeased, satisfaction extended from his chest and spread throughout his body.

"I'm sorry," he said again.

She exhaled and fitted her body more snugly against him. "Me, too."

"You don't have anything to apologize for. I never should've left you alone, not on your first night home."

"I was so afraid."

Light couldn't travel through the space between their bodies yet he still had to strain to hear what she'd said.

Leighton afraid? He pictured the woman who'd walked into *Sedici* like she'd owned the place. "Why?"

"How often have I stayed here? Do I know anyone in this neighborhood? Are they friendly?" She shook her head, her hair soft against him. "I had no idea who I could trust. I felt alone."

Though it wasn't his promise to make, he told her, "You're not alone. If I have anything to say about it, you never will be."

Shudders wracked her body and warm tears seared his skin.

Aw hell.

A lump materialized in the back of his throat. "No. Leighton, please. Don't cry."

"Sorry."

"And for fuck's sake, stop apologizing."

He shifted and bent his arm, urging her to face him. Using his thumb, he brushed away her tears and traced the path of her angular cheekbones.

"You're so lovely." There was no mistaking the reverence in his voice.

Strands of her hair stuck to her cheek and lips. He gently pulled them away and off her face. When said thumb touched the corner of her mouth, she pressed a kiss to its pad, stealing his breath. As she gazed up at him, her expression open and trusting, he knew he'd do everything in his power to ensure he was never again the cause of her tears.

She encircled his wrist with her hand, parted her lips and—God help him!—he was unable to resist her.

Their mouths met, in their first real kiss since the night of the accident, and his heart sighed, as if a hundred years had passed. She moaned, and delved her fingers into his hair, sending a spasm of pleasure rocketing through him. He couldn't believe the sensations she'd engendered or his body's response.

He'd intended to go slow, to savor the fullness of her lower lip, drown in her intoxicating fragrance. But the sweetest fruit couldn't compare to her enticing taste and he could no more resist going deeper than he could stand up and walk away from her.

He crushed her close and swept his tongue into the warm interior of her mouth, swallowing her moans of pleasure. His cock throbbed painfully, and he experienced a searing need to bury himself balls deep inside of her and feel her warmth surrounding him. But he fought the keening demand, intent on enjoying the here and now.

Time stood still as they tasted, suckled and nibbled. Her mouth was made for kissing, her full lips a fantasy come to life. And she knew how to use them. He thought he'd enjoyed kissing before, but kissing Leighton was making his dick harder than it had ever been in his life. Only when red spots bloomed beneath his eyelids, did he succumb to self-preservation and break the embrace.

He rested his forehead against hers, his lungs working like pistons to draw badly needed oxygen into his body.

"Is it always like that?" she asked, their exertions lending her voice a breathy quality.

He'd been so focused on watching her mouth form the words that he missed her question. "What?"

"When we kiss. Is it always like that?"

"Like what?" He forced his attention away from her lips, curious to hear her answer.

"Like . . . everything. Like I could live off your kisses. Like they could sustain me. Forever."

He cupped her cheek. "Yes."

Their lips met again and again, each kiss longer, deeper and wetter than the one before it. Leighton sighed and he breathed it in, reveling in her hands squeezing his shoulders, caressing the nape of his neck, gripping his hair. His heart pounded loudly in his chest, drowning out all the reasons he should push her away and leave before he did anything he'd be unable to take back.

But his attempt at restraint was crippled when she trailed her hands down his back and gripped his ass. She slid her thigh between his, cradling him against her heat.

Damn, she would be his undoing.

Breaking away from her lips, but promising himself he'd be back, he laid small kisses along her jaw, then buried his face in her neck, inhaling her scent until he was drunk on it. She was so warm and soft and responsive in his arms.

And in this moment, she was his.

Goosebumps spread beneath his fingers and she shivered.

"Are you a dream or is this real?" She whispered, her clutching fingers and softly spoken words driving him out of his mind.

He removed one of her hands from his ass, shifted, and pressed it against the front of his jeans. "Does this feel like a dream to you?"

Her fingers caressed the length of his cock through the material.

"Hell, yeah," she said.

This woman . . .

He reached for the hem of her shirt and several seconds later, it—and her bra—was banished to the bedroom floor. He braced himself above her and feasted on the tempting spectacle she presented: blazing eyes, hair a black curtain on the pale sheets, full and rounded breasts with dark brown nipples. Her skin glistened in the light and his palms itched to stroke its softness.

"Damn, sweetheart. How is any man supposed to see this and then let you go?"

"That seems irrelevant now, because you don't have to."

If only that were true. He caressed and squeezed the mounds, and she moaned, arching into his touch. He flicked his tongue against a nipple, feeling the peak tighten against his tongue. He alternated the pressure, mixing little flicks with long laps and then pressing the bud against the roof of his mouth. She burrowed her fingers in his hair and pressed his head to her. Leaving one nipple, his kissed his way across the valley between her breasts to the other, lavishing it with the same attention.

She writhed against him. "Please, babe . . ."

"What do you want?" He murmured around a nipple.

"You. I just want you. Inside me."

He froze. What the fuck was he doing?

He had to put a stop to this right now. Struggling for control, he drew in a shaky breath and rested his head on her chest. Her heart thumped against his cheek. He hadn't meant for it to go this far. It wouldn't be right, for reasons too numerous to list.

"Jonathan?"

But he had to make her feel better, to atone for leaving her alone when she'd needed him. And though he was so fucking hard his dick could drive nails into the hardwood floors at the restaurant, this wasn't about him. It was all about her.

He reached for a pillow. "Lift your hips, sweetheart."

She did as he instructed and he slid the pillow beneath her lush round ass, propping her up to the perfect height.

"Let me make you feel good."

He gripped the edge of her pants and his tongue christened each inch of skin he revealed. He dipped into her belly button, kissed her hip bones, nuzzled the crisp hair on her mons. When he finally pulled the fabric off her long legs, moisture flooded his mouth.

Absolutely gorgeous.

The pants joined her other clothes on the floor.

He ran his finger beneath the elastic of the black lace. She was so wet he could see it through the fabric. His blood sped to his dick so fast it sounded like he was in a wind tunnel.

He slid her panties off and spread her thighs until she was bared before him. Such a beautiful contrast, a pretty pink against the dark cocoa of her skin. He settled between her legs, gripping her thighs and placing them over his shoulder. Capturing her gaze, and holding it, he leaned forward and put his mouth on her.

She bucked against him, but he clamped an arm around her, holding her steady and using his hand to open her wide. He tugged on her flared lips, then flattened his tongue and took a long slow lick from the bottom of her vulva to the top.

She exhaled and dug her fingers into his hair. He teased her folds with his tongue then firmed the tip and moved it in a figure eight pattern until he could feel her clit swell against his tongue.

"You taste delicious." She was the best thing to excite his palate in a long time.

When he drew the engorged nub between his lips, she stiffened. He didn't get the hint at first, but when she tugged on his hair and angled her sweetness away from him, her resistance penetrated his haze.

He raised his head. "Do you want me to stop?"

If she did, he would, but the effort would kill him.

Her fingers softened their grip and she shook her head. "Just don't suck on it."

Thank god! "Yes, ma'am."

He refocused on his task and gentled his actions. She relaxed against him, and entwined her fingers with his on her lower belly. Once again, her cries of pleasure filled the air, making him drunk.

"You are my new favorite flavor."

He slipped one finger in, then two. She was so warm and wet. God, he couldn't even imagine what she would feel like against his cock. He rotated his fingers and used his thumb to gently move the skin back and forth over her clit. Her inner walls clenched his fingers and she began to frantically grind against his hand.

"Babe . . . oh . . . oh, fuck . . . I'm coming . . ."

She arched off the bed, her arms braced behind her, her head thrown back, her lips formed into a silent O.

It was the sexiest sight he'd ever seen.

Gradually, she floated back onto the bed. He couldn't help the warm satisfaction that filled his chest at her dazed expression. He pressed soft kisses to her inner thighs. She sighed and tugged his fingers, pulling him up her body. When they were face to face, she placed her palms on his cheeks and stared into his eyes, before bringing his head down and kissing him, her tongue swirling around his, than across his lower lips and chin, tasting her essence on him.

His cock throbbed in his pants, as if to remind Jonathan that it was his turn, but when she reached for the button on his jeans, he stilled her fingers.

"No."

"It's okay," she whispered. "I have an IUD, remember, so there's no risk of pregnancy. And I got the full range of tests while I was in the hospital. I'm disease free."

"If I was worried about diseases, I probably would've asked before I did what I did. And just so you know, I had a complete check-up done at the beginning of the year and I'm negative for any STDs. But that's not it."

"Then what? You don't want to?"

Oh he wanted to, a hell of a lot. He was so hard he was about to burst. His dick hadn't known anything but his hand since he'd moved back to DC, finding the thought of fucking any woman but her unappealing.

"Of course I do, but now isn't the time. I just wanted to make you feel good."

A thought occurred to him. "Shit." He stood.

She rose up on her elbow. "Where are you going?"

"I'll be right back."

The master, at the other end of the second floor, was the only en-suite bedroom, so he went into the hall bathroom and wet a washcloth with cool water. He was back with Leighton in seconds, climbing on the bed and pressing the cloth against her inner thigh.

"I wasn't thinking. My stubble probably rubbed you raw. This should help."

She stared at him, wide eyed. "I need my memories

back if only to remember what good deed I was doing the moment before you walked into my life."

And that was the moment Jonathan knew he was in a damn sight more trouble than he'd ever thought possible.

Chapter Twelve

LEIGHTON DISCOVERED SOMETHING about herself during the past fifteen minutes: her love for, and proficiency in, cooking hadn't flourished during the six years she couldn't remember.

She stared at the yellow and brown clumps hardening in the pan and spilling over the sides to roast in the fire beneath the grate. How could this be so difficult? It's not like she was trying to make Beef Wellington or Boeuf Bourguignon. She just wanted to scramble some freaking eggs!

And she hadn't wanted to ask Jonathan. Last night had been amazing. Heat flooded her body as she flashed back to Jonathan's skillful use of his tongue and fingers to make her come. If that encounter was any indication of their love life *before* the accident, it was no wonder her body remembered him.

But it'd happened in a moment of comfort. There had been numerous occasions when they'd been close and the situation had practically screamed for a kiss. Yet he'd consistently walked away. Except last night. When she'd been crying over being left alone. How pathetic!

It scared her that he was the only person who sparked some sort of recognition—some awareness!—within her. It's like her body knew him and was urging her mind to trust him. He'd become her lifeline to the world. He grounded her. But she didn't want to be *that* woman. The woman who couldn't function without a man. That's not the dynamic she wanted to bolster between them.

So to prove she wasn't helpless, that she could take care of herself, she'd decided to get up and make breakfast. Okay, so it wasn't exactly a Joan of Arc moment, but she'd had to start somewhere. She'd planned to greet him pleasantly, engage in polite chitchat and resist the urge to pull his head between her legs and ask for seconds—

No! She shook her head. That was the opposite of what she needed to do. She wouldn't be the reason he neglected his restaurant any further. She'd keep her uneasiness to herself and use her time alone to figure out her next move. Only she'd forgotten she couldn't cook. Or, more accurately, a part of her had wished she'd acquired the desire to learn.

Obviously not.

She reached for the stem of the frying pan and yelped when her thumb brushed against the hot rim. Sucking on the injured digit, she pulled the dish towel from the oven handle and used it to awkwardly grab the pan with her left hand, and throw it, plus the gelatinous eggs, in the trash.

A bitter, pungent scent wafted past her nose an instant before the loud blaring of the smoke alarm permeated the room.

Son of a bitch!

"Oh come on! It's not that smoky in here."

She started waving the towel frantically beneath the annoying white circle of doom.

Heavy footsteps pounded down the stairs.

Great! Bang up job on the not-appearing-to-be-helpless project.

"What the hell is going on?" Jonathan's eyes were wide and frantic. "Are you okay?"

"Fine," she said, shaking the towel overhead, her body swaying like a hula dancer having spasms. "Everything's fine."

His gaze skimmed from the smoke billowing out of the front left burner, where eggs were being charred beyond recognition, to the open trashcan lid where the hot skillet sizzled and melted the plastic trash bag, to her uncoordinated and unsexy movements trying to muzzle the alarm. He nodded. "Yeah, I can see that."

He navigated the sun-drenched kitchen in his bare feet and opened the door that led out to the back yard. Leaving it ajar, he crossed over to the stove and pressed a button on the exhaust fan. A loud whirr clashed with the alarm in an annoying cacophony.

"What were you—" he shouted, stopping when the

alarm finally quieted. He continued in a normal-volumed voice "—trying to do?"

"Make scrambled eggs."

He scratched his whiskered jaw and peered into the stainless-steel trashcan. "Is *that* what this is?"

"It's not funny."

"You're right. The crime you've perpetrated on these eggs is not the least bit amusing." He removed the pan from the trash and set it in the sink. "Nor is what you did to my pan. This is a two-hundred-dollar piece of cookware."

For a pot?! She winced. "Sorry. I didn't know."

Jonathan turned on the hot water and added liquid dish soap. "If you wanted eggs, I would've made them for you."

The sun shone on his rich dark hair and she stared at his broad back, brilliantly encased in a gray t-shirt. "I wanted to do it myself. I don't want to be a burden."

He turned to face her, a frown clouding his features. "You're not a burden."

Now that the crisis was over, she wanted to allow herself a moment to study him at her leisure, but her attention was kidnapped by the slogan on his shirt:

Chuck's BBQ! Once you put my Meat
in your mouth, you'll want to Swallow.

"Seriously?" she choked out.

"What?" He looked down at his chest. "Oh. A going away gift from the staff at *Quartet*."

"Charming."

He shrugged, an adorable crinkle appearing at the corner of his eyes. He was too cute for his own good. That smile was a certified platinum "Get Out of Jail Free" card. "You're up early."

"I'm an early riser, always have been. Wait, has that changed?"

"I meant I thought you would sleep in, especially after last night." He headed to the other side of the kitchen. "Would you like a cup of coffee?"

Although her nerves were already hopping, she said, "Sure. Thanks."

He nodded at the peninsula. "Have a seat."

She slid onto the black and white swivel bar stool. "About last night—"

He stilled in the act of adding coffee beans to a grinder. "Yeah?"

"Thank you."

He leaned a hip against the counter and tousled the hair at the nape of his neck. "This is a new situation for me. You're . . . welcome?"

Heat pooled in her cheekbones and she closed her eyes. "Not that! For comforting me."

"Well . . ."

Her eyes popped open at his teasing tone. "Will you stop? I'm trying to be serious. I'm sor—"

His head dropped back. "Don't apologize again!"

"I'm not!" She totally was.

"Good."

She pressed her hands on the butcher-block countertop, smoothed them against the cool surface. "It's just . . . you're opening a restaurant. I can't imagine how much work is involved and I shouldn't have made you feel bad for doing what you had to do. Especially considering the time you've already taken off."

He poured coffee into a mug and handed it to her. "Not your fault."

"It won't happen again. I know how much work you have to do to get ready for your opening, so you don't have to worry about me."

The heat from his gaze vaporized her breath. "Perks of the job. I'll always worry about you." He clapped his hands together. "But not today. I have something else planned."

"Really?" She couldn't help responding to the excitement in his voice.

"Yes. We don't know how long it'll take to get your memory back, but we do know dwelling on it won't make it happen any quicker. We need to take your mind off it."

"My memory has been compromised. It's kind of difficult for me to dwell on anything."

"Smart-ass."

"Not the first time I've heard that about myself."

He winked. "How about I make you some scrambled eggs? Then our adventure can begin."

"Are we going somewhere? If so, you'll need to change that shirt. I refuse to be seen with you in public while you're wearing it."

"We're not leaving the house."

"Then what are we going to do?"

He opened the refrigerator and pulled out the carton of eggs. "We're going to take a break from everyone and everything."

"And how do you suggest we do that?"

"You'll see."

Half an hour later, after a breakfast of beautiful, fluffy and tasty eggs, she settled on the black leather sectional in the living room.

"How large is this TV?" She watched the muscles in his back tense and flex as he drew the curtains closed.

"Eighty-five inches."

"They make them that big?"

He turned, a devilish grin teasing his lips. "That's not the first time I've heard that about myself."

She laughed. "What about the restaurant?"

"I have a really good sous chef. Gib can handle things for a while." He grabbed the remote from the fireplace mantel and plopped down next to her.

Intent on starting Operation Not-So-Needy, she scooted a full cushion away from him and tucked her feet beneath her. "What do you watch on your big TV? Porn?"

He wrinkled his nose. "I'm not into the seventies theater experience. I usually watch sports."

"What kind of sports do you like?"

"Basketball mainly."

Interesting. She would've thought football or baseball. "Favorite team?"

"I've lived in the Bay Area for the past fifteen years. Dub nation, baby."

"Is that supposed to mean something to me?"

"I guess not, especially with—"

"Because if I recall correctly, they haven't won a championship since 1975."

His look of incredulity was downright comedic. "Whoa, what? You watch basketball?"

"I watch it. I played it." She raised her arms, pantomiming taking a shot. "Capitol Prep's starting point guard, sophomore through senior year."

He raised both brows. "Consider me impressed."

"I'm not sure that's a compliment. It doesn't take a lot to impress you. Your favorite team hasn't done much since the 70s."

"Ahh, Sleeping Beauty, you've forgotten a lot. We won the title last year."

She shoved his arm. "You're lying!"

"No need." He grabbed his phone and brought up the information.

There it was: the Golden State Warriors won the NBA Championship in 2015. In her mind, the Lakers had just won. Hell, the Warriors weren't even on the radar!

When she handed the sleek device back, she noticed the scripted *C* engraved on its back. "What's the *C* stand for?"

"Computronix."

"Something else I've forgotten?"

"Only the fastest growing tech firm in the world. But I'll put in a good word for you. My two best friends own it."

"Now consider me impressed. That sounds exciting."

"It can be. I go to all of their product launches, I tend to know about new products before others, but mainly, I get to be their friend. They're great guys."

His esteem sparked her curiosity. What kind of men invoked this kind of affection from her fiancé?

"How did you meet them?"

"You actually want to hear this?"

"I wouldn't have asked if I wasn't interested." Another thought occurred to her. "You've told me this before, right? Humor me."

He stretched an arm along the back of the sofa. "We met when we were in college."

"Where'd you go?"

"Stanford."

Sexy, talented and smart? "Not bad."

"Would've been better if I graduated."

"You didn't graduate?"

"No."

"Why not?"

"Once I discovered cooking, I realized I didn't need a degree to pursue my career of choice."

Leighton couldn't imagine not graduating from college. Since she'd been a child, higher education had been an expectation. Not *if* she would go to college, but *where*. Not *if* she would attend graduate school, but *which* advanced degree she'd pursue.

"How did you end up on the West Coast?"

"I'd applied to Stanford on a whim. I had offers fro

a few prestigious area universities and a full scholarship to a local school, but . . ." He rubbed the back of his neck. "I needed space. So I decided to go to Stanford."

"What did your parents say?"

"They didn't know I'd applied. And when I told them, they weren't happy. I convinced them I could handle it, but I didn't tell them Stanford only offered me a partial scholarship. I was too proud to ask my parents for support. I took my savings, and the monetary gifts I got for my high school graduation and ended up working in a small restaurant near campus."

That must've been hard for him. He'd had a full ride to college but had turned it down and struck out on his own. He was either extremely brave or extremely stupid.

"Did you always want to be a chef?"

"No. To be honest, I had no idea what I wanted to do with my life. My parents had their own ideas, but that involved me being a mini version of my brother. And that wasn't going to happen. I ended up at that restaurant because they advertised an opening and, well, free food. By then, I was running out of money and convinced I'd made a mistake. I thought I'd take the job, save up money and come back home."

"With your tail between your legs?"

"Exactly. But I loved working in the restaurant."

"And is what you told Shaniece true? About how you ended up becoming a chef?"

"Every word of it. Except I made it seem a lot easier than it was. It's hard work. No one would do it unless they had no other option or they couldn't imagine doing anything else."

"And you couldn't?"

"No. After my first month working, I'd earned enough money for a bus ticket home. But by then, I was hooked."

"And when did you meet your friends?"

"Adam, Mike and I were in the same dorm our first year. Adam and Mike met first. Then we all became friends." He smiled softly. "I learned more about brotherhood from those two men than I did from the person who shares my blood. We've been there for each other, always, through good times and bad."

It sounded so affectionate and sincere. The idea that there would be people who'd have your back, no matter what. That's what family was supposed to be. But that same feeling didn't apply to his actual brother. Interesting.

"Who are my best friends?"

His lips firmed into a tight line and his gaze slid away from hers. "I'm not sure."

"You don't know my friends? Didn't we hang out with them? Do things together?"

"We were both—"

"Busy with our work. I know." The refrain of the decade.

"Hey." He tapped her leg. "You're dwelling. This is exactly what I wanted to avoid."

He aimed the remote at the TV, pressed several buttons and an image of a woman in a wedding dress surrounded by five women in tight bubble gum pink dresses appeared on the screen.

She read the title of the movie. *"Bridesmaids?"*

He reached across the space she'd created and took her hand, lacing their fingers together. His hold was firm, his calluses a delicious abrasion against her palm. Inwardly she smiled, pleased at the overture.

"We're going to catch you up on some of the things you've missed."

LEIGHTON LIFTED THE lid off the box and smiled. "Cheese."

"Seemed like a safe bet."

"When I was younger I only liked cheese pizza. If anything else was on it, I wouldn't touch it. And you couldn't fool me by getting a pepperoni pizza and pulling the meat off. I could always tell." She lifted a piping hot slice from the box and took a bite. The cheesy goodness was unreal. "Do you make pizza at your restaurant?"

He chewed his own piece and shook his head.

"What kind of food do you make?"

His tongue darted out to catch sauce on the corner of his mouth and flames of desire licked along her belly. Just like he'd done the night before.

"I can cook anything, but I specialize in Italian and French inspired cuisine."

"That sounds delicious. What's your favorite dish to prepare?"

"Uh-uh. I plead the fifth. That's like asking a parent to name their favorite child." His face darkened for a second. "Although for some parents, that might not be too difficult."

"Hey . . ." She reached out to touch his cheek. "What's wrong?"

He shook his head and smiled. "Nothing."

His smile was convincing, but she didn't buy it and she didn't want to ruin their fun. "What if I tickle it out of you?"

"I'll take you up on that another time. But how about this? I'll make you one of my favorite meals."

"Tonight?"

He shook his head. "Another day."

"You promise?"

"Promise."

"Okay. So, what's next up?"

She hoped it was another comedy. He had the best laugh, genuine and full-bodied. He often bent forward, as if the humor twisted his frame. She found it so endearing that even if she didn't consider the joke funny, the fact that he did made her laugh.

"I might be taking a risk with this one."

Her mouth dropped open as she took in the colorful costumes, the mayhem in the background and the big green monster. "Is this a comic book movie?"

"It is."

"Are you kidding me?"

"Nope."

"Then yeah, you took a big risk and it didn't pan out."

He pointed to the screen. "This movie got great reviews and it was directed by Joss Whedon."

"Joss Whedon directed a big budget action movie?"

"Yup."

She looked at the picture again. "There's only one woman on the cover. And she's not the star."

"Will you give it a chance?"

She pursed her lips.

"You liked the first one we watched, right?"

"It was hilarious. I almost peed myself."

"Thankfully, for my furniture, you were able to contain yourself. So you trust me, right?"

"I do," she said, without hesitation. Then she laughed. "Practice for our wedding. Do you like this movie?"

He hesitated and then said, "I do."

"Then I'll give it a chance."

"Thank you."

He leaned toward her then hesitated.

She experienced a keen sense of disappointment.

Don't pull away. You kissed me in lots of places last night.

He reached up and used his thumb to wipe something from the corner of her mouth.

"Pizza sauce," he said, wiping it on a napkin.

Oh.

Then he claimed her lips. Her heart raced and she yearned to sink her fingers into his hair and pull him

closer, but she didn't. Mainly because she was still holding a slice of pizza, but also because this was a real
moment. He'd decided to push beyond whatever had
held him back in the past.

He ended the kiss and looked into her eyes. "Ready?"

For the movie or more kisses? Hell, it didn't matter.
Her answer would always be the same.

"Yes."

THREE HOURS LATER, he hurried into the room with
snacks and bottles of water.

She motioned the universal "gimme" sign. "Did you
bring a blanket?"

"Of course," he said, pulling a brown one from beneath his arm.

"And tissues?"

"And tissues," he said, brandishing a box.

"Perfect. I want to be prepared. You were right about
the last movie so if you say I'll need tissues for this one,
I believe you."

"Can you promise me something?"

"It depends."

"Can you wait at least thirty minutes before you start
talking to the screen?"

She rolled her eyes. "Sure, if they wait until minute
thirty-one to do something stupid that requires my
comment."

He pressed a few more buttons and a picture of a blue face and vivid yellow eyes appeared on the screen.

She read the title. *"Avatar?"*

"Do you remember this?"

"No. Maybe that's a good thing?"

He laughed. "Come here. I think you'll enjoy this one."

She nestled into his arms, loving the warmth and security that surrounded her. Since waking up in the hospital, this had been the best time she'd had. Which wasn't a high bar to hurdle. Still, she had the feeling that even if she'd had a million memories to compare it to, it still would've ranked as one of her favorites.

There was no talk of memories, of what she had forgotten, and she'd abandoned any thoughts of keeping her distance hours ago. Instead she'd surrendered to the moment, made new memories and started to discover why she'd fallen in love with him in the first place.

Chapter Thirteen

THE FOLLOWING MORNING, Jonathan sat on the edge of his sectional, cell phone in one hand, a cup of coffee in the other. "How's things going?"

"Good," Gib said, the muted sounds of an active kitchen in the background. "They're setting up their stations. I'm going to stand in the pass and call out orders, like a real dinner service."

He smiled to himself. He'd done the same thing at *Quartet* whenever there'd been a menu change. "Sounds like you've got it all in hand."

"That I do. Don't worry about anything. I've got this."

Once again, he was grateful Gib accepted his offer to come to *Sedici*. Having faith in her had made it easier for him to take her up on her offer when he'd realized how much Leighton needed him.

"You've really stepped up, Gib, and on short notice. I appreciate it."

"That's my job, Chef."

"I'll be in tomorrow and I'll expect you to give me your impressions of the staff and how close they are to being ready to open."

He disconnected the call and took another gulp of coffee. He didn't know what he'd expected when he'd suggested a quiet day at home watching movies, but he knew he needed to take a step back from what he'd done the night before. Being with her had been more intimate than any of his previous sexual encounters. Which was a huge ass problem. He shouldn't have touched her, shouldn't have tasted her. But once he had, he'd been a goner.

He'd planned the movie marathon because that's what he should've done in the first place. He should've spend time helping her adjust to being out of the hospital instead of rushing out of the house like a bat out of hell because her nearness had turned him on. It may have taken him a while, but he eventually allowed the correct head to do his thinking. And he was glad he did. He'd had a hell of a good time. She fascinated him and the day had only increased his affection for her. He loved that they had the same taste in movies. He loved that she was a hoophead like him. He loved how much she loved food. He could've spent another day doing the exact same thing, and he would've, except her fear concerned him.

After this weekend, he couldn't afford to take any more days away from *Sedici*, at least not before it opened.

Leighton had an appointment with Dr. Faber on Tuesday to check in and Jonathan was going to encourage her to talk to the doctor about her fears. Her concerns were valid; DC was a big city and it could be a scary place, especially when you didn't know what to expect around any corner. He'd planned an outing that might help.

Any hope he had that Thomas would come back and take responsibility for her and his part in this situation had been frustrated by his brother's neglect. While Jonathan hadn't agreed with Thomas's decision to stay in London, there'd appeared to be some measure of common sense behind it. But it'd been a week with almost daily calls and texts from Jonathan and nothing. It was clear Thomas didn't give a fuck about his fiancée and that notion made Jonathan want to beat his brother's ass.

Leighton came bounding down the stairs, a walking ad for summers spent boating on the lake, in a navy and white striped dress that flared from her waist and ended just above her knee.

"Don't I wear jeans or shorts?" she asked, standing with both arms bent at the elbow, her palms facing up.

He'd wondered the same thing. When packing clothes for her, the only casual attire he'd seen had been yoga clothes, nightgowns and her bra and panties—not that he'd rifled through her underwear, but he knew she'd need some and then he'd gone through them and when all he'd seen had been lacy and satiny bits of scraps—

Desire settled hot, thick and low in his belly.

Crap.

He seemed to be in a constant state of arousal around her. It'd been bad enough when he'd just kissed her. But now that he knew what she looked like when she came on his fingers . . .

He stood and placed his cup on the mantel. "I've never seen you in either, but then you were always—"

She jammed her hands on her hips. "If you say 'busy with my career,' I'm going to punch you in the throat."

The corners of his mouth quirked. "Wow. Violent much?"

"No." Her displeasure deflated, she let her lashes fall. "It's just the more I hear about Leighton one point oh—"

"Leighton one point oh?"

"That's what I call her, or rather, me before the accident. It's how I keep us straight. Anyway, the more I hear about her, the more she doesn't sound anything like me."

"I can see how that would alarm you," he said softly.

She rubbed her forearms as if cold. Improbable in the heat and humidity of a late summer DC morning. "How do you feel about that?"

He frowned. "What do you mean?"

"You asked Leighton one point oh to marry you. Are you regretting that decision? I may never get my memories back. Maybe Leighton two point oh isn't what you signed up for?"

"And Leighton two point oh would be . . ."

"Me." She pulled an invisible thread from her dress, refusing to look at him. "Without my memories."

His heart constricted. He closed the distance between them and with his two fingers, tilted her chin up. "With or without your memories, you're still the most captivating woman I've ever met. That hasn't changed."

Her expression softened and his gaze fell to her parted lips. Lord, give him strength!

He stepped back and grabbed his keys. "Are you ready to go?"

"Yes. I'm so excited." She bounced from one white canvas shod foot to the other, those being the only non-dress or business shoes in her closet. "Where are we going?"

"It's a surprise."

Thirty minutes later they stood in front of the iconic red brick building, bordered by white tents and rows of vendors.

"I love the Eastern Market. Is that something we do every weekend?"

He stared down at her, captivated by the excitement that shone on her features.

"Not as often as I'd like," he said, smoothing away a stray hair that brushed against her cheek.

Her answering smile warmed him. Intellectually, he knew he should be working at the restaurant, but nothing waiting there could eclipse his anticipation at spending another day with Leighton and seeing one of his favorite places through her eyes.

He placed a hand on the small of Leighton's back and guided her toward the Farmer's Line, where local farmers boasted some of the freshest produce available in the tri-state area.

"I want to check out what they have," he said. "Maybe I'll find something to inspire me for dinner tonight."

Strolling down the line of stalls, they paused to sample the abundant fruits and vegetables on display. Jonathan made a mental note of a couple of places to revisit, but he was looking for a specific stand, one of his favorites.

When he spied the familiar white canopy with its blue border, he grinned. "Hey Bob, you bring me something good?"

"Chef J!" Bob's weathered face creased into a smile. "I would've brought you something if I'd known you were going to be here. I haven't seen you in weeks."

The older man ambled from behind his table on bowed legs encased in worn denim. Jonathan shook Bob's outstretched hand, feeling years of strength, hard work and tenacity in the man's big, calloused grip.

"I only show up when you have the good stuff. I can sense it."

"You do have an uncanny knack for coming on the best weeks." Bob's faded brown eyes fastened on Leighton. "And speaking of good stuff . . . Are you going to introduce me to my next wife?"

Leighton laughed. "It's a pleasure to meet you."

A dazed expression crossed Bob's face.

Nice to know I'm not the only one stupefied by her presence.

"You're already married and she's already taken," he said.

"By you?" Bob's forehead rippled into mini hills and

valleys and he shook his head. "Handsome, talented *and* with this beautiful woman? What magical moonshine are you drinking and where can I get a barrel full?"

"Stop flirting and let's get down to business." Jonathan rubbed his hands together. "What you got?"

Bob rounded his display. "Well, I got some nice blackberries, an assortment of cooking greens . . . Here, try some of this raw honey."

Bob dipped two flatbread crackers into a clear, plastic sample cup containing a grayish-white liquid. He handed a wafer to each of them.

Leighton popped hers into her mouth and her eyes widened. "That's really good. It's not just sweet. There are layers of flavor."

Jonathan rolled the rich, buttery texture against the roof of his mouth, activating his palate. "Floral with hints of lavender and a maple finish."

Bob stroked his salt and pepper beard. "Sourwood honey. One of the best and rarest produced."

Leighton pointed to the other samples. "May I?"

Bob handed her another cup. She dipped her pinkie into the nectar and stuck the digit in her mouth, her cheeks hollowing as she pulled the ambrosia off her finger.

His throat forgot how to function as his mind began cutting and pasting what he saw with the image of her sticking something else in her mouth and sucking on it. When she withdrew her finger and dipped it in the cup again, attempting to repeat the process, he intercepted her and slid the finger in his mouth instead.

Her lips parted and reconfigured into an O. His tongue swirled around the elegant digit and while the exquisiteness of the honey couldn't be denied, he much preferred the sweetness of her skin. While he suckled her finger, her gaze fell to his mouth, then lifted to clash with his. In their dark depths, he saw the ache of his own yearning reflected at him.

If they'd been home in that moment, he would've damned the consequences and continued what they'd started the night before.

"Do ya'll need me to step away for a moment?" Bob's dry humor broke the spell.

Leighton's chin dipped down. She lowered her gaze and tugged to free her hand.

Jonathan let her go, but her taste lingered on his tongue. He cleared his throat and faced the farmer. "I'll take a liter of the honey, but I know you've got something special you're hiding down in that cooler."

He kicked the hard-sided container peeking beneath the table cloth.

Bob pulled the white carton out and pried off the lid. "I got my hands on some Amish cheddar cheese and some of the best goat cheese you'll ever try."

Upon sampling the smooth, tangy dairy, he knew the other man was right. He didn't utilize either of those cheeses at his restaurant, but he was eager to whip up something at home that would best highlight both flavors.

"I'll take a wedge of both of those, too. Thanks."

"Anytime, Chef J." Bob set to work wrapping up his

purchases. "Tell me, when does that fancy restaurant of yours open?"

"On the ninth."

Leighton jerked her head around to gawk at him. "That soon?"

"Everything's proceeding according to the schedule." He winked at her then said to Bob, "Why don't you and your wife stop by that night?"

Bob's weathered cheeks reddened. "Oh, we couldn't. You'll need to entertain the city's food critics and celebrities, not some country farmer."

"Yes, but I also need to be surrounded by my friends." Jonathan clasped Bob's shoulder. "For once, don't argue with me. I'm going to put your and Opal's name on the list."

Bob nodded and squeezed Jonathan's arm, then glanced over at Leighton. "He's a good man."

She bit her lip and her eyes tightened at the corners. "So everyone keeps telling me."

Jonathan took the shopping bag from Bob, and with one last wave, continued strolling down the row. Produce, herbs and breads were available and he added a few other items to his purchases, but Leighton was quiet, withdrawn. Maybe sucking the honey off her finger had been too much.

"Did you come here a lot when you were little?" he asked, curious and wanting to get her talking again.

"Yes, but it wasn't always this big. My family moved

to Paris for four years while my father was an ambassador there and when we came back, they'd expanded."

Ah. *"Tu parles francais?"* he asked in French.

"Oui." She stopped walking, heedless of the crowd that continued to surge around them like river water around a stone impediment, and tipped her head to the side. *"Quand est-ce que tu as appris, too?"*

"Je ne connais pas grand chose, surtout les termes de cuisine et de gastronomie." He smiled and switched to Spanish. *"Mi espanol es mucho mejor."*

She frowned and he rushed to translate and ease her confusion.

"I said 'my Spanish is better than my French.'"

"Lo se," she said in Spanish, a cocky smile teasing her lips, *"estaba tratando de decidir si debo dejar que sigas creyendo eso o desafies la afirmacion."*

Bullshit! His Spanish was excellent. Okay, hearing her accent, maybe he'd have to downgrade his own fluency and intonation to pretty good, but he wouldn't admit that to her.

"How many languages do you speak?"

"As far as I know, only three. French, Spanish and Italian."

All places he loved to visit. "Is there anything you can't do?"

She bumped him with her hip. "Don't tell me the amnesia is contagious? I almost burned your house down yesterday."

He laughed and grabbed her hand. "Let's go."

Their fingers entwined and he brushed his thumb against her skin. She smiled at him and for the moment all was right with his world. Being at one of his favorite places with her filled him with joy. They continued, walking and holding hands as the produce, flowers and baked goods gave way to the artisan and craft section.

"Hold on." Leighton's face brightened when she spotted a stall featuring handmade leather jewelry.

Her fingers skimmed the goods and she asked questions, charming the seller and getting her business card with a promise to check out the woman's website.

She didn't purchase any of those items, but that didn't prevent her from stopping to chat with another vendor, this one selling vibrantly colored hand poured candles.

For fuck's sake, did she intend to stop and talk to every vendor there? He'd thought they were leaving. Now that he'd acquired what he'd needed, he was anxious to experiment with his purchases. He had some ideas about how he could utilize the goat cheese and the honey.

When she paused at another stand, he exhaled loudly. "Are you going to buy anything? At this rate, we'll never make it home."

She peered at him over her shoulder, a silver spherical sculpture in her hand. "I'm sorry, was there someplace else we needed to be?"

The soft volume of her question was his first clue that he'd made a mistake. "No."

She replaced the sculpture and picked up a ceramic jar. "You just figured we were only here for the food vendors, since that's what interested you?"

The back of his neck heated. That's exactly what he'd assumed.

She rolled her eyes and held out a tall brown and amber vase. "What do you think of this?"

He shrugged. "It's nice."

"Do you think you'd get tired of looking at it?"

"Why?"

"Because I'm thinking it would look great in the entryway."

"In my house?"

"*Your* house? Oh." She lowered the vase. "So you are a control freak."

Shit.

"I wasn't too busy to decorate and it had nothing to do with our decision to live separate until after the wedding. You don't want me to put stuff in your place. Why?"

He closed his eyes and pinched the bridge of his nose. How could he tell her it wasn't what she thought? It was a vase. If they were in a real relationship and she wanted to buy it for their house, he wouldn't object. That type of thing didn't matter to him one way or another.

But they weren't a real couple. Soon she'd go back to his brother and he'd be left looking at the stupid vase and remembering his time with her.

"I—I just don't like it," he finished weakly.

Leighton's withdrawal was a tangible thing. She returned the vase to the vendor and muscles engaged in her face to raise the corners of her mouth, but no one who'd ever seen the original would call it a smile. Her expression lost its usual animation and leveled out to one devoid of emotion. It was the first time he'd seen Leighton one point oh—as she'd named herself—since she'd awakened in the hospital.

He watched her and the space around him grew bleak, as if clouds had engulfed the sun.

Fuck!

He'd upset her, the last thing he'd wanted to do. He strove to rectify his error.

"What about this one?" He lifted a beautiful, palm-sized sculpture of a surging wave, constructed with two different colors of wood. Easy to exhibit and easy to discard when she left. "We can put this on the fireplace mantel."

She cocked her head to the side and arched a disbelieving brow. "It's your house. If you like it, you should buy it."

She maneuvered around him and proceeded on, her posture stiff, her movements spasmodic and lacking in their usual grace.

Idiot. Idiot. Idiot.

He replaced the piece and hurried to catch up with her. They walked for several minutes in an awkward, tension-filled silence. She no longer held his hand and his palms itched, a physiological rebuke. Gone was her pleasure in their surroundings. Before she'd drifted from booth to booth, asking the vendors about their process and inspiration, admiring their wares, her happiness infectious. Now, her head was aimed forward and she strode as if her eyes were on the exit and her body intended to follow.

They'd had an amazing weekend. He couldn't allow it to end in bitterness and anger because he'd allowed his own insecurities and uncertainty about the pact with his brother to affect her.

A few minutes more and the craft booths gave way to food vendors and music. A trio of musicians playing the guitar, saxophone and violin were surrounded by a crowd of people, clapping and swaying to the well-known jazz melody of a popular song.

Enough was enough. She was hurting and he needed to make it right. He set his bags down on the side of the tent then jogged after Leighton, taking her hand and leading her back to where the band performed.

"What are you doing?" she asked, slightly resisting the pressure of his tugging.

He raised and dropped his shoulders in an alternating pattern in time with the beat of the music and his steps matched the rhythm, hauling them backward.

Comprehension dawned in her eyes and she tried to pump the brakes, Fred Flintstone style. "Oh no."

He paused on the outskirts of the crowd, her fingers lightly clasped in his. "Please. One dance."

Various emotions skimmed over her features too quickly for him to figure out the direction of her ultimate decision. Finally, the tension eased from her stance and she moved with him toward the other two couples on the makeshift dance floor.

Her hips swayed, her body moved back and forth and he couldn't take his eyes off her. She smiled—a true one—and it burnished her features. In her dress, with her hair pulled back into a ponytail, she was easily the most stunning woman there and a tide of male satisfaction washed over him.

She was his.

For now.

It didn't matter. He'd take it.

Her lashes fell, her head dropped forward and she lost herself in the music. She was so fucking sexy! She released his grip and his jolt of dismay was appeased when she raised her arms above her head and shimmied, the epitome of womanly seduction.

Hot damn! His blood sallied south and set up camp in his dick. He lowered his hands and kept them around his waist while he danced in an effort to camouflage what had occurred.

No need to frighten any of the young children present.

The song ended with a flourish and the crowd clapped and expressed their admiration vocally and monetarily. When the band launched into a ballad, some of the spectators moved on, but he and Leighton didn't move. They stood staring at one another until he lifted his hand toward her, palm up.

She glanced at it, then at him, and he swore his heart

went into hibernation before she placed her hand in his and moved into his arms. He slid an arm around her lower back and pulled her close, pressing his cheek against her hair. The soulful notes provided them a cocoon from the world where no one was between them and nothing else mattered. She must've felt it too, because her soft curves melted into him. Relief closed his eyes and he squeezed her tight, inhaling the sweet citrus of her shampoo.

"I'm sorry," he whispered as they moved to the music.

She stiffened within his embrace, but she didn't respond.

"That didn't have anything to do with you. It was all me and the . . . shit I'm dealing with."

Would she acknowledge his apology?

"What's going on?" Her question slid into his ear, her tone hesitant. "Is there something you're not telling me? About us?"

How could he not confess when her anguish was obvious?

Determination galvanized his pulse and he set his jaw. Screw Thomas. He could come clean now. This was his chance, the universe giving him the opportunity to do the right thing. He'd explain everything to her and she'd understand. She had to.

She continued. "Very few things make sense to me right now. I have so many questions about who I was and who I am and the uncertainty is unsettling. It makes me afraid to seek out the answers I need."

She extracted her hand from his and twined it with her other, clasping them around his neck like he was her lifeline.

"But I recognized you. I can't remember anything about my life in the past six years, but I know you and, more importantly, my heart trusts you. And if I can't depend on that—" Her voice broke and her head moved against his.

This scenario had passed complicated and was hurtling toward fucked! Should he tell her the truth and risk derailing any progress she'd made in getting her life back on track? Or continue to lie to her and provide her the stability she needed until she was settled or her memories came back?

He reared back so he could look into her eyes. The faith he saw humbled him. He stroked his thumb along her jaw and when her lips parted, he lowered his head and kissed her, concentrating on pouring all of his concern and tenderness into the caress. He knew he'd succeeded when he felt her soften.

"We're okay," he told her when they'd parted, "and you're going to be fine."

He closed his eyes and hugged her tighter, wishing the song would never end, but knowing it would.

Just like this relationship, built on a lie.

Chapter Fourteen

"An actual phone call. To what do I owe the honor?" Jonathan asked, gripping the phone so tightly he actually worried he might break it.

"I've been busy," Thomas said, defensively.

Was he serious? Jonathan didn't know the measurement of his arms from one hand to the other, but if Thomas had been anywhere within his wingspan, he would've wrung his brother's fucking neck.

He tiptoed over to the railing and heard the water running in the hallway bathroom. Good, Leighton was still in the shower. Abandoning the ingredients for the breakfast he'd planned to make her before heading to the restaurant, he stepped out onto the back porch, closing the door behind him. He leaned against the wrought-iron railing and stared at the alleyway that divided the back of his house from the back of the neighboring Victorians a block over.

This had been going on long enough.

"So have I, and yet I've found the time to update you on the progress of your fiancée who has amnesia."

"I've responded."

Jonathan slid one arm across his chest, tucking that hand against his side beneath his elbow. "I'd hardly call '*Got it*' a viable response."

Silence.

Was he getting through to Thomas? Good. His brother needed to book the next flight to DC. Jonathan couldn't continue to do this. It wasn't even about the time away from *Sedici*. It was the time he spent *with* Leighton. She was sexy, smart, funny and quite unlike any woman he'd ever known. He'd lost all objectivity and his final desperate hope was that Thomas's physical presence would be enough to extinguish his growing feelings. Other than a rejection from Leighton, it was the only thing that could.

"It's not too late." Jonathan pitched his voice low, melodic and persuasive. "We don't have to make this worse. Come home."

Please.

"Not yet. Things are going well for me. That partnership will be mine. I just need to hang in here a little while longer."

That open window to freedom slammed shut. On Jonathan's neck.

"This is bullshit! When you left you said you'd come back in a week. It's been over that. Are you coming home this weekend?"

"No."

Fury at Thomas for not returning home flooded through Jonathan almost felling him. That selfishness meant Jonathan would have to continue this charade. It wasn't fair to him, but it was doubly unfair to Leighton.

Though his anger was fierce, it was no match for the guilt shredding his insides and daring him to complain. His intense initial attraction had progressed into genuine feelings for the woman who was going to marry his brother. The doctor said there was no reason to believe her memories wouldn't return. Was he willing to betray Thomas and risk her going back to him once that happened?

"You've placed me in an impossible position," he said.

His brother wasn't the only one to blame for this situation. Jonathan could've said no. He should've said no. But he'd let the belief of his culpability for her accident lead him to make a reckless decision.

What about now? What's stopping you from making the right choice now?

"Then it can't get any worse, right?" Thomas asked.

Cold fingers traipsed down Jonathan's spine. "What in the hell does that mean?"

"Kimberly Reed."

Why did that name sound familiar? "Your wedding planner?"

"She can see you and Leighton this afternoon."

"You're unbelievable!"

"She's doing us a favor." His brother's voice was calm, as if they were discussing the banalities of the day, not furthering their conspiracy to lie to Leighton. "We would've lost her services, but she's willing to squeeze us in even though we missed the last appointment."

This had to be an elaborate joke.

"Leighton had been in an accident." He enunciated each word carefully, as if talking to a toddler.

"At *your* restaurant." There was no mistaking the accusation in his tone.

And he doesn't even know the full story.

"I've explained our circumstances," Thomas continued, "and made her swear on her reputation that she'd keep it confidential."

"What did you tell her?"

"I told her about the accident, Leighton's memory loss and that you would be there acting as my . . . proxy."

Proxy? Jonathan threw up in his mouth a little.

"And this *Three's Company* caper wasn't enough to turn her off?"

"Apparently not. She's expecting you at four. Please don't be late."

A week ago he'd thought the worst thing that could happen to him was the delayed opening of his restaurant. He'd give anything to go back to that time.

"Thomas, we're digging a hole so deep, we'll never get out of it with our integrity intact."

"This amnesia thing is a tiny setback. When she remembers, she's going to be happy that I stayed on course with our plans." Thomas disconnected the call.

Jonathan didn't move. He was starting to wonder if his brother knew Leighton at all.

PINK WALLS, PINK pillows, pink area rugs on the hardwood floor. He'd taken a meeting in a Pepto Bismol bottle.

"What do you think, Jonathan?" Leighton tilted her head to the side and her hair cascaded over her shoulder.

He loved the way she said his name, loved watching her mouth and tongue utter the word.

So not appropriate right now.

He dragged his focus away from her beauty to the two elaborate flower arrangements on the table in front of them.

"Uhhh . . . Are you sure you want to do this now?" he asked her.

Kimberly Reed slid her glasses from her pale, round face. "I understand your situation and ideally, we would wait. But when we spoke previously and I agreed to do your wedding, you were adamant it happen in the spring of next year. That's only eight months away. If you're still sticking with that timeline, there are some decisions we have to make now."

She'd directed her response to Leighton, as she'd done since they'd shown up for the appointment. Ms. Reed had done everything possible to resist speaking to him or even looking in his direction. He didn't blame her. He couldn't imagine what she must think about him, his brother and this entire fucked up situation.

"Like the flowers?" Leighton confirmed.

"Exactly. You said you wanted your wedding to be luxurious, grandiose. A showstopper. Your choice between these two bouquets will point me in the right design direction."

Jonathan eyed the arrangements. *Bouquet* wasn't the word he would use. More like three feet tall floral behemoths. They screamed conspicuous extravagance to him.

"Now this one," Kimberly said with reverence, touching the stark white arrangement on the left, "would fit in with an elegant, soft-color palette. Think white, blush, coral."

He looked over to gauge Leighton's reaction. She'd tilted her head back, lips parted, to stare at the decoration.

"This one," Kimberly continued, patting the jewel-toned arrangement, "is more vibrant. You can go neutral and let it bring the pop of color or pull your palette from these blooms."

A woman came over to the table and showed Kimberly something on a tablet.

"Excuse me a moment." Kimberly stood, smoothed the fabric of her black dress with large pink blossoms over her hips, and left the office.

Leighton placed her hand on his thigh and leaned

close. "I picked *her*? I keep wanting to call her Elle Woods. What's up with all this pink?"

Her touch seared through his jeans and her sweet whispered breath tickled his ear.

He cleared his throat. "She's *the* premiere planner for the under forty crowd in DC," he said, parroting Leighton one point oh.

"What the hell was I thinking?"

Very good question. If he knew, he'd tell her.

She gestured to the botanic monstrosities. "Seriously, what do you think?"

He held his hands up, palms facing outward. "I'm a chef. You have questions about food, I'm your man. But flowers . . ."

"What kind of details did I give her at our first meeting?" Leighton pulled her lower lip between her teeth, leaving a sheen of moisture behind.

Good God, what had he done to justify such torture?

Oh, that's right.

He rubbed his nose and looked away. "I don't know. I didn't come with you."

"Why not? It's your wedding, too."

Fucking Thomas.

He exhaled and leaned forward. "The flowers look fine to me, but isn't it more important if you like them?"

She fingered a deep purple petal. "Something I said to her made her think I'd love these. They're so pretentious."

Great minds think alike.

Kimberly strode back into the room, grabbing a leather portfolio off her desk. "I apologize. Questions about the wedding we're doing next weekend. Let's talk venues. You said you were anticipating three hundred plus?"

Leighton's eyes widened. "That's a lot of people."

"There are several venues in the area that can accommodate that number of guests." Kimberly flipped open the portfolio to display laminated pictures. "The Four Seasons is a solid choice. They redid their ballroom and lower level and their staff is incredibly helpful."

Kimberly picked out another photo.

"The Ronald Reagan Building is an iconic DC wedding venue. And it's versatile. We can transform any of the spaces into a unique theme for you."

She chose several more pictures.

"But my favorite for you would be the Andrew W. Mellon Auditorium. It's one of the grandest, most beautiful venues in DC. We're talking serious 'wow' factor."

Leighton sat back and pressed a shaky hand to her forehead. Kimberly steamrolled along.

"Something else you'll want to consider. Some venues will say they can hold three hundred people, but that doesn't include space for the band, a dance floor or food stations. If you're not sure of the specific count, it's better to pick a larger venue than one that's too small."

The same young woman approached with a phone. Kimberly flicked her gaze upward but stepped away to take the call.

Leighton turned pained eyes to him. "Are you on board with this?"

"You can pick any venue you—"

"This is *our* wedding. It should be for both of us." She lowered her voice and pointed to the flowers and the laminated photos. "Is this what you envisioned for your wedding?"

He shuddered. "Hell no."

"Then why would I choose this type of wedding for us?"

She touched a hand to the nape of her neck. Her uncertain tone and obvious bewilderment spoke to him. For the millionth time, he questioned whether he was doing the right thing withholding the truth from her.

He stroked a hand along the back of her shoulders, her tension carving knots he couldn't help feeling. Fuck it. He didn't care what Thomas said or what the old Leighton would've wanted. He was entrusted with the care of *this* Leighton and she was clearly distressed by all of this.

"Please excuse me. I needed to take that call. Have you come to a decision?"

Leighton pressed her lips together and shifted in the pink and white brushed velvet chair, increasing the space between herself and the wedding planner. She scooped her hair over her shoulder and smoothed the ends.

"I—"

"No," he said.

Both women risked whiplash turning shocked faces in his direction.

"What?" Kimberly toyed with her pearl necklace. He finally had her full attention.

"We're not ready to make a choice." Hearing no denial from Leighton, he continued, "Not right now."

"I don't understand."

"You said you appreciated Leighton's situation, that you know what she's been through. She's not in any position to be making these choices. Can we reschedule for another time, like in a few months?"

By then, Thomas would be back and they would've told Leighton the truth. Maybe then, her memory would've returned and she'd remember the reasons behind her preferences. Or, she and Thomas could decide to go with something simpler. Either way, the two proper parties could make this decision together. He struggled to breathe through the pain that sprouted in his chest like an oxygen-coating, fire-fighting foam.

"That's not possible. Her—" Kimberly's eyes flickered. "*Your* wedding date is coming up, and between that and my schedule, we have to make these decisions now."

"Then I'm sorry we wasted your time." He stood and held out his hand. Leighton, her brown eyes shining, placed her hand in his. His heart pounded at the trust he saw in her gaze.

She stood and they turned to leave.

"Wait."

Kimberly was staring at him, speculation in her eyes.

"I'll tell you what I can do. I can set your account aside for about six weeks. I have two other weddings I'm working on. Once I clear those from my schedule, I'll check back in with you to see how you're doing and if you're up to continuing." Her sharp gaze cleaved him into pieces, making him fully aware he may have misjudged her. "Maybe some things will have changed."

He nodded and shepherded Leighton out of the office. When they exited the building, he was surprised when she headed in the opposite direction from the valet stand and perched on a brick half wall with a view of one of the city's downtown green spaces.

"What's wrong?" he asked, coming up next to her.

She didn't look at him. "I knew I didn't want to be there, that I wasn't ready to make those decisions, but I didn't know why. So thank you."

"You're welcome." Choosing not to sit, he shoved his hands into the front pockets of his jeans and studied her expression, noting her downturned mouth. "Are you going to be okay?"

"Aaaargh." She clasped her hands together and pounded them against her forehead. "I keep bumping into who I used to be and instead of filling me with peace and security, it's adding to my confusion." She gestured behind her. "Who did I plan that wedding for, a lost Kardashian sister?"

He smiled at her rhetorical question. She didn't have a high opinion of that family, remembering her comment about them the night she'd met the jeweler at *Sedici*.

"And what about my job? Growing up, my parents

were very keen on public service. My father often said we were privileged—it was our duty to give back. For some reason—another one I can't remember!—I left a job I loved at the Women's Defense Fund and ended up a *lobbyist*." She uttered the last word as if it belonged to one of the few languages she didn't know.

"Are they different?"

"Very. Advocates work to change some aspect of society. Lobbying is all about money and efforts to influence legislation. It's a big distinction, especially on the Hill. Why would I do that?"

Good question. "You said your mentor called you the night you were released from the hospital. Did she say anything that would help you?"

"No. But she wants to. Maybe if I push her . . . ?"

"You can talk to your doctors about this, too, but it's important that you do what you feel is best. Whatever you decide, you'll have my full support."

She braced her hand on the wall and finally looked up at him. "This doesn't mean I don't want to marry you. I do. But those choices, those details didn't feel right. I can't remember the person who made those decisions, and until I do, it's not fair to either of us to move forward. Are you okay with that? That doesn't hurt your feelings, does it?"

"No."

But it made him realize he didn't have half her strength. If he did, he'd tell her the truth. Now.

But he didn't.

He took her hands and pulled her to her feet. "You've only been out of the hospital for a few days. Let's focus on getting you better and put off talk about weddings. At least for a while."

She stood and slid into his arms. "I don't know how I would've gotten through this without you."

"And you won't ever have to wonder about it. As long as you want me, I'm here."

It wasn't a wedding vow, but it was a promise he intended to keep.

Chapter Fifteen

LEIGHTON PEERED THROUGH the glass into a meeting room that belonged in a mansion and not in a hotel. Four gold sconces graced the warm yellow walls and a long maroon-skirted conference table took up a majority of the narrow space. Andrea Ferris sat in a beige and gold tufted chair at the far end of the table watching a large TV mounted on the wall, a pen clamped between her teeth.

Leighton opened the door. "Is now a good time?"

Andrea held up her left hand, the light glinting off the simple platinum band on her ring finger.

Recognizing the universal *Give me a minute* sign, Leighton eased down the narrow space between the edge of the table and the wall, taking a vacant seat. She'd meant what she'd told Jonathan yesterday. She intended to learn more about the woman she'd been before the accident and since she'd had the feeling that Andrea had tried to tell her something, this was as good a place as any to start.

After a moment, Andrea pulled the black square frames from her face and tossed them on the yellow legal pad in front of her. "Hey, doll."

She reached forward and clasped Leighton's hand.

The sting of tears burned Leighton's eyes at the amount of affection in that gesture. She squeezed Andrea's fingers in response. "Thanks for agreeing to meet me."

"I'm glad you called." Andrea's shrewd gaze scanned Leighton from her casual topknot down to her plum-colored silk tee and black pants. "You look great."

"I feel great." Leighton smiled. "What are you working on?"

Andrea pointed at the screen. "Do you recognize that lady?"

Leighton stared at the crisp HD image of the tall middle-aged brunette. "No."

"That's because the incident she's known for happened in 2012."

"Who is she?"

"Her name is Catherine Wittig and she's the governor of Oregon."

"What happened to her?"

"She was visiting a school in her state when a shooting occurred. Despite taking a bullet, she personally carried several kids to safety."

"That's amazing."

"She's a remarkable woman . . . and you and I were talking about her the day before your accident."

Leighton sat up straighter. "We were?"

"Yes." Andrea drummed her fingers on the table. "What I'm about to tell you doesn't leave the room."

"I understand."

Andrea inhaled, held it and then—

"When we saw each other that day, it was a chance encounter. Actually, you surprised the shit out of me. The governor and I had met to discuss the possibility of her running in the next presidential election."

The announcement sent Leighton's pulse leaping into action. It was impossible to grow up in the most political city in the world, possess an interest in politics and not be enthusiastic over the idea of working on a presidential campaign.

Her scrambled thoughts coalesced into one focused narrative. "Isn't it a little early for her to be considering that?" Admittedly, she'd missed quite a few years, but it was August 2016, so . . . "Aren't we due for an election in a few months?"

"Oh doll, our party isn't winning this one. It's an election about change and there's a sense our current candidate is too establishment. If I'm right, we'll need to start thinking ahead to 2020, which is what Catherine and I were doing when you saw us."

Leighton studied the woman's image frozen on the screen. Governor Wittig stood in front of a wooden podium, the flags of the United States and the State of

Oregon framed behind her. Even through the digital medium, the governor exuded intelligence and determination.

"What is she doing in the video?" Leighton asked.

"Giving her state of the State speech in April."

Andrea pressed a button on the remote and the governor continued speaking. Leighton was impressed with the clarity of her thoughts and the apparent strength of her convictions as she put forth solutions to solve the top issues she believed plagued her state.

"She's good, but she's too wordy," Leighton observed. "She'll need to be more concise when the time comes to deal with the national media."

Andrea planted her elbow on the table and caressed her chin between her thumb and curled index finger. "Anything else?"

"If she decides to proceed, when will you declare?"

"We won't officially announce until a year and a half before the election. That gives us two and a half years to gauge how the current president will do, take the temperature of the country, discuss strategy and determine if it's her time."

Leighton shifted onto one hip in the chair and crossed her legs. "And she'll do that while she's still governor?"

"She's in the last year of her second consecutive term. This is the perfect opportunity for her to explore running for national office."

"So any talk of PACs, Iowa and New Hampshire . . ."

Andrea shook her head. "Way premature at this point. That's not to say we won't visit those states, but no fundraising and no speeches at county steak fries."

"Let me guess—it's time for a nationwide 'get to know you tour'?"

Andrea smiled. "Exactly."

"Sunday news shows, late night TV—"

"I'm considering something different. There are over five hundred television channels and most of them speak to a specific audience. That's a tremendous number of opportunities to talk to people in a comfortable setting, away from the polarization inherent in certain news outlets. Catherine's determined not to take any demographic for granted."

"Does that mean you're not going to have her write a book?"

Andrea laughed. "Oh, she's already working on the book. The book is necessary. It'll allow us to highlight her accomplishments, remind the public of her heroism and give them some of the details they never knew before, all without the appearance of bragging. Plus, the advance will help fund her life when she begins this next chapter."

While it may be too early to declare her intent, it was clear that the governor and Andrea had already spent significant time pondering the venture.

"What are her issues?"

"Gun control, obviously. Economic opportunities for women and the poor, health care, infrastructure."

Infrastructure. The political equivalent of the beauty queen's "world peace."

"What's going to work against her?" Leighton asked.

"Other than the fact that she's an outspoken woman? A few years ago, she attempted to increase the state sales tax by one percent to fund equal access to early childhood education, but the initiative failed. Her heart was in the right place but she underestimated the power of the big business lobby in her state. It was a valuable lesson for her."

Is that the type of case I handle at Faulkner? The thought brought forth a sour taste in her mouth.

"Does she have any foreign policy experience?"

"No, and that's a weakness we'll need to address." Andrea pursed her lips. "Having someone like you on the team would help."

Ha! Leighton pounded the table with the palms of her hands. "Are you kidding me? I'd get to work on a presidential campaign with Andrea Ferris, living legend? Sign me up."

She expected to see the excitement she felt reflected on Andrea's features. But the creases dotting the other woman's brow and her averted gaze made Leighton reconsider her assumption.

"I said something different that day, didn't I?"

Andrea's gaze was steady. "I offered you a position on the team—"

Her brain snapped its fingers.

"And I said no," she finished softly.

"Exactly," Andrea said.

"No." Leighton shook her head, slightly dazed. "I remember."

"What?" Andrea's pale blue eyes widened and she jumped to her feet. "You have your memory back?"

"Not all of it. Not even most of it." She was finding it difficult to hold on to the gossamer-thin strand of memory while trying to breathe around the tightness in her chest. "It's like my mind was reaching for the memory and instead of the usual nothing, there was something."

"What do you remember?"

Leighton closed her eyes, straining to make the blurred pictures in her mind clear. "Bits and pieces of our conversation in Tysons Corner. About work. You're lecturing me about . . . Concord Tires and the safety issue. And before that I was at the State of Affairs gala, talking to Congressman Ramsey, and . . . oh."

When Leighton opened her eyes, Andrea sat watching her. "Are you okay?"

"I've got to call my doctor, see if he wants me to come to the hospital." But her hands shook so badly, the phone slipped through her fingers and smacked against the table. She left it there, deciding to wait a few minutes and see if she could get herself under control.

"God, I need a cigarette," Andrea muttered. "Is that all you remember?"

Leighton nodded.

"That's got to be a good sign, right?" Andrea asked, her sharp gaze scanning Leighton's features.

"I think so."

"Then why aren't you happier?"

"Because I don't know who the fuck I am?" Tears stung the back of her eyes. "The emotions that came with those memories . . . I was so cold, so ruthless, so ambitious. There's a safety issue with the Concord valve. In three percent of the trial cases, the valve over-inflated the tires, causing a blowout and a serious accident to occur. I knew it, but I was trying to hide it. I can't imagine doing that, but for some reason I did. How did I get from me to her?"

"You're getting therapy to deal with this, right?"

Leighton gathered her hair over her shoulder and smoothed the ends. "I started this morning. I saw several doctors and they all told me it's called the healing *process* for a reason. They've told me to give it some time—that none, some or all of my memories may come back. And some have. But is that all I'll remember or will there be more? The unknowing will kill me. I'll be living my life constantly waiting for the other shoe to drop."

Andrea touched her hand. "Y'know, I was impressed with you from the moment I first met you. You're a smart, capable young woman. You need to trust yourself. The essence of who you are is the same."

It seemed so simple, so zen, but—"What if my memories return and I change back into who I used to be?"

"Your memories will give you context to the decisions you made. They don't define your identity. Your morals and behavior determine what kind of person you are. So you get your memories back?" Andrea shrugged. "You'll understand why you decided to move from one job to another. But that choice doesn't make you a bad person. In fact, you'll be in the enviable position to decide, with everything you know, if you want to abide by that choice, or make another one."

"Just like that?"

"Just like that," Andrea echoed firmly. "You haven't done anything that's irreversible."

Frustration welled up within her. "I don't know that!"

It was just as she feared. She'd gotten some memories back and instead of clarifying her life, it'd made her confusion worse.

"Say no more memories return this week, or the next or the one after. Are you willing to spend the next one, two or five years waiting around to see if they'd return? Living as if your current situation is temporary?" Andrea pressed.

Professionally, Leighton needed to make a decision. She could either go back to work at Faulkner, even though she couldn't imagine working for them, or go back to working at the Women's Defense Fund, although she didn't know the reason she'd left. There was a third option now, but if she accepted Andrea's offer to work on the campaign, wouldn't that count as running away? Especially if she did so without definitive answers about Faulkner and WDF?

And what about Jonathan? She couldn't put their relationship on hold forever. Based on what she told him yesterday, if she was waiting for her memories but they never returned, that meant she'd never marry him.

"I can't," she whispered.

This was her life. Not what might have happened a few years ago or what might occur in the future. Now. And she intended to make any choices necessary based on that fact. Andrea was right: if she got her memories back, she'd adapt.

Andrea's pale blue eyes softened. "*You* decide who you are. *You* decide what your life will be. You survived a serious accident and were given a second chance. Not everyone is as lucky. Don't waste it."

"I won't. Thank you."

Andrea's chin quivered. "Anything for you, doll. You gonna try your doctor now?"

Leighton picked up her phone, grateful her hands seemed more stable. "Can I get a rain check for lunch?"

"Absolutely. If you need anything, give me a call. And you don't have to give me your answer about the campaign right now. Take your time and then think about it."

Leighton smiled. "If I remember correctly, that's what you said last time."

UNABLE TO CONCENTRATE on anything other than Leighton, her first appointment today and his decision to cease keeping his distance from her, Jonathan put Gib in charge and headed back to his office for a break. Placing his cell on the phone stand, he leaned his elbows on his desk and initiated a video call. A few seconds later, Adam's handsome, stern image appeared on the screen, a wooden bookcase acting as his backdrop.

"Hey, man. Can you talk?"

Adam's dark blue eyes narrowed. "Hay is for horses."

"Seriously, dude?"

"I understand it's a colloquialism, but it's one of my least favorite greetings."

"Fine. Hello, Adam." He exaggerated the syllables and his politeness. "How are you doing this evening?"

"I'm well. Thank you for asking. And you?"

Something rang false in Adam's tone. "Are you fucking with me?"

"While I wouldn't word it that way . . . yes, I am," Adam said, finally allowing a smile to break through.

Jonathan laughed. What a difference a year made. Twelve months ago, they would've had the same conversation except Adam wouldn't have been joking. Opening himself up to love with a wonderful woman had made a huge difference in his efforts to work on improving his communication skills.

Speaking of—"Where's your better half?"

"Chelsea's working late tonight." Chelsea, Adam's wife, was a partner at Beecher & Stowe, one of the top PR firms in the country.

"Are you still in the city?"

In addition to their house in the San Mateo Mountains, Adam and Chelsea also had a place in San Francisco, close to Chelsea's office.

"Yes. We'll leave for the mountains tomorrow afternoon." Adam leaned back in his chair and crossed his arms over his chest. "Mike told me about Leighton's accident. You were with her when it happened?"

His stomach churned like the ocean during a storm. "That's what I wanted to talk to you about."

"Are you worried about the restaurant's liability? Give Sully a call," Adam said, referring to Computronix's general counsel. "He can brief you on your options."

"I'm not worried about her suing me—"

"From what Mike said, you should be."

"Well I'm not." He clenched his hands into fists. "Can we change the subject?"

Adam shrugged. "It's your phone call. How *is* Leighton?"

"They released her from the hospital on Friday."

"That's good news." Although Adam was focused on something off screen, Jonathan knew he was listening.

"Yeah, but she did sustain some lingering injuries." He swallowed. "She has amnesia."

Adam's gaze swung back to fixate on him. "Amnesia? That's a rare diagnosis. Are they certain?"

"They are."

"How severe is her condition?"

"She's lost her memories. Does it get more severe than that?"

"It can. Is her amnesia due to a physical brain trauma or

is it psychogenic, meaning there's no anatomical damage, but a psychological trauma she wishes to repress?"

"There was some physical brain trauma. Swelling in her temporal lobe."

"Are only her memories compromised? Can she remember how to complete tasks, like reading books and tying her shoes?"

"You understand how amnesia works?"

"I'm a genius," Adam said, matter of factly and without conceit.

"So you know everything?"

"Not everything, but my base of knowledge is substantial." Adam lifted a bottle of water and took a drink. "And you know how I feel about sarcasm."

Jonathan laughed softly. "Yeah, man, I do. The doctors believe her amnesia is caused by brain trauma. She doesn't remember the past six years of her life."

Adam's brows shot up. "That must be very traumatic for her."

Recalling her agony, confusion and guilt strangled the air from his lungs. It was all his fault. If he could, he'd envelop her in emotional bubble wrap and protect her from everything she was experiencing. Still, she was taking it much better than he would've if the situation were reversed.

"You appear to be upset, as well. How can I help you?"

Jonathan exhaled deeply. "This is really awkward, but . . . what did it take for you to finally forgive Chelsea?"

When Chelsea and Adam first met, Chelsea had

lied to him about who she was. And while she'd had a good reason, Adam had been furious with her and it had almost ended their relationship forever. Luckily for Adam, he'd realized he was happier with her than without before it was too late.

Adam scratched his cheek. "What does my relationship with Chelsea have to do with your brother's fiancée and her amnesia?"

Leave it to Adam to cut to the chase. At least he hadn't been offended by the question.

Jonathan swallowed. "That's the thing. Right now, Leighton doesn't know she's Thomas's fiancée."

"Because it happened in the past six years."

"Right."

"How has Thomas been dealing with the situation?"

Jonathan rubbed the back of his neck. "He hasn't."

"What does that mean?"

"He's not here."

"Where is he?"

"In London."

Adam's features twisted as if he were trying to solve a puzzle. "Did she send him away because he lied to her?"

"No."

"Did she lie to him before the accident and now she can't remember but he does?"

Jonathan almost laughed. "You're getting very theatrical in your old age. Does your wife have you watching those reality housewife shows?"

"Is that it?" Adam persisted.

"No."

"Then why did you ask me about forgiving Chelsea? And if you don't give me a clear, concise answer, I'm disconnecting this call."

"Leighton is under the impression that she and I are engaged."

"And how did she come to form that impression?"

He winced. "Because I let her believe we were."

Adam sat forward. "Why the fuck would you do that?"

Jonathan closed his eyes and pinched the bridge of his nose, but he went through the whole sordid tale. Afterward, there was silence.

Disapproval carved brackets along the side of Adam's mouth. "That was a bad idea from the beginning."

"I know."

"It's not going to end well."

"I wish I hadn't agreed to it. Especially now that I . . ." He shook his head.

"Now that you what?" Adam asked softly.

"The situation is getting complicated."

"You know how I feel about lying."

Jonathan did know. "Same way you feel about sarcasm."

A result of Adam's Asperger's diagnosis was that reading social cues could be difficult for him. It was the reason Adam abhorred dishonesty.

"Exactly." Adam sighed. "A year ago, if this situation had come up, I would've told you unequivocally that you were wrong and you needed to tell her the truth."

Jonathan believed him. His best friend was never afraid to speak his mind or direct those around him to do the same.

"However, I've learned that a person's intent can make all the difference. I know you. You're a good man. I don't believe you would do this with animus. You must've thought there was a worthy reason for the deception."

"I did."

"The problem is this isn't fair to Leighton."

"I know, but Thomas asked me and we've never gotten along. The fact that he trusted her well-being to me meant a lot."

"Did he entrust her to your care or fob her off on you so he wasn't inconvenienced?"

Damn! Adam could be perceptive. "Initially I thought it was because he trusted me. Now, I'm not sure."

"The longer Leighton goes on believing in your relationship, the harder it'll be for her when she finds out the truth. Now that I think about it, Leighton and I share similar plights. For differing reasons, neither of us can depend on context clues to aid us in sussing out honesty. We have to trust in the people around us. When everything comes out, it'll be a setback. She'll question who she can depend on."

Jonathan understood all of this, but hearing Adam put it in those words, made him realize what an asshole he'd been. "I never should've agreed to this."

"No."

"I have to tell her."

"It'll be better coming from you. Believe me."

"I do. Thank you. And thanks for not hating me."

"You're my friend and I love you, man. But you can also thank Chelsea. She introduced me to the concept of shades of gray."

Jonathan made a note to send Chelsea flowers and have her favorite meal from *Quartet* delivered to her office.

"You guys still coming to the opening?"

"We'll be there." Adam frowned. "How are you working on the restaurant when you've been dealing with Leighton?"

"It's been difficult."

"Will you open on time?"

"I have to. There's no other choice."

"If you need anything, call."

"You've already helped me more than you know. Give my best to Chelsea. And I love you, too."

He touched the screen, ending the call.

So that was it. He was doing what he should've done from the beginning, or at the very least, what he should've told her the night she'd come home from the hospital. He only prayed that when he told her truth, he didn't lose her forever.

Chapter Sixteen

JONATHAN RAN THE final sheet of homemade dough through the spaghetti attachment and let the long, thin cylindrical noodles pool on the countertop. He dusted his flour-specked hands on the dish towel tucked into the waist of his jeans, then lifted the lid off the pot on the stove. The water had reached a rapid boil. He added a liberal amount of salt and dropped the homemade pasta inside.

Nerves fluttered in his stomach. His conversation with Adam this afternoon had given him the clarity he needed. Tonight, he was going to tell Leighton everything: that he wasn't her fiancé and that it was his fault she'd been in the accident. She'd be angry, probably furious, but with his explanation, he hoped she'd understand why he'd agreed to Thomas's plan in the first place. And he wasn't above using everything in his arsenal to earn her forgiveness, including a home cooked meal.

He finished chopping the pancetta and tossed the small cubes in the pan. The pork hit the hot olive oil and hissed, its aroma blending with the garlic and scenting the air.

"Hey, you. When did you get home?"

He looked up as Leighton descended the last few steps and strolled down the hallway.

"Hay is for horses."

Jonathan smiled, recalling Adam's words. "A little while ago. I checked in on you, but you were asleep. I didn't want to disturb you."

She came up behind him and slid her arms around his waist. "I went to the hospital today."

"I know. You had your first follow-up appointment with Dr. Faber. How did it go?"

"It went well, but that was this morning. I ended up going back later this afternoon, because I had a memory flash."

He froze in the middle of tossing the pancetta. Oh, fuck! Her memories came back and now she knew he'd lied to her. He choked on his panic, struggling to get his words out, anxious for the chance to tell her himself, in the hopes it would mitigate some of the damage.

"Leighton—" Her name was a strangled, indecipherable utterance.

She cut him off. "I know I should've called you, but

you didn't need another thing to take you away from the restaurant."

He cleared his throat. And through the waves of dread he noted that she seemed rather calm. "You can always call me." He swallowed. "Do you have your memory back?"

"Not all of it. Just a few pieces and only about my job. But between dealing with the memory, the doctors and a new round of tests, I was exhausted. I came home and crashed."

Relief whisked all his tension away, leaving him boneless. He hadn't lost her. Thank God. Two weeks ago, a life without her hadn't been an issue. Now it was inconceivable.

He turned and enfolded her warm, slumber tousled body in a hug. "How are you feeling?"

"Good. I didn't expect to sleep so long."

"Your body needed the rest."

"Probably. But now my stomach needs the food." She reached around him and stole a cube of pancetta from the pan, popping it in her mouth. "Yummy."

"Just wait until you try it in the actual cooked dish."

She laughed. "Does it matter? It's bacon. It's delicious in all its forms."

"Not bacon. Pancetta," he corrected. "But your point stands."

"What's the occasion? You spend hours cooking at *Sedici*. I'd imagine the last thing you'd want to do is come home and prepare your own food."

"That's usually true. But tonight we're celebrating."

"What are we celebrating?"

He scanned her smiling, upturned face and noted the air of tranquility surrounding her. She seemed happy. And at peace. Probably for the first time since he'd known her. She wore one of his blue V-neck tees, which looked a million times better on her than it ever did on him, and her long legs were encased in black leggings. In her bare feet, with her long hair pulled into a loose knot on the top of her head, she looked charmingly casual and kissable.

So he kissed her.

His lips settled over hers and her gasp of surprise allowed him full access to her mouth. His heart threatened to burst from his chest as he explored her thoroughly, memorizing her taste and texture, achingly aware this may be the last time he kissed her. The thought snatched his breath, like a punch to his solar plexus. He wouldn't let that happen. There was no way he'd ever want anyone more than he craved Leighton.

It would be like serving a man a perfectly cooked Kobe filet mignon and when he was done feasting, informing him he'd have to eat rump roast for the rest of his life.

Fuck that.

No matter what happened with his brother, he couldn't lose her. He allowed himself the pleasure of her kiss for another second before he pulled away. Her lashes fluttered open and her eyes were soft, slightly unfocused.

Good to know he wasn't the only one affected by their kisses.

He smiled. "We're celebrating you."

Her gaze sharpened. "You didn't know what happened to me today, so why did you think I needed a celebration?"

"Look at what you've gone through in the past couple of weeks. Most people would've curled up in a corner somewhere, retreated from the world. Not you. It takes a tremendous amount of strength to keep going, in spite of the hurdles tossed in your path."

"I may have curled up in the corner, if I was alone. But I had you. We should celebrate you, too. Not many men would choose to stand by me as I go through this."

Aware of the information he withheld from her, her praise made him uncomfortable. "Anyone—"

She touched his arm and shook her head. "No, they wouldn't."

A combination of emotions swam through her gaze, but it was the unwavering trust he saw that almost undid him. He had to tell her. The longer he waited, the less his intentions mattered and he needed to be worthy of her faith in him.

"Leighton—"

The smoke alarm shrieked just as the acrid odor wrinkled his nose. They both jumped.

Shit. The lumps of charcoal in the pan bore little resemblance to the ingredient he'd originally added.

Leighton grabbed the towel from his waist and he

rushed over to open the back door. A moment later, the siren ceased its assault on their ears.

He threw an arm along her shoulder. "This is why you could never be in the kitchen with me. You're too much of a distraction."

"I don't want to distract you. I want to eat!" She pointed to his half-empty wine glass on the counter. "Is there more?"

"Sure. On the fourth shelf of the wine fridge. The pinot grigio."

He tossed the pan in the sink, flooding it with water and dish soap. He grabbed a fresh pan, added more olive oil and garlic, and began chopping a new batch of pancetta.

Leighton topped off his glass, poured one for herself and settled on a bar stool. "What are you making?"

"Spaghetti carbonara."

"Is this one of your favorite dishes?"

"It is. I promised I'd make it for you."

"And you're a man of your word." She took a sip of wine. "How are things going at the restaurant? Are you going to be ready for the opening?"

Pancetta in the pan, part *deux*. He grabbed a carton of eggs from the refrigerator and cracking one said, "It'll be close, but we'll get there."

"Close." She lowered her head and trailed a finger around the rim of her glass. "Because of me."

"No, not because of you. You didn't delay permits or

cause our neighbor to get his boxers in a bunch under his balls."

She burst out laughing and bliss rippled through his chest. He'd make it one of his missions in life to invoke that sound from her. Often.

"Boxers . . . in a bunch . . . under his balls?" she managed around fits of giggles.

His lips quirked. "You never heard that expression?"

"No one has. You totally made it up."

"I did not. But I don't mind taking credit for it. It's a good one. And it describes the situation perfectly. That's what delayed our opening."

She sobered. "But having to babysit me didn't help."

Uh-uh. He didn't want those lush lips downturned in remorse. He wanted her laughing and satiated. Because she deserved to be happy.

And it'd help when he finally told her the truth.

Coward.

"If you feel so bad about it, why don't you return the favor and babysit *me*?" He gave the hunk of fresh parmesan one final pass, then sat the cheese down and tapped the grater against the bowl. He winked at her. "That'll fulfill all of my teenage fantasies."

A corner of her mouth lifted in response and her eyes softened. "You are too cute for your own good."

Much better! "Really? I've never heard that one before."

"But seriously"—she leaned forward—"you'll be ready?"

He grabbed a whisk and began incorporating the eggs and grated cheese. "We'll be ready."

"Good." She sagged against the stool's backrest. "When are your friends supposed to arrive?"

"In two days."

"On Thursday? Why so early? The opening isn't until Saturday."

He seasoned the mixture with a pinch of salt and pepper, then removed the pan from the heat. The pancetta survived. "They want to come in early so Indi can get settled before the event."

"Is she okay?"

"She's pregnant. She's actually due in two weeks, though she swears it'll be late, because it's their first baby. They've chartered a private plane for her comfort."

"That's extremely thoughtful of her husband. Which one is she married to?"

"Mike."

"Right. Mike and India. Adam and Chelsea." She repeated the couplings like a mantra. "That's sweet of Mike, but didn't they consider staying home?"

"That's what I said, but I realized I was wasting my breath." He used tongs to add the cooked pasta to the pan, swirling it in the meat, garlic and oil. "They wouldn't miss the opening. It's become a tradition."

He combined all of the components and when the noodles were sufficiently sauced, he plated the meal. He twirled the pasta with the tongs, grated on some additional cheese, wiped any excess off the outer rim and . . .

Voila!

When he straightened, she was standing beside him. She rested her hand on his back, the touch branding him as hers.

"This looks incredible," she said.

He inhaled and his chest expanded with satisfaction. "Thank you."

She kissed him. "Will you re-think your rule about having me in the kitchen? I love watching you cook."

He had to bite his tongue to refrain from promising her anything she wanted.

Not yet.

He lifted the plates and nodded to their glasses. "Grab those and follow me."

Though she was only a few seconds behind him, he'd reached the dining room, deposited the plates and was setting the electric lighter down when she appeared in the doorway.

She gasped.

Flickering tapered candles sat in sterling silver holders and, with the dim overhead lighting, imbued the space with a dreamy ambience. The dark wood of the table gleamed in the candlelight and the silverware shone where it lay on the white cloth napkins. It was simple, elegant and intimate.

Leighton set the wine glasses on the table and reached out to stroke a petal of the floral centerpiece.

"It's beautiful," she breathed.

He'd told her he didn't know anything about flowers, and that was true, but he knew what he liked. And the colorful bouquet of roses, lilies and sunflowers reminded him of a well-balanced plate of food, with different hues and textures combining to create a beautiful work of art.

"These are the flowers I'd pick for my wedding," he said, finally answering her question from their visit with Kimberly Reed.

She nodded, her gaze shining. "Me, too."

He pulled out her chair and when she was seated, he joined her at the table.

She smiled. "This looks amazing."

She took a bite of food and her lashes fluttered shut, an expression of ecstasy coloring her features. His dick immediately hardened.

"This is the best carbonara I've ever had." Her tongue darted out and swept over her bottom lip.

He almost groaned aloud, but he caught himself, transforming it into a cough. He cleared his throat. *Focus, Moran. Keep it light and playful.*

"There's a possibility you're forgetting a meal, but it's okay. I'll take it."

She actually moaned. "Good. Because I meant it."

He loved watching her eat his food, loved the passion and intensity she gave to the task. There's nothing he hated more than seeing someone nibble, or even worse, take a few bites and push the plate away. He knew she liked watching movies, appreciated simple works of art and wasn't shy about enjoying good food. He knew wha she looked like when he was pleasuring her, knew the feel of her pussy clenching his fingers, her clit swelling against his tongue. He knew his hand would always be a poor substitute for what he really wanted.

But there was so much more to learn and he wanted to know it all.

"It must've been fun to grow up the only child of an ambassador."

"It definitely was an adventure. I traveled a lot when I was younger and I thought it was normal. Didn't everyone tour the world, greeted and praised everywhere they went?" Her laugh was self-deprecating. "It wasn't until I was older that I realized how fortunate I was."

"My family didn't do adventurous. Our vacations were limited to the DMV." He used the nickname many locals understood to refer to the DC-Maryland-Virginia region. "Sometimes, if my parents were feeling bold, we'd head down to the Outer Banks or Myrtle Beach."

She paused, her fork halfway to her mouth. "You're kidding, right?"

He wished. He shook his head and took a sip of wine.

"You've mentioned your brother before. Is he older or younger?"

Chilled tendrils wrapped around his heart and squeezed. "Older."

"So you're the baby?"

Her teasing tone abated some of his dread. He linked his fingers with hers and placed her hand on his thigh. "There's nothing babyish about me."

"No, there isn't." She squeezed his hard quad muscle. "Does your brother live here?"

He disentangled his fingers from hers and rested his hand on the table. "Yes."

"It's good to have family nearby." She frowned. "He hasn't been around since I came home from the hospital."

His stomach churned and his internal body temperature rose. The very last thing he wanted to discuss was his brother.

"He's traveling for work."

Leighton had other ideas. "Oh? What does he do?"

"Why the interrogation?" He lost control of his tone and immediately regretted his harshness.

She stiffened. "I understand my questions may be frustrating for you, considering you've probably already told me about him, but—"

"No." He reclaimed her hand. "No, I'm being an ass. I'm sorry."

She didn't pull away from him, but she pinched her lips tight and refused to meet his gaze.

"My brother—Thomas—works in finance."

The tension seeped from her posture. "One brother in finance, one a chef. Two very different men."

No shit. "Yeah, you could say that."

"Who don't get along."

It wasn't a question. "How did you know?"

"It's obvious."

He slumped back in his chair and a familiar numbness stole over him. "I wish it weren't."

"What happened?"

"I don't know. Maybe it's because we *were* so different. I found it very challenging to have the perfect older brother. There wasn't an adventure I had that he didn't have first. A teacher I had who didn't already know about Thomas. A place to hang out that he hadn't already frequented. I wanted to be seen as my own person. Everyone expected me to be like Thomas and I wasn't. I was me."

She rotated her wrist until she was cupping *his* hand. "Is that why you went to Stanford?"

He nodded. "My parents were hurt by my decision. Thomas saw it as a betrayal to the family. He's yet to forgive me."

"And that's why you came back to DC?"

"A big part of it."

"Has it worked?"

He thought about his current situation. "Not really."

She shrugged. "He needs to get over it."

She couldn't have surprised him more if she'd stood and dumped the contents of her plate over his head. "Excuse me?"

"What did you do to him exactly? Choose to live your life outside of his shadow? What was wrong with that decision? Apparently, it was the right one for you. You went away and in doing so, you found yourself. No one who loves you should fault you for that. And I'm happy to share my opinion with him the next time I see him." She picked up her fork and continued eating.

He stared at her, amazed at her support of him.

And you're lying to her.

He'd thought the evening would end with him telling her the truth and his plans hadn't changed, but he wasn't ready. He needed more time.

"If you're not too tired, how about another movie? There's a new Mad Max movie that came out last year—"

She removed her napkin from her lap and placed it next to her plate. "I'm not tired at all, but I don't want to watch a movie."

The husky tone and suggestive quality of her voice clearly telegraphed her intent.

He swallowed. This wasn't a good idea.

"Scrabble, chess, cards?"

She shook her head.

He'd tasted her on his lips ever since their first night together in this house. Although he'd told himself he'd done it for her, it was a lie. He'd wanted to be with her and he couldn't pass up the opportunity, even if he hated himself for doing so.

"We should wait until you get your memory back."

She rose and moved around the table until she was standing before him. "Perfect timing. I got some back today."

Oh, crap, he'd forgotten that quickly. "Leighton—"

She scraped a hand through his hair. "Do you want me?"

Want seemed too tame to describe the roiling need for her that raged within him. "More than you know."

She exhaled. "Do you love me?"

He talked about her incessantly with Mike, Gib and Adam. He'd altered his life for her—Hello, she was now living in his house! He wanted to spend all of his time with her and when they weren't together he was thinking about her. Both the thought of living without her and the thought of her with anyone else was unbearable. Not to mention the fact that she'd stealthily and steadily climbed to the top of the list of everything that was important to him.

Did he love Leighton Clarke?

"Yes."

"Isn't that the only thing that matters?" she asked, staring down at him. "I may not remember how we met or what happened last year, but I know I don't want to go another moment unaware of how it feels to have you inside of me."

Holy fuck! How was he supposed to resist her when she said things like that?

The moment of truth. If he did this, there was no turning back. Despite his past inclination for short-term flings, there was nothing temporary about his feelings for Leighton. He didn't have any illusions that this was a hit it and quit it affair. If he surrendered to what he was feeling, did what his heart and body had been screaming at him to do, it could cost him his relationship with his brother and further strain his family. The very thing he'd come back to DC to mend.

Was she worth it?

She held out her hand. "Dinner was delicious, but I'm ready for my dessert."

Her gaze was direct and fierce, a siren's song calling out to him. And he was incapable of resisting.

Chapter Seventeen

THEY HADN'T TAKEN more than three steps past her bedroom's threshold when she turned abruptly and kissed him, her fingers digging into his shoulders, her tongue stoking the fire raging inside him until he feared his body would go ablaze.

His hands slid down and cupped her hips, pulling her closer. Wanting the ultimate closeness, knowing they needed to slow down for that to happen. He broke their kiss and dragged in lungfuls of air.

"What? What is it? What's wrong?"

She was the picture of confused vulnerability, his fingers having defeated her topknot, the thick strands falling around her shoulders, and against her cheek, her lips moist and slightly swollen. Her skin looked like luminescent silk. He reached out, unable to believe it felt as soft as it appeared, and she angled her jaw and leaned into his caress. Her lashes fluttered close, her lips parted . . .

"Nothing's wrong, but it's been a while and I've thought about this for a long time. Now that it's close to happening, my body is in more of a hurry than I want it to be."

Her dawning smile banished the distress. She laughed and the smoky sound wound its way through him. "Did you know that telling me how much you want me makes me want you even more?"

Really? Then he needed to tell her how much he wanted her several times a day. Hell, what would happen when he showed her?

He trailed his hand along her collarbone, exposed by her t-shirt. The pulse at the base of her neck rippled beneath her skin. He leaned forward and licked the rapidly beating spot. Proof that she felt the same uncontrollable desire he did.

She grabbed his shoulders and her head fell back. "Just promise me you'll be honest."

"What?" His heart stutter stopped.

"If it's not the way you remember or if I'm not doing what you like—"

He pulled her close and stared into her eyes, cupping her cheek in his palm. "There was nothing before this. Right here, right now, *this* is our first time."

Before she could parse his statement and decode

what he did or didn't say, he pressed his mouth against hers, pouring everything he felt into the kiss. He didn't just kiss her with his lips; he kissed her with every part of him, every inch of his body yearning to be part of whatever was causing her pleasure.

His heart pounded in his chest and blood roared in his ears, but everything in him was focused on Leighton. His gaze locked on hers, he backed up until his knees hit the edge of the bed and he sank down on the mattress.

"Come here." He barely recognized his own voice, tangled and rugged with a need he'd never before experienced.

She crossed the distance to stand between his thighs, and he stared up at her, mesmerized by the play of light and shadow over her features.

"You're so beautiful." His hands cupped her waist.

"So are you," she said, and swept away a lock of hair from his forehead.

The billows surging throughout his body were expected, but he wasn't prepared for the rush of tenderness that stole over him. It shook him to the core. He pressed a hot, open-mouthed kiss to her belly, then ran his finger along the bottom of her shirt, oh so slowly lifting it, wanting to give her the best experience . . .

"Jonathan?"

"Yeah, sweetheart?"

She licked her bottom lip. "This is really sweet, but . . . can we fuck?"

His mouth fell open. He was at a loss for words. Then he saw the mischief brimming in her eyes. Moving quickly, he lifted her then dumped her on the middle of the bed, her squeal of delight adding fuel to his blazing arousal. He swiftly followed, his arms bracketing her head, his muscles straining to hold his weight.

"Not feeling the slow and romantic?"

She shook her head and watched him, her eyes feverish, her lips curved in a provocative smirk. She trailed her fingers up his arms, leaving raised flesh in her wake. "Do you know what I thought when I saw you for the first time in the hospital?"

Did he want to know? "What?"

"I thought you were the sexiest man I'd ever seen."

That wasn't what he'd expected. His dick hardened painfully.

"Want to know what I liked?"

Hell yeah.

He nodded.

"Your hands." Her fingers encircled his wrists, braced by her ears. "They looked long, strong and capable. I imagined all the ways they could touch me and I got wet."

Holy fuck. He shook his head, trying to disperse the impending fuzziness as the blood deserted his brain seeking a new home down south.

"You want to know what else I thought?"

Could he take hearing any more? She didn't wait for his response.

"I could see the edge of your tattoo. It intrigued me. I wanted to know where it began . . . and ended."

She turned her head, lifted slightly and traced the inked pattern with her tongue.

He thought his dick would burst through the zipper of his jeans.

He dropped onto one elbow, tangled his other hand in her hair and bent her head back, kissing every surface he could reach: her lips, cheek, jaw and neck. She moaned, her fingers moving just as freely through his hair, down his neck, over his shoulders. She raked her nails across the front of his chest and before he knew what was happening she had his shirt up, over his head and on the floor.

He shuddered. She was no pillow princess, intending to lie there and make him do all the work. She knew exactly what she wanted, which he found sexy as fuck.

He returned the favor, divesting her of her shirt. He pushed back on his haunches and used his hands to trace her rounded hips, trim waist and magnificent breasts that billowed out the top of her black satin bra.

She tilted her head on the bed. "You like the view?"

"Absolutely."

He bent, kissing and nibbling the plump top of each mound. She arched into his embrace and he reached around and undid the hooks of her bra, swallowing as they were freed. When he slid his index and middle fingers into her mouth, her tongue wrapped around them and his hips surged forward.

Good God, he needed to get a hold of himself. If he didn't regain some measure of control, he was going to explode all over the blanket. Not cool.

He dragged the digits from her lips and tracked a wet path down her chin and across her chest until they circled her nipple, plucking and pulling until it stood erect.

But exploding all over her breasts sounded real promising indeed.

Leighton's fingers plunged through his hair, curved around his skull and pressed him tight against her. He didn't need the coercion. There was no other place he'd rather be. Her scent enveloped him. Her taste overwhelmed him. She writhed against his torso, the heat from her core beckoning him.

Not yet. As much as he wanted to get there, he didn't want to stop what he was doing.

He flicked the other nipple with his tongue, then laved it before sucking the glistening peak between his lips and pressing it against the roof of his mouth. She cried out and ground against him.

Her moans drove him wild. He couldn't get enough of them. He delighted in bringing her pleasure, realized he loved it as much as seeking his own.

He explored her mouth again and his hands went to the waistband of her pants. She lifted her hips to help remove them, but he had something else in mind. He didn't take them off. He slipped his hand inside, beneath her panties, and sought her heated wetness. She gasped, her eyes widened and then she was pressing herself into his hand, her hips raised, her weight supported on her arms.

She was so wet his fingers easily slid through her outer lips until they found the hardened nub nestled within. He hooked his fingers and gently massaged the bundle of nerves, remembering the pressure she liked. Her eyes fluttered shut and her breath came in sharp pants.

He wanted to stay present in the moment, but the moment was treating him like a teenage boy who'd just discovered his dick. He took several deep breaths, needing to calm down . . . anything to allow him a few minutes more.

He inserted one finger, two, then three and she bucked against him. He rose, slid an arm around her waist and pumped his fingers in and out of her as she moaned and undulated against him. She was so snug and warm against his digits. That's how it would feel inside her body.

Now he was the one panting and his heart felt like it would erupt from his chest. How had he lived without knowing this part of her? What would he do if he could never have this again? Before that thought could take hold, she jerked and her nails dug into his arm.

"Ahhhhh," she moaned, her voice husky. "Babe, I'm coming."

The walls of her pussy clenched against his fingers

and then she was shuddering in his arms. She fell back on the bed and he shoved her pants and panties off in one fell swoop and pressed his head between her legs so he could taste her. The tangy sweetness was nectar to him, and when his tongue swept against her clit she made a sound that shot straight to his dick. He had to have her.

Now.

He should've known there could be nothing slow or tame about their first time. Not the way she affected him. Her nearness invoked an insatiable craving that only she could assuage.

He grabbed her ankle and tugged her to the edge of the mattress. Hooking her knees over the crook of his elbows, he pulled her to him and slammed into her with one powerful thrust.

"Yes!" she screamed.

He almost lost his shit.

Their joining ripped the breath from his body. But he couldn't take the moment to savor the experience of being inside of her. Longing had him driving in and out of her, quakes from her orgasm trumpeting up and down his dick.

Her hands grabbed his hips before sliding around to cup his ass. Her nails raked across his cheeks causing a stinging pressure. He threw his head back, not sure it was possible to feel so much and still live. At one point, she held him in her and rotated her hips, grinding on him.

His head snapped forward and his eyes rolled back in his head.

"So good," she moaned.

"You like that?"

"Fuck, yeah."

Her words stoked him higher. He sank into her over and over, watching her breasts bounce, and her hips move. When the titillation became too great, he would close his eyes, thinking that *had* to be the best way to savor the feelings. It didn't take long before he realized he was being denied the satisfaction of the view so he'd force them open and the delicious torment would begin anew.

He didn't know how long they remained in the wonder drenched experience but as the pleasure increased he knew he'd be unable to last much longer. He leaned down and tangled his tongue with hers. The feel of her bare softness against him was all he could take. He pressed his head in the crook of her neck, inhaled her scent and lost himself in the sensation that rocketed up his spine and sent stars to blind his vision.

"Wow," she breathed several minutes later, as they lay together on the bed.

Wow was right. Fuck. He had never experienced an orgasm that intense before in his life.

He didn't care how this had started, Leighton was his. He loved her. And there was no way in hell he would step aside when his brother returned. Thomas had given up being worthy of her the moment he'd left her in the hospital to pursue his career in London.

While his actions had been just as bad, Jonathan had been here with her, taking care of her, building something with her. That had to have value. Even when she got her memory back.

"It was my fault." The words were out before he could recall them. The moment, following an almost religious experience, needed some confession, though it wasn't the one he should have given.

Her cheek rose but she settled and combed her fingers through the hair on his chest. "I don't know if *fault* is the right word. You're definitely the *cause* of those orgasms . . ."

He stilled her hand. "Your accident. It was my fault."

Her warm, languorous body tensed against his side. She yanked her hand from beneath his and sat up. "I thought the doctors said some piping fell on my head."

"It did."

"Then I don't understand. Did you throw it on me?"

He pushed himself up on his elbows. "Of course not."

"So how was my accident your fault?" she asked, her earlier gratification replaced with spine stiffening anxiety.

He fell back onto the pillow and raked both hands through his hair. "We'd had a disagreement and you were upset. You ran from the restaurant, you didn't see the scaffolding and . . ."

He shook his head, tears scalding his eyes as the same feeling of helplessness that had inundated him that night.

"Why didn't you tell me before?"

Because I'm a fucking idiot. Already well-established.

"I thought you would hate me. That you'd decide you wouldn't want to see me and I needed to be there for you."

It was a small slice of the truth. He was still keeping a majority of the cake from her.

She sat for a long moment, staring straight ahead. Then she scooped her hair over her shoulders, smoothed the ends. "Did you mean to hurt me?"

He scrambled to sit up, placing his palms on her cheeks. He stared into her eyes. "I would hurt myself before I'd ever hurt you. I love you."

Though he'd answered her question in the affirmative when she'd asked him earlier, this was the first time he'd uttered those words to a woman, and meant it.

Please believe me. Please believe me. Please believe me.

Karma could be a bitch right now and it'd serve him right.

But Leighton nodded. "I know."

And he thanked the heavens, the moons and the stars for her partial absolution. He pressed kisses to her forehead, eyelids and nose before brushing one across her lips. She wrapped her arms around his shoulders and he pulled her close, burying his nose in her hair.

He'd chickened out, but Adam was right, the longer he waited, the worse it was going to get. This weekend the restaurant would open. And then he would tell Leighton the truth. He'd deal with the fallout, whatever it was and prayed it didn't cost him her.

Chapter Eighteen

IF IT HAD been up to Leighton, she and Jonathan would've spent the days following their romantic dinner the same way they'd spent that night: making love until all they had the strength to do was sleep. But with the opening now only two days away, their sexual sabbatical was placed on hold.

That's why she found herself in *Sedici* later that afternoon. She adjusted the bow on the server's waist apron then shifted her weight onto her back foot and eyed her handiwork.

Perfect. The butter yellow popped against the black, adding a bit of elegant whimsy to the severity of the uniform.

"Robby, how is this?"

The Front of the House manager strode over, shoving the digital tablet he was carrying under his arm. His blue eyes raked the server's attire.

"That looks great, Leighton. Thank you." Robby turned and yelled at the assembled waitstaff. "The way Jenny is wearing the uniform is the prototype of how we want you to look. Take pictures if necessary. If you have any questions of how to achieve this style, ask Leighton."

Between one blink and the next, a line of servers had formed in front of her, their uniforms in various stages of disarray. She directed a wry smile at Robby, motioned the first one forward and set to work.

Bedlam reigned all around her. Bodies circulated as servers gathered the components of their uniforms and either figured it out themselves or joined her ever-increasing line; bar staff wiped down everything from the countertops to the blenders to the soda gun holders; and handymen put the finishing touches on last minute projects. It was all hands on deck as everyone pulled together to get *Sedici* ready.

She was happy to help and content to be in the same space with Jonathan, even if they weren't in the same room. He'd been working nonstop in the couple of days since he'd confessed his role in her accident. In fact, she could've convinced herself she'd imagined their romantic evening together if not for the fact that he crawled into bed with her each night when he finally made it home. She was becoming accustomed to waking up to the distinctive weight of some part of him wrapped around her.

But she'd made good use of her time alone, continuing with her required therapies. The doctors had been encouraged by the spontaneous recovery of some of her memories, but they couldn't offer her any guarantees. The rest would either return or they wouldn't.

She'd thought she'd been living her life, but she'd only been existing, like a hamster running on a wheel—active, but never moving forward. She decided the time had come for her to assert some control. She scheduled time next week to meet with her bosses at Faulkner. She intended to apprise them of her situation and get briefed on her employment history with them and her current assignments. With that missing piece of information, she'd be able to explore all of her employment options.

As for Jonathan, just because she didn't remember how their relationship began didn't mean she had no say in how it progressed. She'd made her needs known—and they'd been ably fulfilled!—but what about what he wanted, beyond the physical? If her memories never came back would he still want to be with her? The thought of that conversation twisted her stomach into a tight knot, but it was necessary and she intended to have it.

But first, they needed to get through the opening.

"Run it again. Repetition yields consistency and builds muscle memory. What's going to happen when we're totally slammed with over 120 covers? I won't tolerate a station running short or food dying on the pass because someone wasted seconds figuring out something that should be second nature. Run it until they get it right!"

She'd know that commanding voice anywhere.

"Look at me, sweetheart. I want to see your beautiful face when your pussy tightens around my cock and you come."

She shivered.

Focus, Leighton. Now isn't the time.

She inspected the length of a bistro apron then nodded at the tall, young server wearing it. "You're fine."

"So. Are. You."

She'd already switched her scrutiny to the next person in line, but his amorous tone recalled her attention. "Excuse me?"

Dimples made their appearance. "I said, you're fine, too. How about drinks later?"

Her lips quirked and she clamped them together to repress her emerging smile. He was good-looking and she was flattered, but there was no need to encourage him.

"How about drinks never?" Jonathan interrupted them, sliding an arm around her waist.

The young man's complexion turned ashen, quite a feat considering his warm brown coloring.

"Sorry, Chef," he murmured, slinking away.

"That wasn't nice," she said, despite the old-fashioned thrill that zipped through her.

"Good. Then I achieved my goal." In one controlled, deft motion, Jonathan curled his arm and brought her body flush with his.

The genetic lottery could be so unfair. He'd been at the restaurant all day but his tousled hair and scruffy jaw didn't cast him in a messy or unkempt light. Instead, he came off looking like a sexy, naughty bad boy on the prowl.

"No one told me you were here," he said, nuzzling her neck, his hands locked at the small of her back.

She wrapped her arms around his broad shoulders and snuggled into his embrace. "There was no need to bother you."

"You are never a bother." He sighed and placed his forehead against hers. "I've hated leaving you home by yourself these past couple of days, but it can't be helped."

"Don't worry about me. I'm getting better every day. I can take care of myself."

"I know. You're one of the strongest people I've ever met." He straightened and raised a concerned brow. "And you're okay? I wanted to be with you your first time back here after the accident."

"I did worry how I would react—that's why I came before Saturday. The last thing either of us would want is a meltdown during the opening."

The anxiety hadn't been necessary. She'd taken a deep breath, opened the door . . . and been so taken aback by the beauty of the place that she had no apprehension about what might have happened before. And as a bonus, no disturbing memories came surging forth. She'd grabbed the first person she saw who appeared to be in charge—that turned out to be Robby—and introduced herself. He'd put her to work immediately.

Jonathan stroked her hair. "And?"

"Nothing." She turned her shrug into a hip-shaking dance of joy. "But, babe, it looks amazing. You did it!"

"We did." He slid a lock of hair behind her ear. "I'm glad you're here. Seeing you is the pick-me-up I needed."

Their lips met in a kiss that began casually and quickly shifted gears into something fierce and arousing. The hard muscles beneath her palm, his scent that drove her wild, the skillful way his tongue invaded her mouth with purpose and tangled with hers. She shivered again. She'd never get enough of him.

"Umm, excuse me . . . Chef, it's —oh, hell!"

They broke apart, both breathing heavily. A man in a stained white t-shirt and khaki-colored tool belt grabbed the rim of his baseball cap, pulled it off his head and with that same hand, scratched his hair, his gaze glued to the stunning Brazilian Cherry hardwood floors.

"No problem." Jonathan gave her one last lingering kiss then transformed back into his all-business persona. "What do you need?"

The handyman jerked his thumb over his shoulder. "The signage is up."

"It's about time!" Jonathan clasped his hands together. "Let's go see this fucker."

Grabbing her elbow and bellowing to anyone within hearing distance to follow, he pushed through the front door. Outside, a worker was descending a ladder. Jonathan shifted to shield her with his body, hurrying her out the street—and away from the possibility of any falling is.

Not by hesitating or speaking or glancing at her did he convey his awareness that he'd sheltered her. But she'd noticed. That had to mean something, right? Everything he'd done proved how much he cared for her, even if he hadn't yet said the words. Inside her, an inferno blazed bright.

The custom ironwork sign was impressive and eye-catching with spotlights strategically placed to emphasize the gold-plated script. Wolf whistles and claps filled the air. Drivers who figured out the reason behind the commotion honked their horns, adding to the moment.

Jonathan released her arm and executed a courtly bow with a double-handed flourish. "Thank you. Thank you."

The restaurant's door opened and a striking woman, with large light-colored eyes and a mop of jet black curls, poked her head out. "They're plated, Chef."

"Come see the sign, Gib."

She jammed her hands on her hips. "Later. Go."

"Jeez, so pushy." He winked at Leighton. "Duty calls."

"No worries. I'll continue to pitch in where I can."

He shuffled backward, pointing his finger at her. "Don't leave without saying goodbye."

"Wouldn't dream of it."

His responding broad smile stoked her inner inferno.

Everyone followed him back inside *Sedici* everyone followed him, like a foodie pied piper. She took one last look at the eye-catching sign and then she joined the captivated masses, bringing up the rear.

"How are you feeling?"

Leighton stalled mid-stride at the husky, honeyed voice. The woman who'd first summoned Jonathan had remained by the door. This was his sous chef, Gib? She hadn't expected his trusted second-in-command to come in this package.

"Better. Except for the occasional headaches."

"I'm glad." Gib's lashes fluttered. "That you're on the mend, not that you have headaches."

Leighton found the retraction charming. She smiled. "I know. You're Gib?"

"That's me. It's short for Gibson. Nyah Gibson."

"Nyah. That's a beautiful name."

"What?" The shrill cackle grabbed both of their attention.

In the small group of women encircling Jonathan, a young redhead patted her chest above her low-cut shirt and laughed, revealing the source of the original sound. Fire Crotch tilted her head and swayed back and forth. Leighton firmed her lips. The girl couldn't be more obvious.

"She won't last," Gib said.

"Who?" Leighton asked, trying to play it cool. Apparently FC wasn't the only one being too obvious.

"You don't have to worry about that." Gib nodded toward the groupies, er, grouping. "He's a celebrity in the food world. Women fawning over him isn't a new occurrence, or men for that matter."

Heat flared through her. Why was she jealous? Jonathan loved *her*. Didn't she believe him?

A sudden pain arced behind her eyes. She pressed a hand to her forehead. "Will he fire her?"

"That's not his style. They usually quit when they realize their attentions won't be returned."

"So it happens a lot?"

"It comes with the territory. But he takes his work very seriously. He'd never get involved with one of his employees."

Leighton scrutinized the beautiful woman standing next to her. "You've worked with Jonathan for a long time?"

"I have. I started out at *Quartet* and when he decided to open *Sedici* he asked me to come with him."

That required a huge commitment from both parties. "What does being his sous chef entail?"

Gib crossed her arms over her chest. "I'm his second in command. Chef has a vision for his restaurant. It's my job to carry it out. I manage the kitchen staff, prepare the food and ensure the customer's experience is the way Chef intends it."

Leighton lifted both brows. *Wow.* "You must work closely with him?"

"Twelve to fifteen hours a day, six days a week. I'm like his right hand. But only in the kitchen." Her lips twitched. "I'm not touching anything else."

Leighton laughed. "I didn't ask."

"You didn't have to. It was written all over your face."

"Never?"

Gib shook her head, her eyes bright. "Never."

Leighton returned her attention to the women fawning over Jonathan. He made eye contact, his smile was open, and his posture appeared relaxed. Friendly but professional. There was nothing in his behavior to indicate he was flirting.

"He cares for you, Leighton." Gib's voice was gentle.

"I know."

"We were three weeks from opening. Nothing could've dragged him away from here. Then you had your accident. He went to see you at the hospital every day and when you regained consciousness, he chose to be with you. I didn't think anything would take precedence over his restaurants. But you did."

A booming voice intruded before Leighton could process Gib's words. "Someone told me this restaurant was owned by a famous chef, but there must be some mistake. The service is seriously lacking."

A tall, handsome blond man waited just inside the door, holding hands with a delicately beautiful pregnant woman. Beside them stood another couple: a gorgeous woman with a mass of black curls, and an incredibly attractive man with dark tousled hair and an intense gaze, his hands resting on her shoulders.

Jonathan's smile threatened to split his face in two. He hurried across the restaurant. "What the fuck are you doing here? I wasn't expecting you until tonight."

"Adam realized the restaurant was near the hotel, so we decided to stop." The woman blessed with the curls said, jerking a thumb at the man standing behind her.

Handshakes, hugs and kisses on the cheek accompanied the various greetings and exclamations and she realized these must be Jonathan's friends and their wives. He looked so relaxed and happy in ways she'd only recently seen in their quiet moments together.

"You haven't checked in yet? Indi, that's not good for you."

"Really, Jonathan? I already have two husbands and a wife," the pregnant woman said, motioning to the three people surrounding her. "The position of 'worrying about Indi' has been filled. Besides, we couldn't drive past without stopping to see you."

Mike's blue eyes softened and he placed a hand on his wife's belly. "Don't worry. When we get to the suite, I'll make sure she rests."

Adam walked around, studying the interior. "The decor is clearly different from *Quartet*, but there are elements that bind the two restaurants. Congratulations, this is impressive."

"Thanks, man." Jonathan looked around as if searching for something, but when he caught sight of Leighton, he smiled and held out his hand for her to join them.

When her palm slid against his, a wave of certainty crashed over her. This is what she wanted. Always and forever.

Jonathan brought their joined hands up and clasped them to his chest. "Everyone, this is Leighton. Leighton, these are my best friends, hell, they're my family. Adam and his wife, Chelsea. Mike and his wife, Indi."

As if they'd practiced it, all four pairs of eyes zeroed in on their clinched hands then swung to her face.

She could feel the blush sweep across her cheekbones, though thankfully her dark complexion hid the evidence of her embarrassment. She'd never been a self-conscious person, but in that moment she wished she'd had the opportunity to smooth her hair, re-apply her lipstick and straighten her sleeveless black top and white wide leg pants. Jonathan loved these people and she loved Jonathan. She wanted to make the best impression possible.

"Hi. It's a pleasure to finally meet you."

Adam and Mike both nodded and shook her hand. The women regarded her with open curiosity.

"So you're the reason he's abandoned us." Indi's tone was serious, but there was a teasing warmth in her light brown eyes.

"I don't think I'm to blame for him leaving San Francisco," she said, ever the diplomat's daughter and able to fake confidence when required, "but I'll definitely take credit for persuading him to stay."

"Damn right," Jonathan said, his suggestive smile actually making Leighton's knees weak.

Chelsea nodded approvingly. "As you should."

"Too cute," Indi said. "But this is a restaurant, right? Can a sister get some food?"

Chelsea nudged her. "Queen, thy name is drama! You ate on the plane."

"I'm not dramatic, Chels. I'm passionate, emotional and fifteen months pregnant."

"I'll take care of it, Chef." Gib stepped forward, laughing. She looked at Indi. "Anything in particular?"

"Nothing major. I'm just feeling a little peckish." She scratched her chin. "Some chicken, pasta, bread, obviously and, ooh, if you have any of the duck with the chanterelle mushrooms, like you have at *Quartet*, that would be perfect."

Gib's eyes widened. "I'll see what I can do," she said.

"Sorry, Gib," Mike said, calling to the sous chef's retreating figure. He shook his head and turned to Jonathan. "Is Zach here?"

Indi playfully smacked her husband's arm and said, "Don't apologize for me. Gib and I are cool."

"He's in New York," Jonathan answered, smiling, "but he'll be at the opening."

"When you told us you were forming a restaurant group with an eye toward opening more establishments, I was concerned," Adam said. "But seeing what you've accomplished . . . we're proud of you."

"Just make sure you never get so big that Computronix can't get *Quartet* to cater our events," Mike added.

Jonathan shrugged. "I don't know. You might have to start using our official request process like everyone else."

"Oh, that's how it is? No problem. And when I get to the part of the form where it asks how we heard about your services, I'll be sure to mention how we've been friends since you plastic-wrapped your freshman roommate to the dorm couch when he passed out after party."

"You're going to bring that up?" Jonathan asked. "The little prick started it by peeing in my shampoo bottle."

"But you could've stopped. You didn't have to replace the kid's conditioner with hair remover," Adam said.

"Motherfucker, you helped," Jonathan began, pointing at his friend.

They were three wildly successful men and yet, in that moment, they'd reverted to the college kids they'd once been, bantering, teasing and name-calling. Leighton shared an amused look with Chelsea and Indi.

"You've got an audience," she told the boys, in case they were interested.

While no one stood around gawking at them, everyone, from the servers, to the bartenders to the construction crew, was overt in their efforts to keep one eye on their task and the other on their little comedy troupe.

Jonathan waved them away. "Nothing to see here. Let's get back to work."

Indi winced and placed a hand on her lower back.

Mike instantly sobered. "What's wrong?" he asked his wife, rushing to her side and ushering her into the nearest chair.

"I'm fine. My lower back aches, but I think I may have overdone it today."

"Why don't you head over to your hotel and check in?" Jonathan suggested. "Indi probably needs to rest and I'm headed for another late, tiring night."

The fact that Indi didn't argue with the notion spok volumes about the other woman's exhaustion.

After his friends left—with the food Gib provided—Jonathan gave her a quick kiss. "I'm sorry, but I've got to get back in the kitchen. Make sure you come see me before you leave."

Several hours later, she found him in his office going over paperwork with Gib. Though he looked tired, he perked up when he saw her. Without a word, she slid him a folded note, kissed his cheek and smiled at Gib.

When she reached the door, she turned in time to see his mouth drop open and his gaze lift to meet hers.

Something told her that while he might be late getting home this evening, he wouldn't be too tired for her plans.

Chapter Nineteen

"LEIGHTON?"

Jonathan's voice pricked the balloon of anticipation lodged in her chest, causing tingles to cascade down her body. His keys hitting the wooden bowl, his messenger bag hitting the floor, each thump acted as a soft tap to her quivering pussy. She clenched her thighs together and savored the sweet ache of the movement.

"Where are you?" he called out.

She smoothed a hand down the front of her dress and took a deep breath. "In the kitchen."

She blinked. Sweet Jesus.

He was standing in the doorway, a visual treat for her starving senses. His hair was mussed and tousled and she envied his fingers for their ready access to the thick, dark strands. Stubble coated his jaw, his lids sat at half-mast and his lips were slack and pouty. A bad boy, made all the more irresistible because he was such a good man.

She was going to scale him faster than an expert climber mounted an indoor rock wall.

"Why is it so dark in here?" He reached for the overhead light.

"Don't," she protested, from her spot next to the back door.

He frowned. "What's going on?"

She nodded to the dim illumination emanating from above the sink. "Turn that off."

"Leighton—"

She didn't wait for his compliance. She slipped out the door onto the porch. Though it was almost midnight, the air still retained a balminess that in no way suggested they were a week into September.

The light gleaming through the window switched off and Jonathan appeared a few moments later. "What are you doing out here?"

Trying not to look like an imbecile.

She braced her arms against the wrought iron railing and glanced at him over her shoulder. "You ask a lot of questions."

"I know. So . . ." His previous unanswered query hung in the air.

She turned back to look out into the night. "I'm getting some air."

"From where? Not in this swamp. Please tell me. I'd like to get some with you."

She laughed. He was sexy and adorable. Was it any wonder she was smitten?

He came up behind her, slid his arms around her waist and she shivered from the contact. "What are you wearing? This isn't what you had on earlier."

She leaned into him. "Do you like it? It's a new dress I picked up."

The black shirt dress was made of a soft jersey fabric and hung in a straight silhouette to her knees.

"It's very . . . roomy."

She smiled to herself, and bumped him with her backside.

"This . . . uh, isn't what I expected from your note," he said, his voice tentative.

"What note?"

"*You have no idea how much I want you in me. Are you* up *for it?*'" he quoted. "That note."

Her mouth dropped open. "You memorized it?"

"Are you kidding?" He pressed a kiss to her shoulder, bared by the dress's loose boat neckline. "It was etched on the back of my eyelids from the moment I read it. Every time I blinked, I could see the words. I don't know how I managed to finish my work."

Her fingers clenched and released around the top rail. "If you didn't expect this dress, what did you expect?"

He bit her earlobe and liquid heat pooled between her thighs.

Steady, Leighton.

"You. Waiting in my bed."

She wanted him, too. The bed, not so much.

"Want something else unexpected?" She slipped two buttons free on her dress, took his hand and placed it between the folds.

His hands skimmed over her breast, down her torso and across her belly. She gasped and arched her back at the exquisite sensation of his fleeting touch on her skin.

He froze. "Are you naked beneath this dress?"

Bingo! "Mmmmm."

He groaned. "Oh, sweetheart, you're killing me."

"That's the last thing I want to do."

She turned her head, her chin grazing her shoulder, and met his lips in a searing kiss. He was an intuitive kisser. He knew when she wanted soft, sweet pecks or when she was in the mood for something harder and rawer.

With lots of tongue.

He palmed her breasts, kneading the mounds, squeezing them together, pulling them apart. His caresses drove her wild, building a cauldron of tension and pleasure that left her unable to remain still. She writhed against him, greedy for more, wanting everything he had to give her.

He trailed his mouth along her jaw and nibbled down to the sensitive spot where her shoulder met the base of her neck. When he bit her there, his forearm was the only thing keeping her from dissolving into a puddle of lust on the ground.

She raised her arms and clasped her hands around his nape, tilting her head to offer him greater access. His strength and desire consumed her and elicited a responding passion that threatened to incinerate everything around her.

His thumbs and index fingers encircled each nipple and alternated between rolling and pulling the engorged peaks. She moaned and captured his lips again, riding the streaks of pleasure that flowed straight to her core. Nothing felt better than when she was in his arms. He made her feel safe, protected. Loved.

He withdrew his hands from inside her dress and tried to tug her back toward the door. "Let's go in the house."

That wasn't part of the plan. She resisted, holding onto the railing. "Why? I'm happy right here."

"Here? Outside?"

She lifted the corner of her mouth in response to his surprise. "I didn't take you for a bedroom-only type of guy?"

"I'm not, but—"

"The lights are off in the house, there's no streetlamp, we're perfectly hidden. Mostly . . ."

He slid his hand between her legs and delved his digits in her slick folds. She sighed.

"And that turns you on? The possibility of being seen?"

She ground her ass against him. "God, yes!"

He smiled against her neck. "You're a bad girl. And I'm one lucky man."

He had no idea.

Her pussy throbbing in anticipation, she turned, grabbed the folded dishtowel she'd placed nearby and dropped it at her feet. Kneeling on it, she unbuttoned his fly and pulled his dick out.

There you are.

He had a beautiful cock, long, veiny and thick enough that when she wrapped her fingers around him, her tips barely touched. She stroked him, long, slow pulls, loving the hardness that pulsed beneath the soft skin. His lashes fluttered and his head fell back. His hands hung loosely at his side while he thrust into her grip, his hiss of pleasure filling her with a potent sense of power. She basked in the knowledge that she made him feel this way, that her hands were bringing him bliss.

A bead of pre-cum formed on the tip and she used her thumb to spread it around the meaty head. She licked her lips. She wanted to taste him, to draw his hardness into her mouth and evoke more reactions. The walls of her pussy swelled as moisture coated her entrance. Gripping his thigh with her left hand, she palmed his cock with her right and massaged the underside of his dick with her tongue.

He groaned and widened his stance, holding onto her shoulders. She lavished his cock with little flicks and gentle kisses, making her way down the seam that ran from the head to his sac. She cupped the balls in her hand, pressed her tongue into the space between them, then gently drew one into her mouth. He hissed again and tilted his pelvis toward her. Her lashes fell as she alternated between both testicles. The skin was so soft and she loved the way they felt in her mouth.

Apparently he did, too. "You're driving me insane."

Her breath coming heavily, she stroked her hand up and down his length, then took him into her mouth.

"Fuck!" He clutched her hair between his fingers, the slight sting turning her on. She clutched his hips, her nails digging into his ass and pulled him in and pushed him out, signaling that she wanted him to fuck her mouth. When he finally took over the motion—at first with caution and then more smoothly—she sighed. Her body was a bundle of ecstasy that she wanted to both stoke and slake. She lifted the front of her dress and dipped her fingers into her wetness.

"Yeah, sweetheart, that's it. Touch yourself. Play with your clit . . ."

Her lids fell shut and she concentrated on all the sensations sweeping through her. His low, erotic words, the feel of his shaft sliding against her tongue, the musky scent of arousal permeating the air, the—

Her eyes flew open. Jonathan stood several feet from her, his chest rising and falling rapidly, one hand gripping the base of his cock.

Why had he stopped?

"Enough," he said, once her eyes met his. "I've been thinking about being in you all night and I don't want to come in your mouth."

It took a moment for his words to penetrate the sexual fog clouding her mind.

"What about on my tits?" She pushed them together and offered them up.

His Adam's apple bobbed and he licked his lips. "You'd let me do that?"

Yes. Please. Now.

She glanced at him from beneath her lashes and nodded.

"I . . ." He swallowed. "Not this time. But I will. I'm going to spread you wide and lick, suck and finger your pussy until you come, screaming my name, your heels digging into my back. And then, when you're spent and I can't hold it any longer, I'm going to come all over those beautiful breasts."

Her eyes widened and she shuddered at his words.

Bring. It. On.

He clenched his teeth and closed his eyes. "I shouldn't have said that. But it doesn't matter. I have no control left when it comes to you."

He pulled her to her feet and wrapped her in his embrace, fusing his mouth to hers. Her heart thundered like a locomotive in her chest and her hands developed wanderlust, skimming all over his body, unwilling to settle in one spot for long.

He bent to grab her leg, but she shook her head.

He straightened. "No? Wh—"

She turned around and bent forward, grabbing the railing. Rising up on her toes, she reached behind her for his cock, then arched her back and pressed the head of him just inside of her, before pulling him out.

"Jesus, Leighton . . ."

She rubbed the head against her lips, letting the evidence of her desire coat him, teasing him—and herself!—in the process, before she slid him completely inside her.

"Ahhhh . . ."

She widened to accommodate him. He stroked deep into her, every hot, pulsing inch of him abrading her internal nerve endings, making her want to scream out in pleasure. She bit her bottom lip to resist the temptation.

It was so delicious being out here. The darkness hid them from prying eyes, but they were still outside, in the open. Anyone could see them. Someone could be watching them now . . .

She pushed her hips back. "Harder," she moaned.

He lifted her, encircled her waist with his arm and pounded into her. The friction was so good she wanted to pull her hair out. And even though it was rawer and filthier than the times they'd made love before, the intimacy between them was stronger than ever, binding them, adding a layer of affection to the dirty words and crude joining. He was literally part of her. She never wanted it to end.

"You feel so fucking good," he whispered into her ear, putting words to her thoughts. "I swear your pussy was made for me."

It started then. She'd been simmering on low for hours, but now . . . Tension coiled tight in her lower belly. She clenched her pussy, undulated her hips, and reached out to the tidal wave of sensation that hovered just beneath her reach. When it finally crested, it pulled her under with a strength she'd hadn't expected, reaching into her chest, squeezing her heart and stealing her breath.

"Jonathan!"

Her knees buckled and the stars floating in her vision wasn't from the night sky. She gave herself up to it and it delivered her sated, satisfied and fulfilled.

With one final stroke, he stiffened and then came with a roar. If no one knew what they'd been doing before, a few of them must have an idea by now.

He rested his forehead on her back. "We're still fully dressed," he said.

She exhaled and lifted a shaky hand to pat his cheek. "I know."

"What am I going to do with you?"

She put her most fervent wish out there. "Love me."

"Always." He squeezed her and kissed her shoulder. "Can we please go inside now?"

She laughed. "Yes."

Upstairs, she followed Jonathan into the large, well-decorated and very masculine master bedroom. When he continued into the adjoining bath, she spread her arms wide and fell back onto his large king sized bed, with its dark duvet and messy sheets.

Orgasms, take me away.

That had gone well, if she did say so herself. She wondered if he'd be up for an encore. Just one. And then she'd let him get some sleep. He had a busy couple of days ahead of him.

The shower roared to life and she popped up, eager to share her idea. She sauntered into the bathroom. "Now, about you coming on my tits—"

Her brain snapped its finger, and a spark flared inside her head. She swayed and dropped onto the tiled rim of the large garden tub.

"Leighton?" He turned off the water and hurried to her side. "Sweetheart, what's wrong?"

She stared at him, dazed, waiting for the fog to dissipate. "It happened again."

"What happened?"

"Remember when I told you about getting pieces of my memory back when I was with Andrea?"

He tensed and scraped a hand through his hair. "Is that what just happened?"

"Yeah." She looked at him, sadness clinging to her like heated tar.

He swallowed. "What did you remember this time?"

"My father. He died six years ago."

He frowned. "I thought you knew that already."

The pain was there, waiting, and it greeted her as a childhood frenemy, rushing over her in waves, the strength of its torment diluted by time and new experiences.

"I did. But it's what happened *after* his death that I'd forgotten."

She turned her gaze inward as the scene unfolded in her mind like a movie, wincing as she faced the harsh words she'd hurled at her mother, relishing their malicious precision.

"Sweetheart, you're scaring me. My imagination is working overtime."

She exhaled. "My entire life my father told me we were blessed. We had so much; it was our duty to give back. He was my hero, until I discovered he was pretending to be something he wasn't. I found out my father wasn't the fine upstanding man, a pillar of the DC community and the US diplomatic corp. He was a liar. He'd been having an affair with a woman he met in Paris. For years."

"Shit." His eyes softened. "Come here."

He pulled her onto his lap, but she didn't relax. She couldn't until she'd told him all of it.

"It gets better. My mother knew about it. Not in a she-found-out-made-him-break-it-off-and-stayed-with-him way. More like he carried on his affair until the day he died and she let him."

She'd never understood that reaction. What woman would let her husband cheat on her? Leighton remembered the years she and her mother hadn't traveled with her father. The events, games, and recitals he'd missed, explained away by her mother as their family sacrificing for their country.

Sure.

Her father got to have his side piece; her mother retained her position and status in DC society. It seemed to Leighton that she'd been the only Clarke who'd suffered. Fuck that! She'd given in to her hurt and anger and unfortunately, she'd made some important personal and professional decisions based on those destructive emotions.

"It changed everything for me. It's the reason I left my old job and went into lobbying, the reason I stopped talking to my mother." She looked at him. "That explains why she didn't know about our engagement."

The tears came then, streaking down her face, overwhelming her senses. Not because she experienced the dishonesty anew, but in sympathy for the shock, pain and betrayal she'd felt all those years ago. When they ended she felt cleansed. Like she'd finally be able to put what happened behind her and move on.

Was that the silver lining? Could the accident and her resulting memory loss be a possible blessing in disguise? She mentioned the idea to Jonathan.

"How so?"

"For the first time in years I wasn't living with the heavy weight of that anguish. It sounds weird, but without my memories, I was able to reclaim the woman I used to be and take a break from the cold, unforgiving person I'd turned into. I'd come to believe there was no such thing as altruism or giving back. That everyone acted in his or her own best interest. I guess I must've started rethinking those beliefs."

"Why do you say that?" His gaze searched hers.

She kissed him on his lips. "Because of you. The damaged person I'd been would never have allowed you into her life. She wanted to feel nothing. You're too vibrant, too passionate, too sexy and you make me feel . . . everything."

God looks out for babies and fools. Considering she was well into her twenties, she was grateful her insanity hadn't caused her to miss having him in her life.

"You should call Dr. Faber and make an appointment."

"I will." She laid her head on his shoulder, wishing this particular memory had stayed buried, peeved it had tainted an otherwise perfect evening. "After the opening."

"Hold on." Jonathan stretched for the towel hanging on the bar, but couldn't grab it.

"What are you doing?" she asked, standing to shift out of his way.

He hauled her back to his lap and tightened his hold on her. "Don't move."

Executing the sexy-guy-disrobing maneuver, he reached over his head, grabbed his shirt from the back and yanked it off, using it to wipe away her remaining tears.

"Everything will be okay," he said, kissing the top of her hair. "No matter what you remember, we'll get through it together."

Not long after she'd first seen him in the hospital, she'd instinctively surrendered her heart to him. But there, in his bathroom, clutching his tee between her fingers, she made a conscious choice to entrust him with her soul.

Chapter Twenty

THE FOLLOWING AFTERNOON, everyone gathered at *Sedici* to taste dishes off the menu. Jonathan, Gib and his crew had spent the entire morning making several show plates of each dish, then they'd invited the waitstaff, bartenders and a few special guests to sample and offer their opinions.

People buzzed around outside of the restaurant as if the entire city was excited about the opening tomorrow. After the tenth person walked in, acting as if they were supposed to be there, Robby ordered one of the servers to cover the windows with brown butcher paper and to lock the front door. Anyone who needed to be there would know to come around to the back kitchen entrance.

The tasting had gone well and while there were still a few minor issues—the restaurant's ordering platform refused to sync, the credit card machine didn't work an the blown glass votive candle holders hadn't arrived—it looked as if the opening tomorrow would go off without a hitch. Most of the staff had already left and Jonathan stood at the bar talking to Adam and Mike about *Quartet*'s opening and how Jonathan had been so nervous he'd thrown up right before the doors opened.

Leighton pivoted, totally not interested in that story. She'd never understood people who could talk about vomit or poop in the presence of food. And they were in a restaurant, for Christ's sake!

The staff had set up long tables in the main dining room and as she passed, she was struck by how much food was left over. Surely, they wouldn't throw it away? Maybe they could box it up and take it to a homeless shelter?

She headed into the kitchen hoping to find Gib before she left and ask about donating the food, but she found Chelsea and Indi instead.

"What are you two doing?" Leighton shook her head, knowing she'd find the answer entertaining.

She liked both women immensely, finding them intelligent and witty with strong, distinct personalities. Their care and concern for Jonathan had been evident, but they hadn't approached her with skepticism and suspicion, choosing warmth and friendliness instead. Leighton learned that though they bickered like sisters and referred to each other as such, they weren't actually related by blood, having met each other growing up in the foster care system.

"It's a long story," Chelsea had warned, "and we'll be happy to share it one evening over a good bottle of wine."

"After Nugget makes his entrance," India had added. "I'm so ready to have this baby. He has a couple more weeks to vacate these premises before I institute eviction procedures."

Now Chelsea stood with one hip propped against the stainless-steel workstation, her arms crossed over her bright yellow sheath, the color radiant against her skin tone. "Ask her."

Indi, glowing in a short floral print sundress, was heading toward the walk-in pantry. "Jonathan once gave us a tour of the kitchen at *Quartet*. He told us the chefs always hide the good stuff back here."

Leighton pointed behind her. "There's a truckload of food out there."

Indi waved a hand. "I had that. Now I want something different."

Leighton looked at Chelsea. "Maybe she's had enough."

Indi pointed a finger at her. "We welcomed you into the sisterhood, Leighton. Don't make me regret it."

"Don't make me tell *you* what *I* regret," Chelsea said. She raised her brows at Leighton. "Since she got back to the States, she's been . . . grazing . . . everything in sight."

"Where did she go?" Leighton asked.

"Mike took her on a three-month trip around the world."

"Nice."

A worldwide voyage was out of the question, but

once Jonathan felt comfortable leaving the restaurant, maybe one across the country? She wanted to drop by *Quartet*, visit the Computronix campus and see where he'd lived before moving back to DC.

"Pay dirt!" Indi exclaimed, followed by, "Oh shit!"

"Whatever you found, put it back!" Chelsea said.

Indi's lips trembled and she lifted light brown eyes gone wide with panic and fear. A stream of liquid flowed down her leg and puddled by her right foot.

Oh shit, indeed!

"That's not pee, is it?" Leighton asked to no one in particular.

Chelsea hurried to Indi's side. "Take deep breaths. You're going to be fine. Let's get you to the hospital."

Indi shook her head and clutched Chelsea's forearm. "Not happening. I can't move."

Chelsea winced, but her voice was composed when she asked Leighton, "Can you grab Mike for me?"

The adrenaline that spread through Leighton's chest made her a little light-headed but not enough to hinder her speed. As she rushed out of the kitchen she heard Indi moan, "You know I was kidding about the eviction notice, right Nugget?"

Four men stood in the dining area but she was focused on the only blond head in the bunch.

"Mike! It's Indi. Her water just broke."

Her hair fluttered against her cheek when Mike raced by, his face carved into determined lines.

"In my kitchen?" Jonathan's voice was horrified.

Adam raised his brow, transforming into a dark, sexy autocrat. "The juices of raw chicken have dripped on numerous cooking surfaces back there. A small amount of amniotic fluid on the floor won't contaminate the space or cause an outbreak."

"I serve squab, not chicken," Jonathan retorted, returning his attention to the other member of the group.

Leighton's laugh trailed off as her gaze followed his to the man who was staring at her—

Her brain snapped its finger, and a spark flared inside her head, but this time it felt like a punch in the middle of her back. The force of the impact caused her to stumble forward and she gasped as an army of memories swarmed into the mental breach and flooded her mind.

By the time Jonathan reached her, she'd recovered. Better than recovered. She thrived. Her heart thundered in her chest and pure happiness shimmered from the top of her head to the soles of her feet.

She threw her arms around Jonathan's neck.

"Are you okay?" His furrowed brow telegraphed his concern.

Thomas took a step toward them. "Don't touch her!"

She spared him a brief glance before responding to Jonathan. "I remember!"

His head flinched back. "What?"

"I remember everything!" The excitement and relief was intoxicating. "My name is Leighton Clarke."

One corner of his lip quirked up. "You already knew that."

Information erupted from within her like a volcano science fair project.

"I'm a lobbyist. I work at Faulkner & Ingersoll. I just made the Top One Hundred Lobbyist list. Because I'm a rock star! Your name is Jonathan Moran. You've won a James Beard award and you have a restaurant in San Francisco that has three Michelin stars, which is insane."

She could barely catch her breath as the facts poured from her. She pointed to Adam. "You're the CEO of Computronix." She turned to the last man present. "And you're Thomas Moran, banker, Jonathan's brother and"—her heart stopped—"my fiancé."

Those last words trickled from her.

She noted Jonathan's sudden stillness, the way his eyes darted to his brother and the remorse shading his features.

He'd lied to her.

Her lungs shut down, making it difficult for her to breathe. She pushed out of his arms and backed away from him, wrapping her own around her waist. For weeks she'd believed she was engaged to Jonathan. She'd lived with him, trusted him, made love to him. She'd shared parts of her family history she'd never told another soul, save Andrea, and the entire time, he and his brother had been laughing at her behind her back, passing her around like it was a fucking Olympic sport.

And last night . . .

Jonathan reached for her. "Leighton—"

Chelsea strode out of the kitchen, her voice overriding his. "Leighton, do you have your phone? Call 911!"

"That won't be necessary." Mike followed behind her, Indi cradled in his arms. "I'll drive her!"

"In what?" Chelsea flung her hands. "We don't live here and you have no idea where to go."

"Fuck!" Mike's eyes were wild.

"Already on it." Adam held up his phone. "I called 911 four minutes ago after Leighton told us Indi's water had broken. The ambulance should be here shortly."

As if to bolster his claim, sirens wailed in the distance.

Chelsea blew him a kiss. "One of the many reasons I love you."

Mike tried lowering Indi into a chair but she wasn't having it.

"Don't you dare put me down!" Indi hooked her elbow around his neck and crunched her knees, holding on for dear life. "You can't leave me!"

Mike's face ripened to an alarming shade of pink. "Indi, if you don't take it easy, I'll have to tap out."

Indi winced and pressed her free hand against the side of her belly. "When your moments away from pushing something the size of a watermelon out of something with the give of a turtleneck, then you'll have the right to lecture me about taking it easy!"

"As soon as I saw those props, I knew we should've skipped that last childbirth class." Mike gently shifted

Indi and pressed his cheek against hers. "Listen to me. You can do this. You've been an incredible wife. You will be an *amazing* mother. And I will never leave your side."

Their display of love, support and devotion would've been beautiful to witness, but she couldn't appreciate the sentiment. Not when she was teeming with bitterness and a sense of betrayal.

She was keenly aware of the Moran brothers: Jonathan, standing next to her—invading her personal space, actually!—his expressions tag-teaming between concern and fear; and Thomas, stewing in annoyance and impatience, on the periphery, but not part of the gang, hands clenched into fists at his side.

Fuck them. They'd both have to wait. While this *could* be the place, it definitely wasn't the time.

Adam draped an arm around Chelsea's shoulders. "At least we know Mike's genes will dominate with this baby."

Indi shot him a pained look. "Why would you say that?"

Adam's tone was candid. "I can't recall one instance when you've managed to be on time, but Nugget is coming a week early."

Another event to seal their bond. This group had shared joys and tragedies, successes and failures, adventures and quiet moments and now a new experience would be added to the collective.

It was all so touching. Only a few minutes earlier, Leighton had looked forward to being in their ranks. Now—she was going to be sick.

"You wait until I have this baby, Adam. I'm going to kick your ass."

"You'll have to catch me first." He softened the starkness of his words by reaching out to squeeze her hand.

"You're dangerous, genius boy. My sister is a lucky woman." A groan distorted Indi's laugh. "We have to go. Now! I will need *all* the drugs."

She buried her head in Mike's neck and then no one could be heard as an ambulance screeched to a stop at the curb and two uniformed technicians burst through the doors and they were able to see the small crowd that had gathered on the sidewalk.

"Finally." Mike hastened to the door, Indi still in his arms. He didn't seem winded. Of course, even pregnant, Indi probably weighed a buck-oh-five.

"Chelsea!" Indi reached out for her sister. "You're coming?"

"Right behind you."

Mike glanced over his shoulder at Adam and Jonathan. "I trust you two can make it to the hospital?"

Chelsea looked at Adam, who nodded and checked with Jonathan—

Who was focused on Leighton.

She could feel his concern, but if he expected a public outburst from her, he wasn't going to get it. She wasn't on some reality TV show. She refused to let what she was going through ruin this occasion. Her father's actions aside, she possessed some "home training," as her elder relatives called it.

Leighton lugged an *Everything's cool* smile into place. "He'll be there."

In the space of a few minutes, Indi and Mike were in the ambulance and Adam and Chelsea were climbing into the backseat of the Uber Adam had summoned.

"I've got to lock up." Jonathan gave her one last beseeching look before running into the kitchen. "Please don't leave."

As soon as he left the room, Thomas gripped her elbow. "This has nothing to do with us. Those are his friends. Let's head someplace quiet where we can talk."

Was he joking? She yanked away from him. "Talk? About your trip?"

"Exactly." The bastard actually smiled. "It's going well."

"Congratulations. I know how much that meant to you."

He either missed the sarcasm, or chose to ignore it. "I knew you'd understand. That's what I told Jon—"

She shook her head and held her hand up, palm out. A palm that itched to smack that smug, shit-eating grin off his face. "You're free to go wherever you want. Jonathan and I are going to the hospital."

The lights suddenly went out, though the glow from the setting sun, filtering through the brown paper on the windows, prevented the space from being totally dark. And then Jonathan was back, leading them out the front door. Thomas passed, giving his brother a murderous look. When she followed, Jonathan grabbed her arm and lowered his voice. "Will you let me explain?"

"Later." Although she mentally challenged him to find any words that would make this right. "Your friends are on their way to the hospital about to have their first child. We will not spoil this for them."

Thomas laughed and the sound was a bit off. "Really? Leighton Clarke is allowing someone else to have the limelight? Doesn't sound like the woman I left three weeks ago."

"Sounds about right, since I'm *not* the woman you left three weeks ago. And that's a good thing." She ignored her seething stomach and motioned to Jonathan without looking at him. "Let's go."

Leighton vaguely remembered hearing birth stories where it seemed labor was divided into two camps: long, excruciating ordeals that took thirty plus hours of pushing or "I didn't know I was pregnant until I went to the bathroom and this baby popped out."

Mike and Indi's experience ended up being nowhere near as dramatic but twice as wonderful. Indi did not scream at the top of her lungs and she did not curse her husband. The couple did utilize the breathing they'd learned until she was able to get "all the drugs."

It was a battle, but Leighton put aside her own hurt feelings and passed the next few hours ignoring Jonathan, talking to Chelsea and Adam and watching Mike hover lovingly over Indi during the brief periods she managed to rest. When the time came, Leighton, Jonathan and Adam withdrew to the waiting room. And a little while later, Chelsea came out to announce that at 12:02 a.m. on Saturday, September 9, Sylvie Jane Black made her entrance into the world.

In the birthing room, Indi cradled Sylvie in her arms and stroked a finger against her golden-colored cheek. Mike sat next to Indi on the bed, his arm thrown along the headrest, his glassy gaze fixed on his family. He kept saying, as if he were a playlist on repeat, "I can't believe what happened. It was the most astonishing thing I've ever seen. One minute there were five people in the room and then there were six!"

His phone rang and when he checked the caller ID, his threatening tears materialized.

"Congratulations, you're grandparents." Mike held the phone in one hand and covered his tear-drenched eyes with the other. Then he switched the call over to video chat and she had the distinct honor of watching Mike and Indi introduce little Sylvie to her "Grandma, Pop-Pop and Auntie Morgan."

Leighton bit her lip, the scene touching her more than she'd ever expected. Her fingers sought and found Jonathan's, locking together. She caught his eye, smiled.

And then she remembered.

Liar. Just like her father.

The joy melted from her face and she turned away from him. He tried to recapture her gaze, but she resisted. She'd share this moment with him and then they were done. She'd let him in, given him first her heart, then her soul and had them crushed into jagged little pieces.

Again.

Chapter Twenty-One

BY THE TIME they'd returned home at 2 a.m., the quaking inside of Jonathan had reached eight-point-zero on the Richter scale and he'd rubbed the skin on the back of his neck raw.

He'd be forever grateful to have been a part of the birth of Mike's baby. The experience would enrich his life. But his anxiety over the reveal of Leighton's recovered memories hadn't allowed him to fully enjoy the occasion. He'd kept one eye on her, trying to suss out her mood, like a boat captain eyeing an impending storm on the horizon.

She was furious. He could tell. In addition to not speaking to him, the air around her was colder than liquid nitrogen and her closed posture screamed danger with a skull and crossbones.

But there had been one moment at the hospital, when

she'd dropped her guard and allowed him to hold her hand. He'd savored that small win more than his first Michelin star because it was the moment that gave him a small measure of hope.

She dropped her purse on the credenza in the hallway and started to the stairs.

Fuuuuuck!

She wasn't going to her room to sleep. He had no doubt that she'd be down those stairs in less than ten minutes with all of her belongings and if he let her, he could kiss any chance of exoneration goodbye.

"Leighton, let me explain—" He sounded like a fucking parrot.

His doorbell chimed. *What the hell?*

She frowned at him over her shoulder, one foot on the bottom step. "Are you expecting anyone?"

"No. Mike's staying at the hospital with Indi and Sylvie. Adam and Chelsea went back to their hotel."

Another chime, followed by persistent knocking, and then—

"Leighton! I know you're in there!"

Thomas!

He was here to plead his case and Jonathan was sure of his plan: shirk his responsibility and blame it all on Jonathan.

Was *he* any better? Pretending to be her fiancé while she'd been in a coma and then not correcting the fallacy when she'd regained consciousness? It'd been a stupid plan and he'd been an idiot to go along with it. And now he'd do whatever it took to gain her forgiveness. And he would. They could get through this. He couldn't bear to consider the possibility that she'd decided to go back to Thomas because their feelings had all been one-sided.

His.

By now, Thomas was pressing the doorbell at one second intervals. Leighton rolled her eyes but, thankfully, she stayed put. Jonathan clenched his jaw and strode back to the entryway. He flung open the door.

"You're being an asshole," he said.

Thomas stood with one arm braced against the doorframe, his brow lowered and his usually tamed hair taking a walk on the wild side.

"Where is she?" Thomas brushed past him. "Leighton!"

Jonathan followed. "This is not a Lifetime movie. Ease up on the drama, okay?"

"The third side of the triangle arrives," Leighton said from her perch on the staircase.

Thomas snorted, his hands jammed on his hips. "You've made yourself at home."

Her lips twisted and a hardness he hadn't seen since the accident crept over her features. "For a while I thought it was."

"It's not, so gather your things and—"

"What, leave with you!" Her laugh raised goose-humps on Jonathan's flesh. He'd forgotten this side of Leighton existed.

Thomas scowled. "Yes, where you belong."

She crossed her arms over her chest. "If I belonged with you, why weren't you here?"

Heat stained Thomas's cheekbones and for the first time since crossing the doorway, his older brother addressed him. "Didn't you explain it to her?"

"When? You were there when she got her memory back and we spent the past six hours at the hospital. We'd just gotten home when you started banging on our door."

"Do it now," Thomas ordered.

"Don't mind me," Leighton said, with a biting tone. "It's not like I'm the subject of this conversation."

"I hate to burst your self-involved bubble," Jonathan told Thomas, "but Leighton and I have more to do than discuss you."

"What do you mean?" Thomas's eyes widened and he curled his upper lip. "You bastard!"

"Boys!" Leighton stepped between them, the warmth of her hand flat against Jonathan's chest. "You're not doing this. I am not a rawhide chew toy. You do not get to fight over me. In fact, you have ten seconds to explain yourselves before I go off. And I'm iffy on those ten seconds."

Jonathan didn't wait to see if Thomas would call her bluff.

"In the chaos of everything going on at the hospital, you have to tell them who you are in relation to the patient. Before they tell you anything or even let you ride in the ambulance. I had to make a split-second decision and it was going to affect whether you were going to be alone or if I'd be able to see you and I didn't want to take the chance of doing the wrong thing."

She focused all of her attention on him. *Good. Thomas doesn't even exist. This is between you and me, sweetheart.*

"Why didn't you correct everyone later?"

"That was the plan. We thought you'd wake up and the deception would automatically end. By then you'd be able to inform whoever you wanted about your condition. The day they'd called me and told me you had awakened, I'd thought this was it. But when I got there, I found out about your memory loss and then you remembered me."

She looked away embarrassed.

"Even before you were discharged, I talked to Dr. Faber. He's the one who said I shouldn't tell you at that point, that it could hinder your recovery."

She wavered and he thought he had a chance. He pressed forward. "My intention was always to do the best by you. I didn't expect to fall in love with you."

"Love? You son of a bitch!" Thomas's face flushed a frightening shade of red. "How could you do this to me?"

Leighton rotated wide eyes in Thomas's direction. "You? How could *you* do that to *me*? I was in a fucking coma. You had to know I'd be confused and scared when I'd awakened, yet you still chose to leave me alone."

"I was in London!"

"And I was in the hospital. Now that we've established our venues, can we get back to how you abandoned me?"

"I didn't abandon you! I asked my brother to look after you until I could return."

"And yet it took you three weeks to get here. What happened? You somehow ended up on the no-fly list? This was the earliest first class seat available? Or you had to come back to get something from your office?"

Thomas's nostril's flared and he flicked an angry look in Jonathan's direction.

Jonathan shrugged. "On the last message I left for Thomas, I told him I was going to come clear to you after the opening. I was going to tell you everything."

Her beautiful but wounded eyes probed his and he bared his soul, willing her to see everything within him, his guilt, his remorse, but most of all, his deep and unwavering love for her.

Her shoulders wilted briefly, before she straightened. Her lips tightened and she tilted her head to the side and shook it. She lowered her lashes then directed her words at Thomas.

"So you didn't come back for me? You came because your plan was in danger. You thought you could fly in, smooth things over and fly back out? Get back to London before your first business meeting of the day?" Leighton asked Thomas, all softness now crusted over.

"Dammit, Leighton, it was a work trip, not a vacation! You knew what it meant for my career."

She opened her mouth to respond and then closed it.

Jonathan staggered a step back. No way! She wasn't going to let him get away with that shit, was she?

"Don't you see how that's a problem?" she asked, her voice calm.

"What?" Thomas asked, rubbing his brow and looking just as confused as Jonathan felt.

"I was in a really bad accident and you didn't think twice about leaving me. For work."

"Work is very important to us. Our careers are everything."

She shook her head. "Not everything. Mike Black is one of the most successful businessmen in the world, and his wife is in the hospital. After spending only a few days in his company, I feel completely comfortable saying he would never leave Indi. Not for any business deal. Neither would Adam."

"Neither would I," Jonathan said quietly.

Leighton finally looked at him and he straightened at the heat he saw in her gaze before she masked it. "Neither would you," she confirmed.

Good. At least she recognized he wasn't like his brother.

"I thought you got your memory back," Thomas said.

"I did."

"Then you know that's not the way our relationship worked."

"So I was naive to believe the man I intended to marry would place a high value on my well-being? You don't have to be in love with me to care about me."

"You've never been naive," Thomas said. "But I thought we had an understanding. We have our own priorities."

"You wanted to marry me because you thought I was selfish."

Thomas lowered his chin and took a step back. "No. I'm not going to let you use your lobbying tricks on me to make this my fault. I wanted to marry you because you knew what you wanted, you weren't afraid to go out and get it, and you didn't let anyone get in your way."

Perseverance was an admirable trait, but that's not the one Jonathan would trot out to convince a woman to marry him.

"I don't know what happened, but the Leighton I left three weeks ago would've made the same decision," Thomas said stubbornly.

She was in a coma, you asshole.

Her expression tightened. "How many times do I have to say it? I'm not the same woman. The old Leighton may have agreed with your decision, but I don't."

"And because you've changed, I'm the bad guy."

Yes, motherfucker! He wanted to yell.

She gathered her hair over her shoulder and smoothed the ends and exhaled loudly. "No. But because I've changed, our relationship is no longer acceptable to me."

Thomas blinked rapidly. "So you're ending our engagement?"

"I am."

Jonathan closed his eyes and released a huge sigh of relief. There was a part of him that worried her composed reaction meant she might actually reconcile with Thomas.

Maybe Thomas had thought that, too.

"For him?" Thomas pointed an accusing finger at Jonathan. "Isn't that what this is about? You've chosen *him*."

Leighton rolled her eyes. "You work out your issues with your brother on your own time. I'm not in this position because of anything I did. I'm in this position because of choices the two of you made when I wasn't able to make them for myself."

"I wasn't trying to be callous," Thomas said with a half-hearted shrug. "I honestly believed I was doing the right thing for us. That doing well in my career, benefitted us both. That's what we wanted, right?"

"It was. But I've discovered that I need a partner who can prioritize me on occasion."

"And you don't think I can do that?"

"After how you handled this situation, I'm not willing to find out."

For a brief moment, Thomas's face fell, and Jonathan wondered if his brother's feelings ran deeper than he'd thought or if he was starting to realize what his decision to stay in London had cost him. But he recovered.

Thomas walked over to Leighton and kissed her cheek. "You should probably see a doctor."

Jealousy burned a hole in Jonathan's chest. His hands clenched into fists at his side, his nails digging into his palms, but he didn't move. As hard as it was to see, this moment hadn't been about him.

"I will."

"Good." Thomas squeezed her shoulder. "Be happy, Leighton. Although, you could do better."

He left without a look back or another word.

Perfect. Now that Thomas was gone, they could finally talk.

Leighton rounded on him. "Why did you do it?"

"I—"

"Did you do it to get back at your brother?"

"Of course not."

"To get back at me?"

He hesitated and that was a mistake.

She shook her head. "You're sick, do you know that?"

"I didn't do it to get back at you. I did it for you."

"Are you kidding me? You really expect me to believe that you lied to me, laughed at me, fucked me for my benefit?"

"I never laughed at you."

"But you admit that you lied?"

"Would it make you feel better to know that I'd made a mistake by not telling you the truth sooner? That the guilt has gnawed at me daily?"

"Yes."

"Then fucking feel better!"

Jonathan braced his arms against the fireplace mantel and dropped his head. His fingers clenched the wood as emotions churned through him. He had to calm down. If he didn't, he was afraid he would blow it. And he couldn't. Some instinct told him he had to get this right.

"What did you get out of it?"

He raised his head and turned to eye her. "What are you talking about?"

"There must have been some benefit to you? What did you get?"

"Are you quoting that bullshit to me? I'm not your father, Leighton."

Her chin trembled. "You bastard!"

"You've got to stop viewing everything through the lens of his actions. You know what I got out of it? I got *you*. I did what I did because I love you. Because I was born for you. Because I get excited when I know I'm getting ready to see you. Your smile lights up my day because you're mine. And I bask in the privilege of being yours."

He grabbed her arms and slanted his lips over hers. When she stiffened, his heart shrank, but he released her, knowing force wasn't the answer. But she wound her arms around his neck, opened her mouth and let him in. He groaned and gathered her close, wanting every part of his heart, body and soul to fuse with hers. He couldn't lose this. He couldn't lose her His heart wouldn't survive it.

They were both breathing heavily when they finally broke apart. He pressed his forehead to hers.

"I know you. I know how you pull your hair over your shoulder and smooth the ends, how you tilt your head when you're considering something—"

"Jonathan, please—"

"It's never like this. That kiss we just shared, the time we spent with each other, the way we loved together . . . It doesn't feel like that with anyone else. Only you."

"Listen to me!" She pushed against him. "I have to go!"

Panic welled within him and he struggled to breathe. He could barely hear her over the sound of his heartbeat thrashing in his ears. "Wait, what? No!"

"You were in a tough situation. I get it. When I woke up in that bed scared and alone, you were there and you gave me something to hold on to. To focus on."

He grabbed her hands, but he was too slow to prevent her fingers slipping through his. "I was happy to do it. I wanted to do it. Because I love you."

She moved away from him. "Looking back on everything, on the kiss before the accident and that bullshit Thomas pulled, I can see why you did what you did."

He shook his head. She was saying the right words but her tone inspired dread. He reached for her again but she shook her head and held her arms out, gesturing for him to stay away.

"I don't blame you for the accident or even for pretending to be my fiancé."

He should've been filled with joy. Instead—"Then why are you leaving?"

Her dark eyes filling with tears were like an eleven inch, carbon-steel sujihiki to his heart.

"For weeks, you acted like you cared for me. But you lied. You made me look like a fool. Like a goddamned idiot. And *that* I can't forgive."

Chapter Twenty-Two

HIS PERSONAL LIFE might be in the toilet, but professionally, he was on top of the world.

Sedici's opening had been a success.

From the moment he'd crossed the restaurant's threshold, it had been *Game on, bitches!* Deliveries of food had to be put away, there was glassware to be cleaned and silverware to be rolled and all of it needed to be recorded by the photographers.

It had required every ounce of Jonathan's skill as chef to empty his mind and focus on the tasks at hand. Not easy when his heart was crushed as if it had been through a pulverizer and he was operating on zero hours of sleep. But there was no time to whine and no one to give a shit. Blood, sweat, tears and a hell of a lot of money had gone into this moment and he intended to do right by it.

All too quickly, it'd been showtime. After a quick

pep talk with the staff, he'd left the front of the house to Robby and Zach and retreated to his domain, waiting for the printer to roar to life and give him his first dupe.

Receiving it, he got down to business. "Ordering, first course . . ."

Service was flawless. The cooks stepped up and he couldn't have been more proud. The comments coming into the kitchen were incredible, giving the cooks an in-the-moment review of the food. Gib did her job masterfully, so much so that thirty minutes after the first seating began, he was able to leave her in command and head out to the floor.

He shook hands with Bob from the Eastern Market and gave his wife, Opal, a kiss on the cheek.

"Where's that beautiful girlfriend of yours?" Bob asked. "I wanted Opal to meet her."

Jonathan's heart twisted painfully. "I'm not sure, but hey, thanks for coming. Enjoy your evening," he said, moving to the next table, trying to dodge any follow-up questions.

Zach was a blur. He spoke to all of their guests, reporting back that there was a great deal of interest in their next venture. People were already inquiring about investing. Music to Zach's ears. Jonathan made sure to personally greet each food writer, restaurant critic and blogger and thank them for attending. He did brief interviews, directed requests for longer meetings to Zach and even received a fair number of propositions, phone numbers and profile names for dating websites.

The verdict was in: *Sedici* was the most exciting DC restaurant opening of the year.

Whoop-de-fucking-doo.

His head throbbed, his cheeks hurt from smiling, and his mouth was dry. He stole away and hid in his office.

From the moment he'd realized his calling as a chef, he'd wanted to open a restaurant in DC. Tonight, he'd achieved that goal, more successfully than he could ever have anticipated and yet it had meant nothing.

Because Leighton wasn't there to share it with him.

His brother had stopped by earlier, when Jonathan had been in the middle of butchering for the dinner service, still angry about last night and ready to lay the blame squarely at Jonathan's feet.

"I guess you're proud of yourself," Thomas had sneered.

Jonathan hadn't looked up, his attention focused on breaking down the squab. "No, actually, I'm not."

"It's your fault all of this happened."

Jonathan had set down his knife, wiped his hands on his towel and given Gib command of the kitchen. He strode out of the back door and past the loading dock. He'd be damned if he'd allow Thomas's energy to pollute his kitchen, especially considering the importance of this occasion. If his brother wanted to have it out with him, he'd follow.

He did.

"You know," Jonathan said, turning to face Thomas,

hands jammed on his hips, "I know what I did was wrong and I take full responsibility for my actions and decisions. At some point, you're going to have to do the same."

Thomas scowled. "I take responsibility for assuming you'd changed. That was my mistake. I ask you to take care of my fiancée and you decide to move in on her. All you've proven is that you're as selfish now as you were when we were kids."

He was like a broken record.

"Dude, just stop! You've been blaming me for shit that's gone wrong in your life since I was born. I'll admit I was attracted to Leighton from the moment I met her, but I didn't set out to take her away from you. I tried to keep my distance, but couldn't, and because of that I'll have to live with the consequences. But I want you to think about what would've happened if *you'd* made another choice. Instead of focusing on what everyone else did wrong, consider how things might've been different if *you'd* stayed behind. If *you'd* made the decision based on your heart instead of your head. If *you'd* chosen Leighton over your career."

Thomas's head jerked back. "Choose her over my career? You think that's the type of man she needs? When did you get soft? You won't keep her if that's what you believe. She's a strong woman. She'll walk all over you, then leave you behind."

"What kind of Cro-Magnon shit is that? Don't misconstrue my easygoing nature with weakness. I know who I am and I'm comfortable enough in my skin to achieve my goals and support her as she pursues hers. I don't know if that's the type of man she needs, but I hope it's the type of man she wants."

Thomas twisted his mouth and his expression tightened, as if he'd tasted something sour. "Fuck you. I'll never forgive you for this."

When Thomas strode past, Jonathan grabbed his arm, halting him. "We can't let it end this way. A big part of why I came home was to work on our relationship, so we can act like the brothers we are."

Thomas had jerked his arm out of Jonathan's hold. "Then you shouldn't have tried to steal my woman."

Thomas was never going to accept his own culpability.

Jonathan leaned his elbows on his desk and dropped his forehead into his palms. He'd irreparably damaged his relationship with his brother, which would only make the tension during family gatherings worse. And once again, something he'd done would be the source of heartache to his parents.

A knock roused him from his musings. He smiled when he saw Mike standing in the doorway.

He stood up, clasped the other man's hand and brought him in for a quick hug. "What are you doing here? Shouldn't you be at the hospital?"

"I can't stay long, but I'm doing what I said I'd do," Mike said, dropping into a chair. "Supporting you."

"How's Indi?"

"Tired, hormonal and amazing," Mike said, lips parting as his expression softened.

The gaping hole in the middle of Jonathan's chest ached.

"And the baby?"

"Sylvie is incredible. It's hard to believe that something so little can be so perfect. Last night I spent an hour holding her and looking at her lashes. She has a head of golden brown curls and she smells so sweet—" Embarrassment turned the tip of his ears pink and he cleared his throat. "Sorry, I probably sound like an idiot."

He did, but it was the sweetest thing Jonathan had heard from his friend in a while.

"Adam told me Leighton got her memory back."

Another painful stitch—

"Yeah, just before you guys went to the hospital."

Mike studied him. "That had to be pretty distressing, yet she still came to the hospital with you. That was extremely gracious of her."

"It was."

"Everything looks amazing out there. It appears you have a success on your hands."

Jonathan nodded. "It does."

"Then why don't you look happier?"

Adam chose that moment to pop his head in the room. "I thought I'd find you both back here "

"You, too? Where's Chelsea?" Jonathan asked.

"I dropped her off at the hospital to be with Indi and the baby," Adam said, leaning his big frame against the filing cabinet in the corner. "She asked me to relay her congratulations and let you know how proud she is of you." He frowned. "But I refuse to give you a kiss or a pat on your ass."

A good belly laugh had been just what he needed. "Thanks, man."

Mike leaned back in his chair. "So what are you going to do?"

"About what?"

"Global warming," Adam said.

Jonathan was sure his mouth dropped open in shock.

Mike twisted in his seat to stare at Adam. "Was that sarcasm?"

Adam frowned. "He's being a dick. He knows we're asking about Leighton."

Mike chuckled softly and shook his head before turning back to Jonathan. "We know what's going on—we both recognize that look. It's the look of a man who fucked up royally and is in danger of losing his woman."

"If you truly love her, it won't get better," Adam said. "I lasted a day and a half."

Mike raised his hand. "One week, but only because I had to set up a few things first. But any time spent in relationship limbo is hell. Whatever you have to do to get her back, do it."

Jonathan shoved his fingers through his hair. "You didn't see her last night. I want to be with her more than anything, but she doesn't feel the same about me."

Adam smiled. "Then change her mind."

LEIGHTON'S GAZE SWEPT the late lunch crowd at OEG, the well-known restaurant on Capitol Hill. Since it was almost two o'clock, the mostly-politico lunch crowd had already hustled back to work, but a few still lingered and it didn't take long to spot her target. He sat alone, his head bent over a half-filled tumbler.

There you are.

She thanked the sous chef for letting her sneak in through the kitchen and strode past some local businessmen, who talked and laughed loudly, their cheeks flushed with the telltale stain of too much alcohol.

"Well, Congressman, it appears you still like a stiff one in the afternoon."

The Honorable Mr. Fred Ramsey from the State of Illinois flinched and the blood drained from his face.

"You've got to be kidding me," he muttered. He craned his head to peer out of the high backed, forest green leather booth. "Where the fuck is my security?"

"Don't blame George." The bodyguard was all brawn with very little brain. "I created a little diversion and snuck in the back door."

"What the hell am I paying him for?" He demanded into his drink.

Leighton winced. Ramsey was responsible for the consequences that flowed from his actions, but this new depressed demeanor didn't sit well with her.

"Congressman, I don't need a lot of your time."

A wry smile crooked his lips and his head bobbed

as if to acknowledge their previous interaction hadn't exactly matched the runtime of Lawrence of Arabia.

She pressed him. "Unlike last time, I think you'll like what I have to say."

Those must've been the magic words. Ramsey narrowed his red, bleary eyes, then motioned for her to join him.

She slid onto the facing banquette. "Thank you."

"The DC gossip mill had it wrong. Word was you'd left politics with a brain tumor." Ramsey took another sip of his drink.

"You can't believe everything you hear on the Hill."

He curled his lip. "I guess it was too much to hope it was true."

Ouch.

His demoralization was palpable and, surprisingly, she took no pleasure in it. Certainty coursed through her. She'd made the right choice.

Leighton placed her phone down on the table. "Now that Congress is back in session—"

"You want me to ensure the tire amendment makes it into the final version of the bill." He dragged a hand down his face. "I'm working on it."

Leighton shook her head. "You don't understand. I'm no longer on the Concord Tires account."

He stared at her for a prolonged moment. "What does that mean?"

"Basically, you don't have anything to fear from me."

She had no idea who Faulkner would assign to the

case, but since the idea to approach Ramsey had been her own strategy, she didn't feel any obligation to share the plan with the new lobbyist. There was still the issue of the leak, though Leighton had her suspicions, but it was no longer her concern.

"Is this a joke?"

"No. The amendment can either pass or die without any action on your part, and no reprisal on mine."

"What about Brad Bagley?"

"What about him?"

"You're not backing him for my seat?"

She pursed her lips. "I never said Mr. Bagley filed the papers, only that he'd had them prepared. But in the end, he decided not to declare his candidacy. He has enough on his plate with his family and his business."

Ramsey leaned his head against the back of the booth and let out a shaky laugh.

Considering her task completed, she grabbed her phone and scooted off the seat. "Don't get too comfortable. I've given up this case, but I'm not leaving politics. Our paths will cross again."

"I'm sure. Brian . . ." he signaled the waiter for a new drink.

She narrowed her eyes.

You've done what you came here to do, Leighton. You've given him a reprieve. It's not your fault if he's too stupid to take advantage of it.

She frowned. "You're turning into a cliché, Congressman and you're doing a disservice to the people who elected you to represent them. Give the booze, gambling and women a break. Don't make it so easy for the next 'me' to grab you by the balls."

As she left, she passed a large agitated man, who stumbled to a stop when he saw her.

"Lovely to see you again, George."

His gaze switched from her to the congressman. "Fuck!"

Smiling, she stepped from the restaurant's dim interior into the bright afternoon sunshine and made a call. "It's done."

"How do you feel?" Andrea asked.

Leighton took a deep, satisfied breath. "Like I'm ready to get to work on a certain governor's presidential campaign."

Five minutes into the meeting with her bosses and Leighton had realized she'd lost her taste for lobbying. Her recovered memories had helped her to understand why she'd initially made the professional change—she'd been reacting from a place of pain. But she didn't want to spend the rest of her life making choices to spite her parents instead of doing what would make her happy.

Andrea cleared her throat. "And we're good?"

When Leighton had contacted the other woman to see if the offer to work on Wittig's campaign was still viable, Andrea had sought forgiveness for her part in their argument the day before her accident.

"You were being my friend," Leighton had told her. "There's nothing to forgive."

"We're good," she confirmed now. "When do we start?"

"After the new year. We need to get through this election first. Take some time off. I'll be in touch, doll."

Leighton ended the call and strode down Fifteenth Street. She felt a measure of peace having taken the necessary steps to get her professional life back in order.

That still left her personal life . . . and Jonathan.

She missed him terribly, constantly experiencing the phantom pain of his absence. Everything reminded her of him. Any billboard or ad about an upcoming film brought to mind the day they'd spent together watching movies. Anytime she was in the Capitol Hill neighborhood—which was often—she recalled their time at the Eastern Market. And food—seeing it, eating it, smelling it, all made her think of the sexiest man she'd ever known.

With her recent neurological trauma, she wouldn't have blamed her brain for a mental hiccup. She actually would've considered it a serious solid if she lost all of her memories of Jonathan. But her brain was like a recently re-hired eager intern, determined never to let her down again. It brought all of her remembrances of them to the fore, whether she wanted them or not.

And for the record, she didn't

And DC wasn't helping, either. This was *her* city and yet he was everywhere: on the news, in the paper, on freaking bus shelters, his handsome face taunting her.

"Remember this? It could be all yours."

What was she supposed to do? He'd lied to her. Played her. She couldn't forgive that, no matter how much her heart begged her to reconsider. Anytime she weakened and pondered going back, she thought of her mother and how her father had made a fool of her.

Why had Beverly Clarke allowed it?

Leighton stopped in the middle of the sidewalk and set her jaw. Maybe it was time she asked.

Chapter Twenty-Three

LEIGHTON JUMPED WHEN the doorbell rang, which was ridiculous considering she was expecting her guest. But with every minute that passed, she'd grown more and more tense until she'd become a human version of a guitar string, ready to emit a chord if someone strummed her. She closed her eyes and counted to five—slowly—before rising.

The late day sun shone through the expansive windows in her living room and cast shining beams on the white oak floors, creating a lit path to her door.

Auspicious or ominous?

The bell chimed again before she reached it. Her heels clicked on the floor as she hurried across the last several feet and opened the door.

Beverly Clarke was a tall woman, with dark skin,

sparkling dark eyes and her trademark thin dreads pulled off her face to flow down her back.

"Mom."

Beverly stared at her for a long moment and some of the sparkle faded from her eyes. Her mouth tightened. "Leighton."

She stepped to the side and opened the door wider. "Please, come in." When she'd closed and locked the door behind her mother, she turned to find herself subjected to a thorough visual examination.

"How are you feeling?" Beverly asked.

"Better."

"Tell me everything."

"I will," Leighton said, "but first I want to discuss something else."

A week later and Jonathan's words continued to echo through her mind.

"I'm not your father, Leighton . . . You've got to stop viewing everything through the lens of his actions."

She gestured to the gray sofa. "Have a seat."

Her mother perched on the cushion's edge and placed her purse in her lap, crossing her legs at the ankle and sweeping them to the side. "What's going on? Are you okay? You're scaring me."

Leighton sat on the wide stool at one of the windows, sweeping views of the Potomac River at her back. "Physically, I'm fine. I saw my doctors earlier this week and went through a battery of tests. Other than a small scar on my scalp, there's no permanent damage from the accident."

Beverly placed a hand against her chest. "That's a relief."

Here goes . . .

Leighton moistened her dry bottom lip. "I need to understand."

"Understand what?"

"You and Daddy."

Her mother's face tightened. "I haven't seen you in months and I just confirmed for myself that you're okay after your accident. I don't want to argue about this again."

"I don't want to argue, either," Leighton said, leaning forward. "But it has affected *everything* in my life. I need to talk about it."

Beverly's chin trembled but she responded with a slight nod. "Okay. Whatever you have to say to me, it will be better than silence. We've had too much of that between us."

Leighton exhaled. She'd hoped to get this far but, to be honest, she'd expected her mother to shut her down.

"Did you always know about it?"

"Not from the very beginning, but, early on. He didn't keep anything from me."

Leighton tried to swallow around the boulder lodged in her throat. "How could you let him do that to you?"

"I let him be who he was and he did the same for me. We both sinned." Beverly clasped her hands together. "I forgave him and he forgave me. That's what marriage is."

Leighton's mind reeled. Instead of answering her questions, this discussion was creating more. Her mother had cheated on her father, too? And her father had known?

Beverly stood up and walked over to her. "There's a lot that goes on in a marriage and I won't answer all of your questions about ours. That will remain between your father and I. But it's not his perceived betrayal of me that's hurt you all these years. I think the real question you want to ask is how could he do that to *you*?"

As soon as her mother voiced the words, tears pricked the back of Leighton's eyes and her hands flew up to cover her opened mouth.

Oh my God, she's right.

"Your father was handsome, brilliant, driven, charming," Beverly said, a tender smile curving her mouth, "but he was not perfect. He was just a man. But you were Daddy's little girl, and to you, he was a god. When you found out your idol had feet of clay, it seemed to destroy all the goodness you saw in him. You not only judged that one aspect of his life, you let it color your feelings on everything about him."

Leighton's mind was pushed to its fragile limits, trying to keep up with her mother's declarations.

Beverly pried one of Leighton's hands away from her mouth and held it between hers. "Your father and I had grown up attending Jack and Jill together. We'd gone to the same schools, our families moved in the same social circles. We had a lot in common, including a drive to give back to our country and our community. We weren't head over heels in love with each other—and to be honest, I don't think either of us thought love like that existed—but we were good friends who liked and respected each other.

"Over the years, I grew to love your father and the life and legacy we built together, for you. But in his later years, he met and fell in love with someone else."

Leighton's heart broke for Beverly, as her mother and as a woman.

"By then we were already one of DC's top political families, with all the privileges and restrictions that entailed. If he'd left me, the scandal would've consumed everything in its path, including you. Do you know how much harder your life would've been living under that cloud of infamy?

"And so he stayed with us and when he had the opportunity, he'd spend some time with her. Your father didn't do what he did as some kind of 'having his cake and eating it, too.' He gave up a part of his life for us. Can you understand what that must've cost him? And yet, until the day he died, he was an incredible father to you."

Leighton's tears refused to be confined. They spilled from her eyes, ran down her face and dripped off her chin.

Beverly swept both thumbs across her daughter's cheeks. "We're people. None of us are perfect. And we make mistakes. I've made them. Your father made them. We made them with each other. With you. And I'll probably make more in the future. But our mistakes weren't malicious. I love you. And when you start with that premise, we can figure out everything else."

"You know what I got out of it? I got you. I did what I did because I love you."

The easiest thing in the world for Jonathan would've been to leave her in that hospital. But he hadn't. He'd disrupted his life, risked restaurant failure and his relationship with his brother, all for her.

Because he loved her.

And she loved him.

Like Beverly said, they could figure everything else out. She needed to find him. But first—

Leighton enfolded her mother in a hug. She gave comfort to her and received comfort from her for the first time in six years, lifting a load she hadn't been aware of carrying.

When the embrace ended, Beverly smoothed Leighton's hair behind her ears. "Let me get you a glass of water."

Her mother crossed the open floor plan and entered the kitchen. "I didn't know you liked flowers this much," she said, remarking on the colorful bouquets of roses, lilies and sunflowers residing on the marble countertops.

Leighton's smile was shaky. "I didn't, either."

But every day for the past week a new bouquet of flowers, like the ones he'd gotten for their dinner together, showed up on her doorstep, each one bearing a card containing a handwritten quote from the movies they watched together.

"These are the flowers I'd pick for my wedding."

"From your fiancé?"

"That's a long story."

"One I hope you'll share with me. Being on the margins of your life for these past six years has been difficult."

"I know. And I'm sorry. But I know how I can make it up to you." Nerves fluttered in her belly and she pressed a hand there to quell her growing excitement. "Would you like to go out to dinner with me? There's this great new restaurant that just opened . . ."

"Is HE COMING?" Leighton asked her mother.

From Beverly's seat at the bar she had a clear, unobstructed view of the path to the kitchen. Leighton sat on her other side, facing slightly away. She smoothed her hand down the front of her red, fitted dress and tried to refrain from bouncing her leg against the rail beneath the bar.

"I don't know. A tall white man with dark tousled hair just came through the door, but he's not dressed like a chef. He's wearing a t-shirt and jeans," Beverly said, whispering like they were on a stakeout. Then she gasped. "Good Lord, is that *him*?"

Leighton recognized the wonder in her mother's tone.

"It's him."

She took three quick breaths. She could do this.

"Hello! We don't open for another couple of hours but my sous chef said you *had* to speak to the chef? I'm Jonathan Moran. How can I help you?"

She almost slid from the stool. It'd only been a week,

but his deep voice affected her the same way it had the first time she'd heard it. It was just as smooth, just as charming as before, but it lacked a measure of warmth it used to have, a heat that had placed it, and him, on a whole other level.

Was that because of her?

He hadn't noticed her yet. Suddenly, wings fluttered to life in her belly and moisture fled her mouth. She needed to just do this. What's the worst that could happen? He'd toss her out on her ass, laughing at her pitiful apology and high-handed assumption that he'd take her back?

She blew out a breath. Okay, not helpful.

She'd given presentations to some of the most powerful people in the country and had greeted foreign heads of state in front of hundreds of people in person, while millions watched around the world. Why was she so nervous?

Because this was the man she loved and her future happiness depended on getting this moment right. So . . . She swallowed and swiveled her chair.

Sweet Jesus, he was beautiful. She drank in the sight of him, appreciating the way his body filled out a pair of jeans and a basic t-shirt, this time in an olive green color that deepened the brown of his eyes.

She'd missed him and hoped to hell he'd missed her. But more than that, she prayed that he'd forgive her.

She stood and stepped around her mother. "Hi."

Jonathan's eyes widened and his expression blossomed into surprise and pleasure before he cleared it, his lips tightening into a thin line.

Beverly cleared her throat. "I'm going for a walk around the neighborhood. It may take a couple of hours. Give me a call if you need me," she murmured.

"Thanks, Mom."

He didn't say a word. He just stood there, staring at her. *Shit, he must really be angry.* Of course he was. Expecting anything else had been wishful thinking. He'd told her he loved her and she'd thrown it back in his face.

She gestured around. "I saw your opening went well. Everyone's talking about it."

"We had a great turnout and good reviews from the press."

Look at us, having a nice civil conversation, as if we hadn't come apart in each other's arms a little over a week ago.

"I know. The article I read said, 'Chef Jonathan Moran proves that simplicity can still triumph over the increasingly forced and chemical.'"

He tilted his head. "You memorized that?"

"Your success means a lot to me."

Brackets formed on either side of his mouth. "What are you doing here?"

She took a deep breath. God, this was harder than she'd thought. She'd taken for granted his warm way of speaking to her. She missed it. Even before her accident, when they'd both been battling their attraction, their interaction hadn't been this tortured. "I—I wanted to see you. To talk to you."

He took a step closer. "Are you okay?"

"I've never felt better." Physically.

"What did Dr. Faber say?"

She shrugged. "The same way he couldn't explain why it happened to me, he couldn't explain how the memories came back."

Jonathan nodded and took a step back.

Dammit, this was ridiculous. It was time for her to woman up and find out if they had a chance or not.

"The flowers were beautiful," she offered.

He shoved his hands in his pockets. "So you got them?"

Here we go . . .

"I did. They gave me the courage to come here and tell you I love you. So much I could burst from it. When I realized I'd lost my memories I couldn't imagine ever feeling whole again. But then I saw you and you lent me your kindness, your strength and your heart. I only hope you still feel the same way."

Her heart twisted in her chest as she waited for his response.

And waited.

And waited.

Slowly, like man's evolution, his blank expression lightened, degree by degree until it resembled the charming, gorgeous face that featured heavily in her dreams of happily ever after. He reached her in two long strides and claimed her mouth with a swift passion-filled precision that left her breathless.

"Just so you know," he said, smoothing her hair back and gazing into her eyes, "next week you were set to receive daily deliveries of vases from the Eastern Market. All shapes and sizes."

She laughed. "I would've preferred you."

"You always had me. I was just waiting for you to figure that out."

Relief flowed through her, making her giddy. It was going to be okay. "Don't take this as a complaint, but you're too easy, babe."

He skimmed his hands down her arms and over her hips. "Only with you."

"No, seriously. I thought I'd have to bring out the big guns to get you to forgive me."

"Aren't you glad it wasn't necessary?" he murmured, trailing his fingers along the neckline of her dress.

Her nipples hardened and she tried to focus. "I am. I'm not so sure you'll feel the same."

His hands stopped and he narrowed his eyes. "Why? What did you do?"

"Nothing bad! It doesn't matter now, since you forgave me so quickly, but I called one of my sorority sisters. She lives in California now, Oakland to be more precise. She's married to an assistant NBA coach . . ."

He gasped. "No!"

A smile teased her lips. "And if you can find the time

in your busy, Michelin-starred schedule before basketball season is over, we have a standing invitation to stop by a practice, meet some of the players and have dinner with the coaches."

He stared at her, a dazed expression on his face. "You're amazing. I love you so much."

He kissed her again, reinforcing her belief that all would be right in their world.

"Thank God you came around. And not just for me. Gib has already threatened to go back to *Quartet* if I didn't 'chill the fuck out.' Her words." He blinked. "Gib was in on this, wasn't she?"

Leighton couldn't hide her huge grin. "Yes, she was."

He enfolded her in a bear hug. "I do believe she's earned a day off."

"A day?" she asked, her tone teasing. "Is that all I'm worth to you?"

She didn't expect his serious response. "You are worth everything to me and don't you ever forget it." He buried his nose against her shoulder and nuzzled her neck. "So . . . that was your mother?"

His question was pure innocence. "Yes."

"Wow."

"Hey, watch it," she said, slapping his arm. Happiness leant her spirit buoyancy. She couldn't believe she wasn't floating several inches off the ground.

He laughed. "I'm just getting an interesting glimpse of thirty years into the future, that's all." He sobered. "Did you have a chance to talk?"

"We did. And I learned a lot. Things I hadn't been expecting, but that I needed to know. And I promise to tell you all about it. Another time. Just know that I'm making peace with my father's actions. I'm not going to live my life or base my decisions on things that happened in the past and frankly, that don't concern me. All that matters is you and me and the promises we make to each other. We'll decide what our life will be."

"Come here." He held her close. "I'm not imagining this, right?"

Her hands trailed over all the muscles in his back, grateful for the chance to do this as often as she wanted for the rest of her life. "No, you're not."

He lifted his head and stared at her. "And this isn't some elaborate revenge fantasy, is it? You're not lulling me into a false sense of security only to yank the football away from me, are you?"

She laughed. "Of course not."

"Good. Because when I look at you, I can't imagine a time when I don't have the right to hold you in my arms. I love you, Leighton, more than anyone or anything in my life and I will never withhold anything from you again. We went through a lot to get here, but if this is the end result, then it was worth it." He took a deep breath. "Will you marry me?"

She thought he'd never ask. "Yes!"

"Wait here."

She laughed and cried at the same time. "You just proposed and you're leaving me?"

"It must be something in the Moran blood." When she gaped at him, he winked. "What? Too soon?"

She was too blissful to be annoyed. And he wasn't gone long. When he returned, he had a dark blue velvet ring box in his hand with the initials W and G stamped in scripted gold lettering on the top.

She opened it and stared at the beautiful but simple oval cut diamond set in an elegant rose gold band. "This is the ring you picked out that night."

"The moment I saw it on you, I knew it was meant for you. And Mr. Bridge agreed."

Jonathan slid it on her finger. "Feels even better to do it this time around."

"Speaking of Thomas—" she began.

He pulled her into his arms and nibbled the side of her neck and up her jaw. "Were we?"

"I think we should. Have you talked to him?"

"He stopped by here the night of the opening. It wasn't pretty. He seems hell-bent on blaming me for everything." He sighed and tightened his arms around her. "He needs to figure some things out. I hope he can find a way to be happy."

She didn't share Jonathan's same forgiveness of spirit towards Thomas. Not because of what he'd done to her, but because of how he'd treated Jonathan. Having her own revelatory experience allowed her to see how much silent rage and resentment Thomas nurtured inside. He'd never achieve peace until he dealt with it. Lucky for her, he was no longer her problem.

"You make *me* happy," she told Jonathan, staring into his deep brown eyes. "Have I told you lately how much I love you?"

"It's been a few minutes. I'm going through withdrawal." He kissed the tip of her nose and leaned his forehead against hers. "Given everything that's happened, do you still believe your accident was a blessing in disguise?"

"Absolutely," she said. "But the next time either of us needs to learn an important life lesson, let's find an easier way to do it, okay?"

Want more Tracey Livesay? Turn the page for an excerpt from her wildly romantic

ALONG CAME LOVE

Available now from Avon Impulse!

When a silly, impulsive decision lands free-spirited India Shaw behind bars in San Francisco, she has no choice but to call the only person she knows in the unfamiliar city—the very man she abandoned after a steamy two-day fling. The fact that she's pregnant with his child is something she'd rather not divulge.

Tech executive Michael Black never thought he'd hear from the quirky beauty after she left his bed four months ago, much less be called upon to post bail. He's got his hands full with a corporate merger that could make or break his career, but his honorable nature—and an overwhelming need to see her again—means he can't just leave her in jail. And when India reveals the truth about her pregnancy, Mike insists she stay with him until the baby is born.

India doesn't want to depend on him for anything, but their constant proximity stirs up feelings she can't ignore. She's never desired a family before and she knows a future with Mike isn't possible . . . but then along came love and shook up all her plans.

INDIA SHAW'S STOMACH twisted into a Gordian knot. She pressed a hand to the still-flat surface, cursing the unfortunate mingling of nerves and nausea.

Settle down, Nugget. Please.

She lifted the starfish pendant that hung from the long silver chain around her neck and brought it to her nose. She inhaled, grateful when the sweet, bracing aroma of peppermint had the desired effect. Exhaling, she squinted against the bright San Francisco sun and watched the uniformed doorman assist the exiting man pushing twins in a top-of-the-line stroller, a leather messenger bag slung across his body. Sending them on their way with a wide smile, the doorman turned back to Indi and the indulgent expression melted from his countenance.

"Was there something else?" he asked, his tone managing to convey his disinterest in her response. He eased past her and reclaimed his post behind the chest-high amber-colored glass cubicle.

Indi cleared her throat, choking on the *Asshole* that yearned to escape her lips. "About that list—"

"You're not on it."

"That's not possible." She took a deep breath, pushing back the panic that threatened to overwhelm her. "Can you check again?"

He ignored her and continued studying the large computer screen in front of him.

She braced her hands on the rich wood-grained counter and shifted her weight forward, trying to see the spellbinding monitor.

The man tightened his thin lips and shifted the screen, further obstructing her view of the list. "I don't need to check again. Your name isn't on the list of approved entrants for Penthouse A."

Her stomach churned again and she slid back to the ground, her boots knocking against the bag at her feet and echoing on the marble floors. This couldn't be happening. What was she going to do? Where was she going to stay? And how could she have forgotten that Chelsea and Adam wouldn't be home?

Because from the moment she'd seen those contrasting pink-toned, parallel lines, her brain had been as disordered as a greasy diner's breakfast scramble.

Sorry, Nugget. Bad analogy.

But how else to explain her sudden resignation

from her job as a craft beer server at the brewery, her mad dash to the Seattle train station, and her having endured loud one-sided phone conversations and bone jarring bumps and rocking for the thirty-five-hour trip? She'd eschewed freshening up at the train station before heading to the apartment—preferring necessity over propriety—and assumed she'd sidestep her sister's interrogation, take a much-needed shower, grab food and a nap, *then* talk to Chelsea about her situation.

Not for one second had she thought gaining entrance to the apartment would be an issue.

Looking at the stack of brochures proclaiming the expanded hours of the restaurant off the lobby, she straightened them, making sure the edges lined up neatly and all the papers were facing in the same direction. "Clearly there's been a mistake—"

"This may be new to you, especially if you live in the Tenderloin," he said, scanning her braids, cable-knit sweater, long floral skirt and leather ankle boots, "but here at the Hermitage at Avalon, we take pride in protecting the privacy of our homeowners."

Indi frowned. She didn't know what "live in the Tenderloin" meant—how could someone inhabit a piece of meat?—but his arched brow, curled lip and eau de condescension was enough to clue her in to his opinion of her.

Did this man think he could intimidate her? She'd been thrown shade by people more elite and more proficient at it than him. She plastered on a bright smile.

"I'm sure Chelsea and Adam appreciate that, but it's not required in this case. You've met Chelsea, right?"

"Mrs. Bennett?"

Indi rolled her eyes. "Technically, but she's keeping her last name. We used to talk about it when we were younger. She'd say she wasn't going to work hard to establish her career and name only to give it away when she got married. So, see? How would I know that if I didn't know Chelsea? We're sisters."

Lines creased his forehead. "Mrs. Bennett doesn't have siblings."

She swallowed. "Why would you say that?"

He narrowed his eyes. "Because I heard her mention it to Mr. Bennett."

Why would Chelsea tell Adam she didn't have family? Was it happening already? And if it was, could Indi blame Chelsea for wanting to embrace the happiness in her future and forget everything—and everyone—who reminded her of the past?

Indignation battled with anxiety and disappointment.

And nausea. These days there was always nausea.

"You were eavesdropping?" she challenged. "Is that part of the service the Hermitage at Avalon provides?"

"Maybe not," he said, his gaze darting away from her, "but a good concierge uses whatever tools are at his disposal to help him do his job. That's how I know you're not related to Mrs. Bennett."

"Your tools are a little dull. Chelsea and I aren't sisters by blood, we're sisters by circumstance. Foster sisters."

The doorman smirked and turned his back to her, but Indi reached across the desk and grabbed his arm. "Don't underestimate the bond we created. We're very close."

She couldn't imagine loving a biological sibling more. Her chest tightened at the invisible wound created by that bond being severed.

He looked down at her hand on his arm and then back at her. She unclenched her fingers and removed her hand, holding both up in a gesture of peace.

"Look, I appreciate you're just doing your job, but Chelsea and Adam would want you to grant me access to their house."

"I'd have no problem doing so, despite my personal opinion, if they'd put you on the list. But they didn't, so . . ." He shrugged, not bothering to finish the sentence.

"So if Chelsea or Adam called and said it was okay, you'd put me on the list?"

His eyes remained glued to the screen as his fingers flew over the keyboard. "*If* they called *and* used their password, then yes, I'd put you on the list."

She couldn't even bask in the fleeting moment of satisfaction she'd experienced at his acquiescence. They wouldn't call because they were on their postponed honeymoon. She didn't remember where they'd gone, or even how long they'd be away, just that Chelsea had mentioned something about a resort in Fiji where Adam wouldn't be able to use his devices and they'd be free from any contact with the outside world for at least a week.

Dammit. She bit her lip and stared at the profession-ally garbed patrons dining next door. What if . . .

"Does it have to be Chelsea or Adam?"

That got his attention.

"Excuse me?"

"You said 'on the list,' so one must already exist for them. Is it fair to assume it contains other names?"

He crossed his arms tightly across his chest and stared down his nose at her. "Possibly," he said, drawing the word out into several syllables.

Indi nodded. If this list granted access to their house, it would be populated with the names of people they trusted. If Chelsea had set it up, Indi's name would've occupied the top slot. Their stint through the foster care system solidified their relationship. They'd experienced ordeals that either caused people to never speak again or bond for life.

Chelsea trusted her. Of course she did.

Are you sure?

Indi refused to take notice of the splinter of doubt that implanted itself just beneath her skin.

That meant Adam had probably established the list and moved on to his next task, not thinking Chelsea's input was necessary. To say the gorgeous genius and CEO possessed a single-minded focus understated his intensity. And suddenly, Indi was certain of who was on the list. Adam's two best friends, Jonathan Moran and Mike Black.

Sensation bobbed and weaved in her belly.

Oh, so you recognize the name, huh, Nugget?

Mike.

Memories she'd tried desperately to suppress came skipping to the fore of her mind. His brilliant blue eyes holding her gaze while his hands learned the contours of her body. His unruly blond curls clutched between her fingers, while his lips skimmed across her skin. His lean muscled body nestled between her thighs as he coaxed back-arching orgasms from her.

He was Adam's best friend and Chief Operating Officer of their immensely successful technology company, Computronix. He'd played an instrumental role in Chelsea and Adam meeting and almost losing each other forever. The man was tenacious, ruthless and self-righteous. But after three tequila body shots, she found him charming, fascinating and panty-meltingly sexy. Why hadn't she learned her lesson in five semesters of college?

Nothing good *ever* comes from tequila.

She refocused on the point she wanted to make. "If a person on the list called you, could they verify that I should be on the list?"

"No."

Crap. She twirled one of her long braids around her index finger. But—

"If a person on the list showed up and requested entrance, you'd have to let them in, right? Even if they were with a guest?"

His face contorted as if he'd swallowed something unappetizing.

Score! *It's your birthday, it's your birthday. Go Indi, go Indi.*

And yet, once again, she had to deny herself the taste of victory. Jonathan, a James Beard Award–winning chef wasn't in the city. At Chelsea and Adam's wedding he'd informed everyone that he'd be spending the next year in DC, opening a new restaurant.

That left Mike as her only option.

She couldn't call him. The last time she'd seen him, she'd been leaving his bed at the crack of dawn after a sex-filled—and-fueled—weekend. The last time she'd spoken to him had been the night before she'd crept away: she'd screamed his name and dissolved into an orgasm when his tongue pushed against her clit. She couldn't call him now and say, "Hey, I know I disappeared on you and ignored your calls and texts, but can you put that behind you and help me?"

And that would be the *easiest* part of their conversation.

No, she couldn't contact Mike. Not yet. So what was she going to do? Despite her travels, she'd never been to San Francisco. Besides Chelsea, Adam and Mike, she didn't know anyone else in the city, and she'd spent most of her cash on the train ticket and the cab from the station. If she'd stayed in Seattle and worked in the brewery until the weekend, she could've made more than enough in tips to—

Her lips parted on a gasp.

Her stash.

Sporadically over the past few years, she'd entrusted some of her earnings to her sister. A personal savings account that earned no interest because Indi refused to let Chelsea deposit it in a bank. And Chelsea always had it, no matter where she'd been living. It was here. Indi could take some of that money and get a nice hotel room until Chelsea and Adam returned from their honeymoon.

"When does Barney's shift begin?" she asked, changing tactics. "He was on duty when I stayed here three months ago during the wedding."

The doorman blinked. "Barney is on indefinite leave."

"Oh no!" she gasped. "Is he okay? Was it his wife?"

The doorman's eyes bulged briefly before receding back into his face. "I cannot discuss his private information." He hesitated. "But how did you—"

"The last time we talked she'd just been diagnosed with Parkinson's. I volunteered at a hospital where they'd had successful trials using a cancer drug to treat some of the symptoms. I gave him some information so he could mention it to her doctor."

"Oh," he said, tapping his thumb against his bottom lip.

Was that a weakening in the levee? "How would I know that if I hadn't spoken to Barney? And I'd only have spoken to him if I was here and spent time with him and that would only have been possible if I actually knew Chelsea and Adam."

She waved her hand with a flourish. That had been a persuasive argument. Surely he couldn't refute that logic?

"If I recall it properly, we had really low temperatures a few months back. Maybe you stepped in from the cold, and Barney, being the nice guy he is, chatted with you while he let you thaw out. Maybe you *have* been here before, but to visit other people. Or maybe you're a stalker and that's how you know the information."

She frowned. *Come on.* She hopped up and down on her toes, attempting to hold off the encroaching exhaustion. "This is silly. I'll only be a second. You can come with me. There's something I need to get—"

"You're not on the list."

"Enough with that fucking list!"

The door to the restaurant opened and the overpowering odor of garlic wafted over and immediately snuffed out her ire. The assault to her senses was devastating. She placed a hand on the counter, bent over at the waist and took several deep, cleansing breaths. She grabbed her scent necklace, willing the peppermint to assist Nugget and the nausea in chilling the hell out.

Most people would've shown her some compassion, some consideration. Not the doorman. He offered no assistance, just delivered his final poisonous barb.

"Did you ever consider that you're not on the Bennetts' list because they didn't want you to be?"

His words were more disruptive then the garlic. They snaked their way through her, winding their way around the handles and flinging open the doors behind which she'd hidden her deepest fear.

Indi was no longer the most important person in Chelsea's life. And she'd continue to tumble down that list as Adam's friends, family and kids arrived on the scene.

Her muscles tightened and her belly fluttered. Indi straightened and pushed her shoulders back.

Don't worry, Nugget. I don't care what that asshat says. I'm getting into that apartment.

**And keep reading for a peek at
Tracey's Avon Impulse debut,**

LOVE ON MY MIND

Available Now from Avon Impulse!

Successful PR executive Chelsea Grant is one assignment
away from making partner at her firm and nothing
will stand in her way. Her big break? Turn a reclusive
computer genius into a media darling in time for his
new product launch. He may have been dubbed the
"sexiest geek alive" but he has no patience for the press—
and it shows. Piece of cake, right? Only problem is his
company doesn't want him to know they hired her.

After a disastrous product launch two years ago, tech
CEO Adam Bennett knows the success of his new device
depends on the media's support. When a twist of fate
brings the beautiful PR specialist to his door, Adam hires
Chelsea to help turn his image around. Their attraction
is undeniable and the more time they spend together,
the harder it becomes to keep things professional.

But when Adam discovers Chelsea's deception,
will she risk everything for her career or
is love the real thing on her mind?

CHELSEA GRANT COULDN'T tear her gaze away from the train wreck on the screen.

She followed press conferences like most Americans followed sports. The spectacle thrilled her, watching speakers deftly deflect questions, state narrow political positions, or, in rare instances, exhibit honest emotions. The message might be scripted but the reactions were pure reality. If executed well, a press conference could be as engaging and dynamic as any athletic game.

But watching this one was akin to lions in the amphitheater, not tight ends on the football field. Her throat ached, impacting her ability to swallow. She squinted, hoping the action would lessen her visual absorption of the man's public relations disaster.

He'd folded his arms across his chest, the gesture causing the gray cardigan he wore to pull across his broad shoulders. The collar of the black-and-blue plaid shirt he wore beneath it brushed the underside of his stubbled jaw.

When he'd first stepped onto the platform, she'd thought he was going for "geek chic." All he'd lacked were black square frames and a leather cross-body satchel. Now she understood he wasn't playing dress-up. These were his everyday clothes, and as such, they were inappropriate for a press conference, unless he was a lumberjack who'd just won the lottery.

Had someone advised him on how to handle a press conference? No, she didn't think so. *Any* coaching would have helped with his demeanor. The man stared straight ahead. He didn't look at the reporters seated before him. He didn't look into the lenses. He appeared to look over the cameras, like there was someplace else he'd rather be. His discomfort crossed the media plane, and her fingers twitched where they rested next to her iPad on the acrylic conference table.

A female reporter from an entertainment news cable channel raised her hand. "Mr. Bennett?"

The man turned his head, and his gaze zeroed in on the reporter and narrowed into a glare. Chelsea inhaled audibly and leaned forward in her chair. His eyes were thickly lashed and dark, although she couldn't determine their exact color. Brown? Black? He dropped his arms, and his long, slender fingers gripped the podium tightly. The bank of microphones jiggled and a loud piercing sound ripped through the air. He winced.

"How does it feel to be handed the title by David

James?" the reporter asked, her voice louder as it came on the tail end of the noise feedback.

The camera zoomed in and caught his pinched expression. "Right now, I feel annoyed," he responded sharply.

"Annoyed? Aren't you honored?"

"Why should I be honored?"

"Because *People Magazine* has never named a non-actor as their sexiest man alive."

"An award based on facial characteristics is not an honor. Especially since I have no control over the symmetry of my features. The National Medal of Technology. The Faraday Medal. The granting of those awards would be a true honor."

The camera zoomed out, and hands holding phones with a smaller version of the man's frustrated image filled the screen. Flashes flickered on the periphery, and he rubbed his brow, like Aladdin begging the genie for the power to disappear.

"How does one celebrate being deemed the most desirable man on the planet?" another reporter asked.

"One doesn't." His lips tightened into a white slash on his face.

"Is there a secret scientific formula for dating Victoria's Secret models? Didn't you used to be engaged to one?" A male reporter exchanged knowing looks with the colleagues around him. A smattering of chuckles followed his question.

"Didn't she leave you for another model six weeks before the wedding?"

"So you're single? Who's your type?"

"What's your perfect first date?"

"Can you create a sexbot?"

Questions pelted the poor man. The reporters had found his weakness: his inability or unwillingness to play the game. Now they would try to get a sound bite for their story teaser or a quote to increase their site's click-through rate. The man drove his fingers through his black hair, a move so quick and natural she knew it was a gesture he repeated often. That, and not hair putty, probably explained the spikiness of the dark strands that were longer on the top, shorter on the sides.

"This has nothing to do with my project," he snapped, then scowled at someone off-camera.

Chelsea glanced heavenward, grateful she wasn't the recipient of that withering look.

"Adam, what do you find sexy?"

The reporters didn't intend to give up easily. They circled, like shark to chum.

"*This* is why you called me away from my home? Do you have any idea what I'm working on? How revolutionary it is? You told me this was important. You neglected to mention I'd be subjected to idiotic questions by reporters from gossip rags." He continued talking to the person off-camera, raising his voice to be heard over the sudden uproar that resulted from his remarks. "I'm done."

He stormed off the stage, his exit allowing Chelsea to see what the bank of microphones had hidden: an enticing bottom half, clad in well-worn jeans. In the wake of his exit, clicks and flashes were the only animation on the screen. A young man leapt onto the platform.

He was dressed in a sleek gray suit, his blond hair perfectly styled, his even, white teeth perfectly bleached. "Thank you all for coming today. Mr. Bennett had to hurry to an important meeting. We'll be taking no further questions." He smiled winningly and headed off, ignoring the torrent of questions.

Across from her, Howard Richter, her immediate supervisor, pressed a button. The image froze on the enormous screen and the lights came up. The blackout curtains whirred along their track, unveiling the unusually rare, smog-free, sun-drenched view of downtown Los Angeles, the famous Hollywood sign a name tag in the distance. Silence blanketed the room.

Chelsea shook her head slightly, as if awakening from a daydream, then stared at the two people who controlled her fate at Beecher & Stowe.

"That was a disaster," she said bluntly.

When the silence continued, Chelsea leaned back in the white leather chair, shifted on one hip, and crossed her legs, her beige Louboutin-clad foot dangling. "I'll admit it was entertaining, in a TMZ sort of way, but what does it have to do with my performance review?"

"What would you have done differently?" Rebecca Stowe asked, ignoring her question. The older woman, and named partner, was a legend in the PR community, being one of the first to understand and predict the impact digital marketing would have on both organizations and consumers as early as the late nineties.

"I would've told him why he was at the press conference, I would have prepped him for the type of questions to expect, and I would've guaranteed that he was dressed properly," she said, extending a finger to emphasize each point. "Publicity basics that eluded Peter Sonic from Kellerman." She waved her hand dismissively, thinking of the man who'd tried to regain control after his client had stormed off.

"What do you know about Adam Bennett?" Howard asked, shifting directions.

Chelsea shook her head. "Not much. That press conference was a year ago, right? I remember all the hype surrounding a non-celebrity on the cover. He's CEO of Computronix and a wunderkind in the tech community. He's known for creating both hardware and operating systems that I use on a daily basis."

"You heard him allude to something he was working on?" Howard asked. "Since the press conference, he's been holed up in his house in the Santa Cruz Mountains and no one has heard from him. Until two weeks ago."

"He contacted us?"

Not surprising. If the press conference was a sample of the type of representation he had with Kellerman, it was little wonder he was interested in Beecher & Stowe, one of the top PR firms in the country.

"No, I did." A voice from behind her.

Chelsea turned her attention to the fourth person

in the room, a handsome, sophisticated, and stylishly dressed man, who exuded an air of authority that commanded respect. She'd immediately noticed him sitting at the back corner of the table when she'd first entered. She was sure she didn't know him, and the lack of an introduction compounded by the press conference debacle had worked to dismiss him from her mind.

"Chelsea, this is Michael Black, COO of Computronix," Rebecca said.

Chelsea held up her phone. "I'm a huge fan of your work."

He smiled, his light blue eyes dazzling. "Likewise."

She tilted her head to the side. "You know my work, Mr. Black?"

"Please, call me Mike," he invited. "And I do. What you pulled off with Ellis York was amazing. You took a girl heavy with talent but low on polish and turned her into a media darling in under two years. She wouldn't have won the Golden Globe without that transformation. And the fact that Leon Bush is now cohosting *Sports Talk Live* is due, in large part, to your handling of the whole cheating scandal last year."

Pride expanded in her chest. Receiving praise from a man with Mike's credentials and clout warmed her.

She loved her work. Controlling a person's or product's image, dictating the way they were perceived—it was her reason for being. She believed she'd been groomed for it from a young age. Unlike many of her colleagues, she hadn't gotten into PR blinded by the glitz and glamour of three-hour lunches and red carpets. She'd been almost clinical in her decision, possessing that critical awareness of the burning need to have people view you differently while lacking the power to make that happen.

That insight kept her going when her entry-level salary was barely enough to cover her rent and student loans, when her workload was so heavy she barely had time for a three-*minute* lunch, and the only red carpet she walked was the one inside the Chinese restaurant around the corner from her apartment. Seven years later, that same insight was fueling her to the top of the industry.

"Thank you. Bush has oodles of charisma . . . and luck. As for Ellis, she deserves the credit for her success. She was willing to make the effort. Working with her was easy."

Mike sighed. "I wish I could say the same about Adam. He's going to be difficult."

She stiffened, her gaze swiveling between Mike, Rebecca and Howard. "You want me to work with Adam Bennett?" Horror coated her words.

Only a rookie would find this assignment appealing. On the surface, it didn't seem like a hardship. The man *was* sexy. There was a roughness and edge to him many would find appealing, especially considering his intelligence. When she thought of computer geeks, the dangerous man she'd seen on the screen did not come to mind.

But his attire and mannerisms? The way he'd handled the reporters? Walking away from the press conference? This would be a nightmare of epic proportions.

As Executive Managing Director of the West Coast Entertainment division of Beecher & Stowe, Chelsea had earned the right to choose her own accounts, and she chose to work with clients who wanted her help, who were motivated but didn't possess the tools to achieve their goals. However, those who needed the help, but didn't want it? People like Adam Bennett? They were assigned to assistant account coordinators.

"Before we go any further . . ." Mike flipped open the cover on his tablet and tapped the screen. A few seconds later, he handed it to her. "This is a nondisclosure agreement. By signing it, you concede that what we talk about in this room, as well as any work you do for us, will be held in the strictest of confidence. You will not divulge it to anyone who is not working with you on this project."

Chelsea scanned it quickly before glancing up at her bosses.

"We've already signed it," Howard assured her.

Nodding, Chelsea wrote her name with the stylus he provided and handed the tablet back to Mike.

He glanced at it, satisfaction gleaming on his face, before continuing. "Adam has created a device that will change the face of personal computing. We'll be unveiling it at a special product launch on April 18. Adam will be a major part of that launch and we need him to be ready. And that"—he pointed to the still image of an empty bank of microphones on the large screen—"is not acceptable."

She agreed. But this couldn't be *her* problem. She turned to Howard.

"I work in entertainment, not tech. I handle actors and athletes, people who understand the business. I've never handled 'real' people. Plus, that's only five weeks away. With the three new accounts I signed last quarter, there's no way I can fit this in."

"We'll reassign those projects to several of your account executives," Howard said. "They can take the lead for the next few months. Right now, Adam Bennett is your main priority. When you've worked your magic on him, you can catch up on the other accounts."

Chelsea's coffee and mid-morning snack seesawed in her stomach. They were pulling her off other high-level accounts?

Rebecca leaned her elbows on the table and steepled her fingers. "Chelsea, I know you came to this meeting expecting an offer of partnership."

Had she blown her chance by hesitating?

The pressure of unshed tears stung her eyes and panic clawed at her chest, threatening to erupt and decimate the mask of calm professionalism she always wore at work. She didn't want to make partner. She *needed* to make partner. There were times she'd thought she'd always be Dirty Diana's daughter. That her childhood, featuring an endless parade of her mother's men, bug-infested apartments, and a short stint in the foster care system, would twist around her ankle like a weed, impeding her efforts to rise above her formative years. Making partner in one of the top PR firms in the country would finally whitewash her past and confer her self-respect.

But if she didn't make partner at Beecher & Stowe, it was never going to happen. Since she'd already achieved upper management status, her options were to continue working for a company where there were no further opportunities for advancement, or leave and start over at another firm. A firm that would hire her for her contacts and skill and compensate her well, but would never offer her a partnership, assuming she was damaged goods because she didn't ascend the final rung on Beecher & Stowe's corporate ladder. Neither prospect came close to assuaging the remembered pangs of hunger that constantly reminded her of her upbringing.

"I've worked hard and paid my dues. I'm the youngest executive manager ever. In the past eighteen months, I've brought in business worth a quarter of a billion dollars." She jabbed her index finger into the conference table to emphasize her words.

"We are well aware of your contribution to Beecher & Stowe. When Mike approached us and requested the best for this account, we immediately thought of you. You've shown us your media relations savvy, marketing and business management skills, and a strong work ethic. Now we need to see your firm-first mind-set. Can you put the needs of the firm above your own? Of course you have the right to work on the clients you brought in. They're important to you. But Computronix is important to us."

A flush of giddiness tingled through her body, causing her hands to tremble. To cover, she pulled them down to her lap and twisted to stare at the abstract paintings on the wall, the only splash of color in the conference room's muted palate. She hadn't lost her opportunity. If she understood what Rebecca had intimated, Chelsea still had a shot.

"To be clear—if I make Adam Bennett presentable for the Computronix project launch in five weeks, you'll make me a partner?"

She held her breath.

Rebecca smiled. "How does Director of US Client Management sound?"

Chelsea exhaled. Like everything she'd been working for her entire adult life. She was so close the honeyed scent of success teased her nostrils. There was no way she would let an obnoxious tech geek prevent her from fulfilling her ambition. "You've got yourself a deal."

"Great." Howard beamed, offering her two thumbs-up.

"There's one small caveat," Mike cautioned.

It didn't matter. She'd do whatever it took to complete this assignment.

"Adam is a brilliant man, but he's . . . demanding. You're not the first professional we've hired to help him.

He says we're trying to change him and he's refused to work with any of them."

That didn't sound good. "Isn't that why you need my help? Aren't you trying to change him?"

"No. We don't want to change Adam. I don't think anyone can. But we can't have him being surly and rude to reporters. Not in this day of instant uploads that go viral in minutes."

"So, what's the problem?"

"If he knows we sent you, he'll be resistant. You'll need to find another way to approach him."

This assignment had left strange in its rearview mirror and was hurtling toward bizarre.

She swung her widened gaze back to Howard and Rebecca. "Is that necessary?" she asked. "You're adding an element of espionage to an already difficult task."

A large part of her success at her job was her insistence on brutal honesty with her clients, a practice she'd embraced after emerging from a childhood of lies generated by her mother. She might spin stories for the media, but she always delivered the unvarnished truth to her clients. Always. She was often the only person who did.

Mike's lips tightened. "Trust me, we've run out of other options."

"We've always had faith in your abilities," Rebecca said. "This wouldn't be the time to make us question that belief."

My brother said your mother is a whore. She must be cheap, because you dress like shit.

"Does your mother take food stamps? What about layaway?"

She blinked away the taunts from her childhood. She'd do whatever it took to ensure she'd never end up poor, used and disgraced like her mother.

"Consider it done."